DISCERNED

THE SAVIORS OF SOULS BOOK 4

SHIRLEY O'NEIL

This is a work of fiction. Names, characters, places, and incidents are products of the author's imagination or are used fictitiously and are not to be construed as real. Any resemblance to actual events, locations, organizations, or persons, living or dead, is entirely coincidental.

World Castle Publishing, LLC
Pensacola, Florida
Copyright © Shirley O'Neil 2023
Hardback ISBN: 9798393918743
Paperback ISBN: 9781960076700
eBook ISBN: 9781960076717
First Edition World Castle Publishing, LLC, June 5, 2023
http://www.worldcastlepublishing.com
Licensing Notes
Cover: Karen Fuller
Editor: Karen Fuller

CHAPTER 1

Hayley Johnson hung her next three choices of wedding gowns on hooks within the spacious fitting room and decided which to try on first. Once she had decided, she removed the white terry cloth robe she wore and draped it over the French tufted chair beside the wide full-length mirror. *Only six more months, and I'll be Mrs. Hayley Franklin.* Love, excitement, and anticipation filled her. *I can't count how many times I've pinched myself.*

Nothing prepared her for the consuming emotions that overwhelmed her the moment she walked into her job interview and met Lee. She had spent her entire life finding a way to control her emotions, a very important feat for someone who's psychic gifts forced her to share the dead's memories of their demise. She learned to block their tear-filled pain, their agonizing endings, their passionate passings, and their emotional states of mind. But her defenses to protect herself from her feelings for Lee failed. Instead, her entire being craved the sound of his voice, the look in his sensitive mahogany-brown eyes, and his masculine mannerism. Her world flipped right-side up when she found he felt the same way about her. *A love affair that would make all romance novels want to rip out their pages. Who knew? It still seems like a miracle that he loves me.*

As she slid into the first dress, its slender silhouette hugged her body, flaring slightly at the knee and flowing to her feet. She fought to steady herself while she attempted to fasten the halter neck's hooks. The ground moved. She glanced up at the chandelier dangling from the coffered ceiling above her. Each teardrop crystal quivered, then slowly swayed to a halt. *An earthquake?*

The sound of the dressing room door opening startled her. In her bare feet, she tip-toed over and peeked out. No one could be seen. *Must've been the earthquake.* She closed the door again and returned to the mirror. *This one's way too tight. It would take me months to walk down the aisle. This is the ninth dress I've tried on.* She sighed. The jetlag from her flight from Sutterville, North Carolina, to London, England, threatened to rob her of her energy. *I'm surprised I'm still tired. I slept most of the way here.*

After removing the dress, hanging it, and reaching for another, again, Hayley saw the door slowly open. She gazed around. Nothing moved. No one stood outside the door. Instinctively, she searched her surroundings with her psychic sense. *Is someone there?* But nothing triggered an alarm. Shrugging off the incident, she shut the door, this time locking it.

I wonder how Laura's doing. It'll be great having a double wedding. I hope she doesn't have to try on as many dresses as I've had to. This is getting ridiculous. Every one of them looks so beautiful on its hanger.

She attempted to maneuver her way into her next choice of gowns when a knock on the door made her jump.

"Need help, Miss?" the store assistant asked.

Struggling to get the dress halfway over her head, Hayley realized a little aid would be useful. "Yes, please."

The door rattled, and she remembered she'd locked it. "Wait a moment. I'll unlock it." By raising the skirt up over her head, she freed herself from the layers of satin and lace and watched the lock's latch turn. *Good, she has a key.*

The assistant turned the handle again. "It's not locked, Miss. May I come in?"

I know I locked it. She glanced around.

"Miss?"

"Yes, please," Hayley replied, gathering herself and focusing on the reason she came to the shop.

The young woman entered and helped Hayley find her way into the gown. Once she slid her arms into the lace sleeves, the rest of the dress settled into place.

"It's beautiful," Hayley said. Looking into the mirror, she gazed at an elegance she had only seen in magazines. Something caught her attention behind her and the assistant.

On a hook on the back of the fitting room door, Hayley watched a hanger gently swing. She quickly glanced up. The chandelier remained still. "Is your shop haunted?" she asked.

"No, Miss." The assistant chuckled. "You must have been fooled by the tremor. It might have made something appear to move on its own. You can trust there are no ghosts in this shop."

Or maybe there are, Hayley thought.

The assistant tugged the zipper up Hayley's back. "There you be, Miss. And I might add, you look glowing. Do you think this could be the one?"

The gown's fit, style, and radiance stunned Hayley. "It looks amazing."

"*You* look amazing, Miss. Would you care to follow me to the gallery, where you can stand back and get a better look? And I believe you'll be needing a pair of high heels to compliment your gown. Would you care for a veil? How about jewelry? Come, let's see what we can find."

Hayley followed her out of the dressing room and down the hall. Fine art lit by brass display lamps lined the walls. To the right, a glass case exhibited platinum gold clips, silver combs, and other diamond and pearl hair accessories.

"Maybe your friends would like to give their opinions," the assistant said. "I can round them up if you'd like."

"No. Everyone is trying on gowns. Let them have fun. Let's start with shoes."

Before she stepped into the front room, she glanced

over her shoulder. She sensed a slight chill in the air behind her. Although she couldn't see anyone, she felt the presence of someone or something close by. After putting on a pair of heels and following the seamstress to the main room, she stepped upon a pedestal in front of a large mirror to have her dress fitted.

CHAPTER 2

Pleased she had finally found the perfect wedding gown, Hayley reviewed her appearance in the bridal shop's seven-foot gold-framed mirror. Behind her, in the front of the shop, large display windows stood beside frosted French doors. Inside this affluent shop, a crystal chandelier dangled above a tufted French circular banquette sofa where normally an audience watched young brides-to-be model gowns.

But on this snowy winter day in London, England, the shop seemed empty as Hayley and her three friends tried on gowns. Although she had the choice of having her gown custom-made, all the time-consuming picky decisions that went with it annoyed her. Going to the store and picking something off the rack fulfilled her needs in her previous life before she'd met Lee. *Why not now? Shopping is instant gratification.* She tossed her long light-brown hair aside to get a better look at the neckline. *It's perfect.*

As she stood statuesque, a seamstress, armed with needles, thread, and scissors, shortened the gown's hem.

While Hayley studied her reflection, she heard an explosion and stared into the mirror in disbelief at the demolished buildings across the street. Bricks rained onto the asphalt while dust billowed toward the bridal shop.

Terrified, Hayley looked over her shoulder, expecting the blast to shatter the window. But nothing appeared out of place. In front of the millinery store across the street, a woman bundled in a coat and scarf admired hats on display. Cars drove by on the uncluttered road. Snow, not bombs, fell from the sky.

It took only a moment before she realized she'd had a vision of the past. *I'll need to brace myself for more of this. World War II residual energy is no doubt infused into every inch of London. A glass of wine sounds good about now.*

"Don't move, Miss," the seamstress said. "I'm nearly done."

Hayley steadied herself and tried to focus on the gown's long lace sleeves seductively streaming all the way up her arm, leaving the round of her shoulders bare. The lace-over-white satin sweetheart bodice adorned with pearls and diamonds hugged her body to the waistline, then flowed into an A-line skirt, pooling around her white satin heels. A train cascaded from the waist and trailed a modest three feet behind her. But she didn't feel as beautiful as she looked. The tide of emotions she'd felt while watching the vision of annihilation still churned within her.

"I don't know why I have to try on wedding gowns if I'm not getting married," Matilda said, exiting the door leading to the dressing rooms.

"A woman should never pass up the chance to look beautiful," Kathy replied, following her.

Matilda, wearing an off-white satin A-line gown, wandered over to Hayley and shared the mirror. "Do you know something we don't? Did you foresee our futures? Or are we playing dress up for the fun of it?"

"I know I told you I can see the past, present, future, and the dead, but I have limits." Hayley clearly remembered that she'd explained what had happened before her birth. While in heaven, she and a group of her friends from past lives had made a pact to be born together into this lifetime and become the Saviors of Souls. Rules were set. And as frustrating as the rules seemed sometimes, they were out of her control.

"Sorry. I forgot."

"There's a good reason for my limitations," Hayley said. "A Divine rule forbids me from seeing my own future. And another stops me from seeing my friends' because our lives are so tightly connected. What affects them affects me."

"That sounds logical."

"As for viewing their pasts," Hayley added, "I was told that because our lives are so uniquely tied together in past lifetimes, it would be impossible for me to separate their pasts from their lives now. For some reason, everything mingles. So, boundaries were set."

"I know," Matilda said. "It just slipped my mind."

"And right now, you look beautiful." Hayley took a calming breath. She sounded annoyed and knew it. Trying to act normal after being shaken out of her wits sometimes seemed difficult. "Sorry, Matilda. I'm just frustrated." She told her about her vision of World War II and the visitation in the dressing room. "It's not that I'm complaining. I see these kinds of things all the time. I just wish I could sit back, have a glass of wine, and not be bothered. I'm on vacation."

"If I had your gifts, I'd be heavily medicated." Matilda peered into the mirror as if seeing herself for the first time. "You're right. I look amazing."

Hayley laughed. "Relax, have fun," she told Matilda. "Try on a few more gowns."

"Okay. You're right. It's not like I get this chance every day." Matilda hiked up her skirt and ambled away.

A smile spread across Hayley's face as she watched her friend stroll off. But when she turned back to the mirror, her mood changed to fright, and she gasped. A child about five or six years old stood staring at her from the other side of the mirror. She wore a dirt-stained dress—Hayley could only guess its color—her face, tangled long brown hair, thin legs, and skinny arms covered in grime. Behind her small body, bombs exploded, buildings tumbled, smoke darkened the sky, and fire consumed

London. *She must have died during World War II nearly eighty years ago.*

Hayley tried to understand when the little girl spoke, but the words didn't make sense. She shook her head and strained to listen as the child repeated herself again and again. In what appeared to be a fit of frustration, the little girl struck the mirror, cracking it, then vanished.

The seamstress's eyes widened, and she jumped up. "Blimey! Mary, come look."

A tall, thin woman darted out of the back room and stood alongside the seamstress. "Bloody hell! How'd that happen?"

Without hesitation, Hayley dashed to a nearby chair, grabbed her purse, unzipped the compartment inside, and took out her cell phone. The women saw that Hayley wished to take photos and stepped away. Quickly, Hayley snapped pictures to show to her fiancé, Lee. *I know he'll be interested to see this. Hopefully, it doesn't mean we're involved in another paranormal case.* Since Hayley, Lee, and their friends had discovered their shared destiny, they no longer hunted for ghosts. Now the ghosts came to them. *If we're lucky, the child just wanted to tell me how she died.*

Memories of Hayley's childhood flashed through her mind. At the most inappropriate moments when Hayley attended elementary school, the dead would come to her — in class, in the lunchroom, in the hallways — and show her visions of their death. This visitation seemed similar.

Kathy joined her. "What on Earth happened?"

Hayley explained what she'd seen, the little girl and the World War II attack on London. She touched the mirror, brushing her fingers across the crack. "The surface is smooth, unbroken."

"I can fix this," Kathy replied in a low voice.

Hayley had no doubts, Kathy, with her recently acquired gift of witchcraft, could repair the break with the wiggle of her finger. "That's a good idea, but the shop owner and her seamstress behind us would freak." A month ago, Kathy had been possessed.

After surviving the ordeal, she had been left with the abilities of the witch who had occupied her body.

"You know this is all your fault," Kathy told her.

The accusation made Hayley want to laugh out loud, but she put her hand to her mouth to suppress the temptation. "I know the weather mussed my hair, and maybe the flight and time difference have made me look drained, but I don't think that would be enough to shatter glass."

"Your face is flawless, and you don't look the least bit tired," Kathy said. "The crack's paranormal. It's obvious to me that you pissed off another ghost."

"It wasn't my intention," Hayley replied. "I couldn't understand a word she said."

"Couldn't understand who?" Matilda asked, sashaying to a halt at Hayley's side.

"A ghost," Kathy said. "Apparently, this place is haunted. She broke the mirror."

"My word," Matilda said. With wide eyes, she glanced around. "Is she still here?"

"You're spooked?" Hayley asked. "Seriously? After all you've been through since you've met us?"

It hadn't been long ago when Matilda had joined their team. With her expertise in historical and evolutionary linguistics, she became an asset.

"It was a little girl," Hayley told her friend, "who died in the 1940s, World War II era. I couldn't understand anything she said."

"There are thirty dialects throughout the UK," Matilda explained. "Unless you have a trained ear, you would have trouble understanding many of them."

"Unfortunately, my ears aren't as good as yours," Hayley said, wishing Matilda shared her ability to hear and see ghosts. "If I could've recorded her voice and let you hear it, we could've figured out what she was saying. Instead, I upset her, and that's the result."

"Kind of an odd crack," Matilda pointed out. "There's lots of curves, and it never trails to the edge."

"Something like this would've been made by thought creation," Hayley replied. "The child had to visualize it in order to create it. It's not easy, and she's very young."

"Come on," Kathy said, taking Matilda's arm. "We still have an hour to kill. Let's try on a few more gowns."

"I'm finished with you, Miss," the seamstress told Hayley while picking up her sewing tools. "You can change if you'd like while I alter your friend's gown."

Hayley thanked her, grabbed her things, and strolled over to Laura, who stood in front of another mirror across the aisle.

"I still can't believe we're having a double wedding," Laura said.

"I never would've guessed." Hayley gazed at Laura's gown. "You look beautiful."

"You do too."

"Isn't this a lot more fun than getting something custom-made? We eliminated all those fittings and saved so much time."

"Good thing," Laura said. "Time goes by quickly."

"June 19th," Hayley said. "I'm surprised you wanted me to select the location."

"It's only fair," Laura replied. "I chose the when. So, you should pick the where."

"I never thought our weddings would be held in the church where Lee's parents had been married," Hayley admitted.

"The beginning of a tradition," Laura said.

"Speaking of tradition and Lee's parents, that's the reason I wanted to come to England. I decided to carry on his parent's tradition of collecting artwork from local painters and craftsmen. In the morning, Lee and I will drive through the countryside to see what we can find."

"Sounds like fun," Laura told her.

Hayley took her cell phone from her purse when it indicated a text had been received. She read the message. "We're to meet the men at the penthouse when we're ready."

***

"Done, Miss," the seamstress said to Laura, putting away her pins and needles. She glanced at Hayley. "Mary will take both your gowns once you undress and will sort out the needs from here on."

After taking care of the purchase and mailing information, Hayley texted Lee and phoned the hotel's courtesy car to retrieve them. They waited inside in the warmth while the snow turned to a frigid rain.

"Oh, here he is." Kathy pointed to a black Jaguar sedan pulling up. Before stepping out of the shop, she gave Hayley a wink and pointed at the mirror. Slowly the crack began to disappear. "That should take care of it."

They filed out the door.

The wind whipped, its gust invading the hood of Hayley's coat. She gripped its fur rim, pulling it forward to protect her face from the icy shards that bit her cheeks.

The driver held the passenger door for them while they climbed into the vehicle and nestled into its ivory leather.

While sitting next to the door in the backseat, Hayley removed her parka's -hood, and through the rain-drenched window, she looked at the store, wondering what the little girl had said, then turned away. "To the hotel, please," she told the driver.

"Yes, Miss." He waited for traffic to pass.

When she glanced nonchalantly out the window again, her heart jumped into her throat. The child stood only feet away from the car door, staring. *Holy....*

Her pulse raced when the child reached toward the window, her ghostly hands icing the wet glass at her approach. An instant before the ghost's gauzy fingers could touch the pane, their car sped off, leaving Hayley's nerves in a disquieted bundle.

CHAPTER 3

After dinner, Lee and Hayley entered the living room of the four-bedroom penthouse and joined Roger and Jim, who were watching the barges on the Thames prepare for the New Year's Eve fireworks.

Roger had been Lee's best friend since they were little. When Lee had turned eighteen, and Roger had been twenty-eight, a great tragedy marred their lives. Lee's parents, along with Roger's, died in a plane crash. Jim, a good friend of the family, had stepped in to become their mentor. Now that Hayley knew about their shared destiny, she could look back with interest and marvel at how they, including Kathy and Laura, had all found one another in this lifetime to become the Saviors of Souls.

"Where is everyone?" Hayley asked.

"Laura and Matilda are upstairs changing," Roger, soon to be Laura's husband, said. "We're going to the lounge to have a few drinks, listen to the band, and dance the night away."

"You both look very handsome," Hayley said, noticing that only Lee remained casually dressed while Roger and Jim were clothed for a splendid night out.

As long as she had known Lee, his face had always been clean shaven. His styled brown hair complimented his mahogany brown eyes. Roger's blond hair had a touch of product added to keep its unruly waves tame. Jim, with his slightly graying manicured mustache, chose a shorter cut for his thinning hair. She glanced around. "Thomas and Kathy aren't going with you?"

"No," Jim, Matilda's sweetheart, said. "They decided to go pub hoppin'. Young fool kids. They don't know what they're gettin' into. A nice pint of beer may look innocent enough, but in England, warm beer will turn ya into a tipsy tourist. I bet they don't make it into more than two pubs. Maybe three, but they won't remember comin' or goin'."

"How are they getting back to the hotel?" Lee asked.

"The concierge provided a designated driver," Jim told him.

"They'll be fine," Lee said. "Kathy's the same age as Hayley. I wouldn't call twenty-nine naïve. And I think Thomas is closer to my age thirty-two. They're not kids."

"I'm callin' a spade a spade," Jim said. "Anyone younger than me still has lots to learn."

"I'm only ten years younger than you, old man," Roger said. "And you're only fifty-three. You sound like you're ready to kick the bucket."

"And when I do, I'm comin' back to haunt the hell outta ya."

"Speaking of spooks, Hayley...." Roger said. "Are you sure the ghost at the bridal shop wasn't asking for help?"

She sighed. "I can only hope that's not the case. We're on vacation."

"Vacation?" Jim said. "That might be as easy as herdin' grasshoppers. Ya know the history of the UK. There're probably more ghosts than the livin' in 'bout any town ya come to."

"True," Lee said. "But not all ghosts or spirits ask for our help."

"I wish I could've understood her." Hayley turned to Roger. "But I didn't get the impression she needed help."

"That's a relief," Roger said. "The last thing we need right now is another case. We're here to enjoy ourselves, not work."

"Odds are you'll never see that ghost again," Lee said.

Hayley nodded. "This is my first time in England, and

work isn't on my agenda."

"I have a surprise waiting for you," Lee told her. "I thought you might like to take a ride and get a glimpse of Big Ben. It's not far from here."

"Sounds fun."

"I've arranged for a car to take us out and about," Lee said.

"So, we won't be taking a rental?" Hayley asked.

"Not tonight. It'll be fun. I asked for Lenny. I talked to him for a while this afternoon. He seems to know everything about England's history. It should be interesting." He checked his cell phone and read a text. "He's waiting in front of the hotel. Let's go."

"Have fun, you guys," Roger said. "It's damn cold out there. Bundle up."

"Have fun yourselves," Lee told them. "We won't be long."

"If we're not here when ya get back, ya know where we'll be," Jim called to them as they turned and walked away.

Before leaving, they put on their coats, scarves, and knitted hats, preparing for the high twenties weather.

Every detail throughout the hotel had a touch of elegance. To Hayley, even something as simple as the elevator's interior oozed chic sophistication. Grandeur and a life of opulence hadn't been the world she knew while growing up. The Divine rule that forbade her from seeing her own future had kept Lee's wealth a surprise. They strolled through the lobby. When they reached the entrance, two doormen held open the tall glass doors.

The sun had set. Streetlights lit the stairs and sidewalk. At the curb, Lenny opened the Jaguar's rear door. Hayley and Lee slid in across the heated plush black leather seats, and Lenny closed their door. Once he climbed in and pushed the start button, he pulled out into traffic.

"This isn't the same Jaguar that picked us up at the bridal shop this afternoon," Hayley said. "The interior is different."

"Spot on, Miss," Lenny replied. "That particular vehicle is out of commission at the moment. One of its windows had to be replaced."

"Why?" Hayley asked. "Everything was fine when we arrived at the hotel."

"Yes, Miss. It's a mystery, really. Before Albert left for the day, he gave the car a thorough going over, as duty requires. He found one of the backseat windows cracked. Odd, since the cars are in a secure location and well monitored. Video footage shows no signs of the perpetrator."

Goosebumps went up Hayley's arms. "Which window was it?"

"Behind the driver's seat, Miss."

Hayley glanced at Lee. "Exactly where I was sitting." *It couldn't have had anything to do with the little girl. She never touched the window. And it would've been a lengthy, delayed reaction, which is ridiculous. It's just a coincidence.* Yet the hairs on the back of her neck that were standing on end didn't seem to agree. She thought a moment. "Is the car still in the lot?"

"No, Miss."

"Hayley is a psychic medium," Lee said. "She might've been able to tell you how it happened."

"I'm gobsmacked. I would've given a week's wages to see that."

"Do you take pictures of the damage to keep on file?" Hayley asked.

"Yes. We do."

"Any chance you can get access to it?" Lee asked.

"I can arrange it," Lenny said. "May I ask why, sir?"

"Hayley has the ability to touch an object and receive impressions."

"I can get it from the gaffer as soon as we return to the hotel," Lenny said. "But if you don't mind, I'd like to keep the reason between us."

"I understand," Hayley said. She had been tormented all her life by nonbelievers. If Lenny tells his boss about her gifts, there would be a good chance he'd be ridiculed too. "There's no guarantee I'll be able to sense what happened, but I'd like to give it a try. No week's wages necessary."

"When we return, I'll bring the snapshot to you straight away, Miss. Do you think the crack is supernatural?"

"It could be," Hayley said. "A ghost broke the mirror at the bridal shop this morning. When we left, she tried to touch that same window you're referring to, but we drove away before she could. Still, it seems odd."

"As you have probably guessed, Hayley can see ghosts and spirits," Lee told him.

In the rearview mirror, Hayley could see Lenny's eyes widen. "What's the difference between ghosts and spirits?" he asked.

"Ghosts are those who had died but linger on the earthly plain," Hayley explained. "Some know they'd died, while others don't. Spirits are souls who have entered heaven and returned either to visit or for other reasons."

"Have you seen them all your life?" he asked.

"Yes. I was born a magnet," she told him. "The *lingerings*, as I used to call them, were the worse to deal with. Some I sympathized with, and I didn't mind helping. Others were bullies. They scared the wits out of me."

"How could you tell the difference between spirits and ghosts?" Lenny asked.

"Mostly, I hid from them when I was little. I didn't care if there was a difference. I just wanted them to leave me alone. I didn't really pay attention until I was six or seven so I could learn to avoid the worst of them. Spirits have a peaceful demeanor. The calm vibration of their essence allows me to sort out who's what."

"So, what was the little girl in the bridal shop?" he asked

her.

"Definitely a ghost. I also had visions of World War II. The war's residual energy is overwhelming throughout London."

"Germany bombed London heavily, more so than any other part of England. I'm not surprised you're having visions, Miss," Lenny said.

"I shouldn't have a problem blocking the energy," Hayley said.

"I know how draining that is for you," Lee told her. "Tomorrow morning, you and I will take off and drive through the countryside."

"If you stay away from the shoreline and major cities, you shouldn't have a problem," Lenny told her. "Before World War II, England knew it had to bolster its defense systems and create a master plan to protect its citizens. So, when it became necessary, the children, expectant mothers, mothers with infants, the elderly, and the disabled were sent to stay with families living in the midland towns where they'd be safe. Those are the towns you should visit, Miss."

The memory of the ghost in the bridal shop still made Hayley uncomfortable. "If the children were evacuated, why would a little girl haunt a store in London?"

"The plan looked good on paper," Lenny replied. "But nearly half the evacuees returned home for one reason or another. In the end, only a third of the children had stayed where they were placed. So, there's a good chance she might have died in the shop or whatever the building was before the war."

Lenny drove down the avenue parallel to the Thames. When he reached Westminster Bridge, he stopped at the intersection. "Do you wish to exit the car and have a looksee, sir?"

Lee glanced out his window. "No, thanks. It's snowing. Let's drive around awhile." He touched Hayley's arm and pointed across the street. "Big Ben and Westminster Palace are right there. Hard to see from the car. This isn't the time of year to sightsee."

"We're only here for New Year's," Hayley said. "We don't have time to see it all."

"There's never enough time," Lee replied.

"I'll drive across the bridge and circle around," Lenny told them. "You'll have a better view of the palace and Elizabeth's Tower on the way back across the Thames."

"Perfect," Lee replied.

Lenny turned.

A vision took Hayley away from sightseeing. Planes flew above the city. The one being chased had narrower wings than the other. A small cross decorated the plane's body and underwing, its nose yellow as well as its tail assembly.

The plane in pursuit had circles within circles on its side and beneath the wings. It flew at high speeds, looping around and shadowing its target. To Hayley, the fight looked evenly matched.

Then her vision ended, replaced by the sight of streetlights illuminating the green seven-arch Gothic bridge. Hayley shrugged off the visual intrusion and mentioned it to no one. *In the morning, I'll block all this residual energy.*

She glanced out the back window at the clock tower. The Palace of Westminster, as well as Elizabeth's Tower, were brightly lit. Big Ben chimed, announcing the time.

Seven o'clock already.

The vision made her wonder. "Lenny, I'm surprised the Houses of Parliament and the clock tower weren't destroyed during the war."

"This area, west central London, wasn't target rich. The bulk of the attacks were in the east end, where most of the docks, factories, and other strategic sites were. That's not to say some places in this area weren't hit. On the west side of the Thames, bombs destroyed St. Thomas's Hospital. Five incendiaries fell on the Abbey just west of the Palace of Westminster. The palace itself was bombed fourteen times. On one of those occasions, the palace took at least twelve hits. A bomb fell in the Old Palace Yard and damaged St. Stephen's Porch. Incendiary bombs fell on the House of Commons and Westminster Hall. And a bomb also hit the Lords Chamber. It went through the floor but was a damp squib."

"A 'damp squib'?" Hayley asked.

"It failed to explode, Miss."

"That's a lot of bombing on a place considered a nontarget," Lee said.

"It's common to find areas that were hit for no apparent reason. I was told the German pilots missed their marks quite frequently. It could have been worse. To this day, we are still finding bombs that never exploded."

"Was Big Ben damaged?" Hayley asked.

"Yes. A bomb strike damaged the tower and broke the glass on the clock's face, but it didn't hurt the bells and mechanisms. Big Ben kept chiming."

Lee looked at Hayley. "Sounds like no matter where we go, you'll experience some visions of the war. Is there any way you can block the negativity?"

"Yes. But not my dreams."

"The England countryside is beautiful, even during Winter," Lee said. He took her hand and kissed it tenderly. "How would you like to buy a vacation home here. It's an idea I've toyed with since I was twelve and came here with my parents. We could travel throughout England. We'd come home to our own manor every night and make love in front of the fireplace. I'd make sure that your dreams were pleasant."

He was right. She knew being intimate with Lee would consume her with desire and not allow another thought in her mind other than his touch and their heated pleasure. "Sounds seductive. You know that would mean we'd have to visit England a number of times."

"Is that a yes?"

"Yes. It sounds exciting."

"You don't know how happy that makes me," he said.

Lenny drove across the River Thames again in the direction of Westminster. He told them tales of kings and queens and the palace's history. After an hour's worth of sightseeing, he returned them to the hotel.

Lenny opened the rear car door, allowing Hayley and Lee to exit.

"Thank you, Lenny," Lee said. "It was a wonderful night. I guess we'll see you in a bit?"

"Thank you, sir. Yes, I'll be quick about it."

Hayley and Lee made their way to the elevator and back to the penthouse. Less than fifteen minutes after they'd arrived, Lenny knocked.

Lee invited him in.

He handed Hayley the photo. "I don't know how it works, your abilities, Miss. I made a copy so you can take your time if need be."

"Thank you, Lenny," she said. "I'll be out of town for a few days. If I have any information, I'll get back to you."

"That will be fine, Miss. Have a safe drive and enjoy England."

Lee saw him to the door.

Hayley studied the photo. The crack's pattern seemed familiar. She searched for her purse, dug out her phone, and pulled up the shot she had taken of the bridal shop's mirror. Chills went up and down her spine. "Lee, come here a minute."

He hurried to her side.

"Take a look at this."

"The cracks are identical," he said.

CHAPTER 4

"It was nice of the hotel to hire us a car this morning," Hayley said as Lee drove the Land Rover out of London.

The spotty rain forecasted for today had skirted by before sunrise, leaving a chilling breeze and random clouds that appeared threatening but moved east without a disturbance.

Once on the motorway, the British-speaking GPS guidance fell silent when Lee discontinued its service. "It's a perk that comes with the penthouse," he said. "Care to drive awhile?"

"Hell no."

"Is that a *hell no*, you might later? Or a *hell no, hell no*?"

"You make it look so easy," she said. "I'd have us in an accident in a matter of minutes."

Hayley considered driving on the left side of the road confusing, not to forget the steering wheel being on the opposite side as American cars. The familiar names she'd been accustomed to, such as freeway and on-and-off ramp, were labeled differently but seemed as natural here as driving at home. Although when it came to the roundabouts, road type classifications, street signs, and even stoplights, she felt relieved Lee had been to England an array of times and seemed comfortable getting around.

"I'm just going to relax and enjoy the day," she said, taking a deep breath and nestling into the leather seat.

"How did you sleep last night?"

"I fell asleep within minutes. As far as I know, I didn't have night visions or bad dreams. It must have been the time change that made me so tired. Otherwise, my mind would've been wrestling with the meaning of the cracked glass."

"Thank goodness for the time change, then," Lee said.

"I decided I can't shield myself from the war's residual energy like I planned. If I do, I may inadvertently block a message from the little girl."

"That's probably a good idea since we don't know what she wants yet," he said.

Hayley grabbed her purse from the floorboard and retrieved the broken-window photo Lenny had given her. She held the snapshot between her palms and closed her eyes, hoping to get a psychic sense of what it meant.

"Any clues?" Lee asked.

"Nothing." She returned the photo to her purse and set her purse by her feet.

"Maybe the two incidents were meaningless," Lee said. "Ghosts are active in haunted houses all the time for no particular reason."

"So, you want me to think of England as being one big, haunted house?" She thought about that a moment. "You should be a director. That would be one of the scariest movies ever made."

But she couldn't deny his suggestion had merit. He had been interested in the paranormal all his life. It had been Jim who had taken Lee and Roger as boys to every haunted house in Sutterville, North Carolina. And Jim knew of quite a few because he'd worked for years to restore downtown and homes in the area. He loved talking about those days, and Hayley enjoyed listening. She'd learned a lot about Lee's childhood from the stories.

"You could be right," she told Lee.

"How's your ability to see auras working out? Have you controlled it yet?"

Hayley thought about the hours she had spent learning

to perfect her skill to see the energy encircling people and other things. She'd been given two new abilities since she began working for Paranormal, Search, and Analysis: the gift of astral projection and one other, the capability to see auras which she had received a little over a month ago. At first, it seemed an annoyance to see every living thing surrounded by a colorful energy field. After studying the meanings of each color, she found it fascinating. She discovered how to disengage the skill and use it only when necessary. Over the last couple of weeks, she had learned to master it, just as she had all her other psychic gifts.

"It's under control, thank goodness. I can see someone in the medical field or even a psychologist using the ability. But why me?"

"That's going to be interesting to find out," Lee said. "So, you're saying you can just look at a person, see their aura whenever you want to, then return your vision to normalcy?"

"Yes. During our trip, I'm planning to practice. It'll take time until I can instantly interpret the colors. It's a lot to comprehend."

"I can imagine."

Hayley glanced out the window. Leafless deciduous trees and easements lined the roadsides, making it difficult at times to see beyond. When she caught a glimpse of the countryside, she saw plots of land or rolling fields neatly separated by hedgerows or stone walls. The sun had peeked through the clouds. Last night's rain had melted most of the remaining snow, leaving only the last of the icy remnants lying in the hedgerow shadows.

"So, what's the plan for today?" Hayley asked. "How many towns or villages are we going to visit?"

"My goal is three. There's no need to rush. I'd like you to buy whatever catches your eye. Since you'll be moving in with me, it'll be *our* house now. So, I want it to feel like your home. It wouldn't bother me if you want to redecorate. I'm touched you want to continue the tradition my parents started by adding to their collection of handmade crafts. We can start our own memories."

She had almost forgotten about giving Kathy her Victorian house as a Christmas gift. Once they returned to Sutterville, she would move in with Lee.

Hayley remembered Lee had said his mansion had been designed after an English manor. Its overwhelming size would give her a challenge to decorate. The three-story, red-brick mansion had two wings extending forward, lengthened by three-story round towers protruding from each wing. Double-hung twelve-pane windows, regimented in size, extended the height of each room.

It'll take me the rest of my life to make Lee's home feel like mine as well. So far, I only have half my wardrobe in his closet, and I've given Kathy everything else. When I move, I'll only have a trunk load of things to bring over. So, he's right. I'll need to get started.

The third floor contained seven bedrooms. And Lee's chambers took up the entire north wing.

The second floor had a music room in the north tower, a ballroom that extended nearly the entire length of the home and overlooked the gardens in the backyard, a dining room, more bedrooms, plus a few other rooms for visitors and social events. The only rooms on this floor she wouldn't attempt to decorate would be Jim's chambers. Jim, whom Lee considered to be his second dad, had taken up residence on the second floor after Lee's parents died nearly fifteen years ago.

"It would be great to look around the house and see *our* home," she said.

Lee smiled. "I'd like that too."

He changed lanes and turned off the motorway. After following the carriageway for a few miles, he turned onto a narrow two-lane road. Amid the hedges and trees lining the road, a fence here and there led to secluded old farmhouses. While they drove, the number of dormant trees became prevalent. More homes,

Tudor style, stone, and cottages, some with thatched roofs, sat on the edge of the village.

When the road ended, Lee veered left toward the center of town. High Road narrowed where cars were parked on one side, making it less spacious. Shops, taverns, and eateries lined both sides of the street.

Lee parked, exited the car, and hurried around to open Hayley's door.

She offered him her hand. The cold wind rustled her long light-brown hair once she stepped out. Striving to keep warm, she adjusted the scarf around her neck and fastened the top button of her coat.

Lee closed the car door behind her, and they walked around the car.

When she reached the sidewalk, she gazed up the street. A gray-haired man, wearing a knitted scarf and a brown coat, walked his beagle and entered a tavern a few doors down. A woman riding a bicycle stopped, climbed off, and propped her bike against the wall of a knitting shop across the street. Three other women, dressed in coats and scarves, walked briskly toward the same shop. *A women's circle, maybe.*

Hayley strolled with Lee to a cottage-style shop where they saw a variety of gifts for sale in the eighteen-pane window. "Do you think any of these are handmade?" she asked.

"I'm sure you can count on it. Maybe not all local, though."

Lee held the door for her. A young woman greeted them while dusting items on a shelf.

"Morning. Out for a drive, are you?" She stepped down from a wooden stepstool. "Don't mind the place. Only a few bits and bobs left after Christmas. Have a looksee. Let me know if you need my help."

"Thank you." Hayley glanced around. Across the room lay an array of quilts, pillows, and lampshades. Doilies, runners, tablecloths, and aprons were displayed near wood-crafted items such as chairs and larger furniture. On the wall to her right, a glass display case featured jewelry, scarves, hats, and leather purses. Paintings and bas-relief carvings hung on the walls. She strolled to sculptures made of clay, wood, and metal.

Lee followed.

"Seems like a lot left over from Christmas," she told him.

He nodded.

A life-sized Labrador retriever carved in birch caught her eye. *It will look good next to the fireplace*, she thought. "I like this," she told Lee. "What do you think?"

"I can picture him in the library. Good choice."

On a shelf next to the statue, a set of rearing-horse bookends looked to have been carved by the same craftsman. She read the name of the artist on its label and found her assumption correct. "And these?" she asked.

"Another good choice."

Hayley tried to picture a place in her soon-to-be home where a painting of an English countryside would look best. Lee's sitting room came to mind. *Twenty inches by sixteen inches would look great on the mantle.* She imagined the color of the room's walls — the green of the apples just before they blushed red on the tree in the front yard of Kathy's soon-to-be home. The room's blue carpet reminded her of a sky reflecting in a crystal pond and the fireplace in white marble. *This will be perfect.* "And this for the sitting room."

"Yes." He glanced over his shoulder. "I'm going to talk to the shopkeeper to make sure they are handcrafted and see about shipping."

"Great."

Hayley wandered to the jewelry display and noticed what looked to be ID bracelets with numbers etched into a piece of rectangular silver-plated metal along with a name and their military rank. A leather strap went around the wrist, and a card attached told the hero's story. When she lifted one from the counter, a vision filled her sight. She stood in front of the headstone of a World War II pilot in a graveyard by a Gothic church. His name echoed the inscription on the bracelet. The last moments of his life played like a movie in her mind. His heart pounded as he flew his Spitfire, diving and looping, trying to escape the German fighter plane on his tail. In a blazing flash, his plane took a hit, and his life ceased.

When Hayley set the bracelet down, the image faded away. She picked up another. She envisioned a different graveyard by a Romanesque-style church and again stood in front of a military grave. This time she witnessed a soldier's death, then released the vision.

Hayley held up the bracelet. "Excuse me. Please, could you tell me something about this piece?"

The young woman left Lee to fill out the shipping information and joined her.

"That's a bit of all right," the shopkeeper said. "Harry Tibbs's son, Finley, makes these bracelets to honor our fallen heroes. Harry himself is a World War II veteran. The numbers are the longitudes and latitudes throughout England where each is laid to rest."

That explains the visions. "What a unique idea," Hayley said, putting the keepsake back onto the table.

"Here you go," Lee said, setting the pen on the counter. "I'll show you what we've decided on so far." He left his written information by the register and showed her the desired pieces.

Once the shopkeeper noted their purchases, she hurried back to the counter and retrieved his mailing details. "Just let me know, sir, if there will be something else, and I'll take care of everything."

"Thank you." He joined Hayley. "Find anything else interesting?"

She told him about the bracelets and visions. "It would be impossible for me to buy one. Each time I'd touched it, I'd have visions of the hero's gravesite." She looked around the shop. "I guess I'm finished here. Let's move on to the next shop."

"That will be all," Lee told the shop keeper. "Thank you for your help."

"You're very welcome," she said. "I'll send these off directly. Have a great day. It's a bit Baltic out there, so keep warm."

"Thank you." Hayley exited the door Lee held open for her.

"How about a hot totty or a glass of wine before we hit the road," Lee suggested.

"Something warm to drink sounds good about now," she replied.

They walked the short distance to the pub. Lee pulled on the brass handle and opened one of the green double doors, allowing Hayley to go inside. The smell of hickory filled the air. The man with the dog Hayley had seen earlier sat at a table eating. A man wearing a pullover sweater and jeans approached them, carrying two menus.

"Good day to you," he said to them. "Would you like a seat at the bar or a table?"

"We'll just have a couple of drinks by the fireplace if you don't mind," Lee told him.

He led them to a seating area in front of a crackling fire. Hayley sat in a butterscotch plaid armchair while Lee eased himself into a brown leather club. The waiter took their order and returned to serve them within minutes.

"Thank you," Lee told him as the man turned to leave them.

"This is perfect," Hayley said. "Where do we go from here?"

"There's another town not far from here that I'd like to visit. There's a gallery there that I think you'll enjoy."

"That sounds promising," she said.

A man wearing gray pants and an off-white cable-knit sweater joined them. "Do you mind if I warm my frost-nipped hands by the fire?" he asked them.

"Please," Lee told him.

The man who seated them walked over. "How's the morning treating you, Chadwick?" he asked the man rubbing his hands together by the hearth.

"I was supposed to meet a prospective client here to entice him into buying the Denton cottage. But he cancelled. Would you mind if I have a cup of coffee, lad? I have a few hours to relax before heading home."

"Would you like cream?"

"Yes, please, unless you have to milk the cow."

"We're milking the goat today, and she's been a fisty beast. Her milk will put hair on your behind, and you're a man who looks like he needs a wide patch of extra fur to keep you warm."

"Then make it black and keep the hair out of it."

"You've made a fine choice," the waiter said. "I'll be back before the nip leaves your bum."

Chadwick chuckled, and the waiter dashed off.

"This is Hayley, and I'm Lee. Are you a realtor by chance?"

"I am indeed. Are you shopping for a new home?" He sat on the love seat across from them.

"A vacation manor," Lee told him. "Five or six bedrooms, a number of bathrooms, something around two or three million US dollars."

"I'm Chadwick Whitmore, by the by." He rose and shook Lee's and Hayley's hands.

"It's a pleasure to meet you," Lee said.

"I think I have just what you're looking for. The manor is 8,000 square feet. It has seven bedrooms and four full baths. Would you like to have a looksee?"

"Yes, please," Lee replied.

"Let me know when your set to go."

Lee and Hayley waited until Chadwick drank his coffee before they grabbed their coats and followed him outside.

***

They drove to the end of a quiet country lane when they arrived at the estate. Chadwick exited his Bentley and drew back the double iron gates. Once in the driver's seat again, he drove them down a long driveway leading to a graveled courtyard surrounded by the manor house, a brick barn, and another outbuilding. He parked, and they got out.

Hayley glanced around.

"It's a 17th Century stone-built home with a stone slate roof. And as you can see, there are many fireplaces throughout. He opened the brown wood door and ushered them inside. "These are the original flagged floors in the entrance hall. Mullioned windows throughout. This staircase leads to the second floor. The oldest construction of the manor is what you see as you drive up. Through the centuries, additions were built, creating a U-shaped floor plan."

Hayley glanced up at the low hand-hewn beams and plaster ceiling as they followed him through a doorway leading to a dining room. Again, beams made the room seem small. *This feels claustrophobic*, she through. A wide fireplace with a stone-carved mantle encompassed the majority of the wall that included a doorway leading into another room.

"In the 17th Century, this would've been the kitchen. This door leads to the present kitchen constructed a century later." He led them into the addition.

They stepped down onto a multi-colored brick floor. And again, wood beams spanned the length of the room as well as across.

"Everything needs updating. The floor will have to be replaced," she whispered to Lee. "And it seems to be closed in."

"I agree," Lee told her. "I just want to get an idea of what to expect as we shop around."

"If you'll follow me," Chadwick told them. He stepped up as he walked through the doorway and into the next room. "Here we have the library."

Bookcases hugged bright green walls on both sides of a fireplace. *The wood and marble mantle and surround would have to go,* Hayley thought. A large area rug covered dark wide-plank floors. And again, beams crossed the ceiling. "Do you think they're structural," she asked Lee.

"It's a good possibility." He glanced out a twelve-pane window overlooking a half-frozen pond. "How many acres does this property sit on?"

"There are two hundred acres of fields and woodlands. Plus, a paddock and stables. And, of course, I must mention the tennis court and inground swimming pool."

"I don't want to take up your time," Lee said. "It's a very nice home, but we're looking for something with less acreage and preferably no stables."

"I understand." Chadwick grabbed his wallet from his pant pocket, rummaged through it, pulled out a business card, and handed it to Lee. "If you'd like to leave your phone number, I'll see what I can find that meets your needs."

Lee responded by handing him his card.

Chadwick read the information. "Paranormal Search and Analysis. Am I correct to assume you hunt for ghosts?"

"Correct," Lee said. "But we're on vacation."

"How utterly interesting. You'd have no trouble finding them in England. We're up to our nickers in them."

"I should add to our property prerequisites. No unseen permanent residents."

"That may be a hard order to fill," Chadwick told him. "Let's head back, and if anything comes up, I'll bell you up."

Once Chadwick locked the front door, they piled into the car and drove back to the pub.

"Thanks very much for your help," Lee said to Chadwick

after they parked and got out.

"The pleasure was mine," he replied. "I'll get back to you if I find anything that you may like."

"We plan on flying back to the States in a couple of days," Lee told him. "My e-mail address is on my card. If you find anything interesting, I'd appreciate it very much if you'd forward the information to me. Thanks again for your time. Have a great day."

"Have a grand day, yourselves, and a nice flight home." He went back inside the pub.

Hayley and Lee walked to the Rover and climbed in.

"I didn't care much for that place," Hayley said.

"Neither did I," Lee said. "But it's interesting to see what we'll be looking at for the price we want to pay." He started the car. "On to the next village."

As Lee drove away, Hayley glanced at the giftshop, remembering the engraved bracelets. In that instant, she clearly saw Harry Tibbs's wrinkled face in her mind, his toothless smile turning to a frown, the color of his eyes covered with cataracts. He leaned forward in his ash wood rocking chair and seemed to be speaking directly to her. *You must hurry,* he said.

CHAPTER 5

Lee drove North on High Road while Hayley told him about her vision of Harry Tibbs.

"I know you're psychic, but are you sure it was him?" Lee asked. "You've never seen his face before."

"I'm positive."

"Who was he talking too? You know anyone you view in the present can't see you when you use your intuitive sight."

"I know," Hayley replied. "But I swear he was speaking to me." She saw the puzzled look on Lee's face.

"You've looked in on me using your gift plenty of times, and I've never felt your presence."

"You're right," she said.

"Did you purposely search him out?" Lee asked.

"No. I don't have to want to foresee someone's past, present, or future before I receive a vision. Information comes to me now and again, especially if I've thought about them or had a question about something in the recent past. That could explain the reason for the vision, but it doesn't explain his talking to me directly. That's unheard of unless he's gifted or has passed away, which I don't think he has, by the way the shopkeeper spoke of him. Or he's a warlock."

"I could be wrong, but I'm more than certain Harry Tibbs isn't a warlock," Lee said. "Why don't we go back and ask how to contact him. If he were talking to you, wouldn't it be a good idea to find out what he meant by *you must hurry*?"

"Yes. I don't need another mystery."

A little way ahead, Lee circled the roundabout and headed again to the gift shop. He parked where he had before. They left the Land Rover and entered the shop.

They found the shopkeeper on the phone.

She finished her conversation and ended the call. "Brilliant. Did you fancy something else?"

Hayley stepped forward. "Do you happen to have Harry Tibbs's son's business card?"

"Oh yes, Miss." She reached under the counter, retrieved a card, wrote something on the back, and handed it to Hayley. "My name's Libby. I've put my name and number on the back in case you'd like to contact me. I'm afraid Finley isn't accepting special orders at this time. His father has taken a turn for the worst."

"Oh, I'm sorry. Is he ill?"

"He was fit as the butcher's dog up until he took a spill."

"Will he be all right?"

"It's early days. He's been in a coma for three days, Miss. Finley's Aunt just belled me up to let me know about the church services tonight. The whole town will be saying a prayer for him."

Hayley felt stunned to realize Harry had been in a coma when he reached out to her. She looked at the card in her hand. *Did he cross over? Was he really speaking to me?* "Tell him we'll say a prayer for his dad."

"Yes, Miss. Is there anything else I can do for you?"

"You've been more than helpful," Lee said. "We'll keep his card, thank you. There's nothing else."

Lee and Hayley turned to leave.

"Cheers," the shop keeper said. "Enjoy your day."

"Thank you." Lee opened the shop door for Hayley, and they walked silently to the car. "Have you ever had a vision from someone in a coma?" he asked while holding open the passenger door for her.

"It's hard to tell." She climbed in and tried to recall.

He hurried around, entered the vehicle, and settled in. "What do you mean by, *it's hard to tell*?"

"It's not always obvious where a vision comes from. But if I had to make a logical guess, I'd say yes, it was highly likely I've had communication with someone in a coma. While the body is damaged and comatose, the soul has the freedom to travel back and forth between the body and Heaven. Foresight and knowledge are obtained whenever the soul crosses over. While Harry's in that altered state, it would be possible for him to relay a message to me. There's no doubt about it."

"So, do you think that's what happened?"

"Yes," Hayley replied. "Too bad the message was so ambiguous." She took a deep calming breath, letting it out slowly. "It's not easy having the gift of insight. Intent, in many cases, is impossible to decipher. Vague visions have confused me most of my life."

"What happens if the message is important?"

"Usually, the message gets clearer. And if I ignore it, I'll be hit over the head, so to speak, until I respond."

"I guess we'll wait and see." Lee started the vehicle, pulled away from the curb, and drove in the direction they had previously traveled before turning around. He followed the narrow road out of town. Fields which would be enriched by crops during the spring and summer appeared bare, the hedgerows surrounding them leafless and gray.

Lee drove for miles before coming to the next town on his list. Along High Street, brick terrace buildings lined the road, each a different color to indicate individual shops, some with canvas awnings. He parked in front of a gallery.

The wind whipped Hayley's hair as she stepped from the vehicle. She crossed her arms in an attempt to stay warm. The sound of the store's canvas canopy shuddering in the breeze muted a dog's bark in the distance, and bells chimed the noon hour from a church down the street. She walked briskly with Lee at her side.

He held the door for her and closed it tightly after entering.

A tall thin gallery steward in jeans and a turtleneck sweater, his long gray hair in a ponytail, stepped out of the back room. "Welcome. Come in out of the cold."

"Thank you," Lee said.

"Americans, are you? Come for New Year's?"

"Yes," Hayley replied. "We arrived early to do some shopping."

"You've come to the right place. Most items are made by locals from a few towns here and about. If you see something that catches your fancy, give me a shout. I'll just get out of your way and let you shop."

"Thank you." Hayley gazed around. Paintings covered the wall to the left, sculptures made from a multitude of mediums were prominently displayed throughout the gallery, and wind chimes of all shapes and sizes hung in the window. A blown-glass vase resting on a shelf near a collection of stained-glass suncatchers caught her eye.

She thought about Lee's gardens and last summer when she'd first strolled down the carpets of grass pathways crisscrossing between manicured boxwood hedges and English holly, which framed colorful flowers. Each day Lee's chef cut beautiful bouquets and displayed them throughout his home.

This vase would be perfect, a masterpiece.

Her eye caught a movement in an oval mirror framed with hundreds of seashells. The image of the gallery in its reflective glass changed. Instead, Hayley saw a graveyard where a child danced among the headstones. In that moment, the child stopped twirling about and glided to the face of the mirror. Panic filled Hayley as she glanced around at all the breakables. "Don't you dare crack anything," she told the ghost.

When the little girl danced away, whirling and swaying around the cemetery again, and the image in the mirror reflected the gallery once again, Hayley let out a relieved sigh. But when she reached out to examine the glass vase that she admired, the room shivered. Nervously, Hayley gazed into the mirror again, and the child with her dirty hair and torn dress stared back at her.

Hayley gasped, stepped back, and looked about. Every artisan's piece seemed to tremble. Wind chimes played their music as if a light breeze had swept through the room. She noticed the concern on Lee's face, as if he waited to see if he would grab her hand and lead her outside or wait it out. In that instant, the movement stopped.

The gallery steward jumped up from the stool behind the rear counter and hurried toward them. "Just a little tremor. We have them from time to time."

"Thank you," Lee said. "We're fine."

"I saw the little girl in the mirror," Hayley whispered to Lee. "Did she do that, or was it really an earthquake?"

"According to the gallery worker, this happens often. I'd go with a tremor, as he called it."

She nodded, not all together convinced. "It was just a coincidence, then. Thank goodness nothing broke."

"Did you find something of interest?" the gallery steward asked.

Hayley pointed to a tall cobalt blue oval vase. "May I please have that one?"

"Champion. Will you be taking it with you or shipping, Miss?"

"Shipping," Lee replied.

The gallery steward lifted the vase. "If you don't mind following me, sir. I'll need a bit of information."

Lee trailed him while Hayley continued to stroll around the shop. A map of England drew her attention. The gilded intricately-carved three-feet by four-feet frame enclosed the painstakingly-meticulous map combining geological details and roads, towns, and scenic interests. She located London and moved her finger across the glass, allowing her to find the vicinity of the hotel along the Thames where they stayed to see the fireworks. From there, she followed the route they drove to the first town they had come to, where they had bought the carved pieces and the painting to put above the mantle in Lee's sitting room. Then she followed the roads to the village where they now perused the gallery. When Lee rejoined her, she showed him her new find.

"Yes," Lee said. "I love it." He called the gallery attendant over. "We'll take this piece as well."

"Splendid." The attendant removed it from the wall and carried it to the back room.

The wind chimes in the window stirred. Hayley jumped and glanced up at the crystal chandelier. It didn't move. The panic she had felt earlier still lurked within her. Her awareness and psychic senses stayed alert, expecting a stronger jolt that would shatter everything in the shop. The emotion, unfounded or not, made her want to dash out the door. "Why don't we get a bite to eat. Aren't you hungry?"

"Famished. There's a little café up the street, or we can get a bite in the pub next door."

"Let's try the pub," Hayley said. "A glass of wine sounds good."

The gallery steward opened the door for them. "Cheerio. Thank you for stopping by. Have a safe trip home. I'll have your purchase sent out directly."

"Thank you," Hayley said.

"Thanks again," Lee told him.

After the door closed, she turned to Lee. "That was unsettling. I'm surprised nothing got broken."

Lee strolled alongside her to the pub. "I've visited England a couple of times when they've had a quake. I've been told that they usually register between 3.0 and 5.0. Enough to make you cringe, knowing how old these buildings are in the UK and not retrofitted for earthquakes. Tremors, they like to call them here."

The tavern's black wood façade encased several multipaned windows. Lee gripped the brass handle and pulled the door open, allowing Hayley to enter, then followed her just as it began to rain.

"Good day to you," a middle-aged man said from behind the rich mahogany bar.

"Good day," they replied in unison, hanging their coats by the door.

Hayley surveyed her surroundings. Wood beams crossed the low ceiling. The warm tones of European mahogany made the atmosphere inviting. Customers at the bar talked loudly and laughed. Only a few tables were occupied. A sign read Please, take a seat. Hayley headed to the empty table in front of the brick fireplace, Lee at her heels. Once they sat, a man wearing an apron approached them.

"Good midday to you. What will you have on this cold day? A pint perhaps, or maybe a bit of hot stew to warm your soul?"

"Does stew sound good to you?" Lee asked Hayley.

"Extremely."

"We'll both have stew," Lee told him. "I'll have a pint of Guinness, please."

"And I'll have a glass of Merlot," Hayley told him.

"Good choice," the waiter said. "Stew's our specialty. Mum's finished cooking a pot just minutes ago." He glanced around the room. "The weather will be warming up as the day goes on. Can you believe it'll be in the high fifties on New Year's? It's a first. I'll be back shortly with your order." He turned and walked toward the kitchen.

"That's good news," Lee said. "The temperature will be rising from the low forties to the fifties."

"That will be appreciated," Hayley said. "Did you pick our bed and breakfast?"

"I left that up to Lewis," Lee said. "He planned our entire

trip. All I have to do is drive. I don't know what I'd do without him."

She understood what Lee meant. Lewis had been hired to oversee Lee's mansion and had a hand in everything. *A man of many talents.* He had asked her for the opportunity to plan their wedding. Hayley couldn't refuse. She didn't have a word for the position he held. The closest term would be family. *Why would I say no?*

"Do you know if the bed and breakfast is haunted?" she asked. "I've heard a lot of them in England are, according to Jim."

"I made sure Lewis found us a place that's ghost-free. Don't worry. Lewis knows you're a spirit magnet."

Hayley reached into her purse, retrieved her cell phone, and answered a call, putting it on speaker so Lee could hear. "We were just talking about you, Lewis. What's up?" she asked.

"I'm in the midst of planning the weddings, Miss, and I need to know where you and Mr. Franklin would like to have the reception?"

She glanced at Lee. "Our house," he said.

Hayley smiled. *Our house.*

She remembered the first time she had seen Lee's mansion. She, Lee, and the team of investigators from Paranormal Search and Analysis had arrived home from a case that had taken them halfway around the world, during which her relationship with Lee blossomed.

They had spent days getting to know one another. But in all that time, Lee had said nothing about his wealth. They returned home, and after a short meeting at the office, she had looked forward to having dinner at Lee's along with Roger and Laura. On the way, Lee took her to a mansion to show her the gardens, hiding the fact he owned the estate. When he tried to tell her it belonged to him, she didn't believe him.

Now it's my home. And we're having our reception in the ballroom, the very room where he proposed to me. The largest of five chandeliers hung in the center of the capacious rectangular room, its width spanning practically the length of the mansion. The walls, painted shades of pale green with gold trim, rose to meet a high ceiling adorned with a fresco depicting the gardens of Florence.

Last October, Lee had thrown a charity costume ball for Children's Hospital, and two hundred people attended. *The number of guests coming to our reception will be somewhat less.* Lee had been an only child, the same as she. His and her parents died in accidents, and all other relatives on both sides of their families had passed away. *That doesn't mean the wedding will have few guests. Lee has an immense number of friends, plus Roger's and Laura's families and friends will be there. And I can't leave out Grams, my parents, Lee's parents, or any other spirits who wish to attend. It's going to be wonderful.*

"To be fair, I will talk to Roger and Laura for their preference," Lee said. "If he agrees with us to have the reception at our home or not, either way, I'll get back to you."

"Yes, sir," Lewis replied. "Also, Miss, have you and Miss Song picked your wedding colors?"

"Yes. Purple, yellow, and white."

"Fabulous. Also, it would be a delight to choose a band to your liking, and of course, I must move quickly, for time is short."

"We'll leave that up to you, Lewis," Lee told him. "I'm sure you know our music preference by now."

"Yes, sir," Lewis said. "I thought the band I had hired for the charity ball would fit the occasion."

"Perfect," Hayley said.

"Splendid," Lewis said. "How is England? I hope you're having a grand time."

"We've had a ghost-sighting, a few paranormal experiences, and an earthquake," Hayley told him. "Nothing unusual except the earthquake. Is England on a fault?"

"I'm on the computer now," Lewis said. "Let me check into it." His research took only a moment. "The UK has about 200 earthquakes a year but only 20 or 30 are felt by the population. The cause is unknown, although they are believed to have been triggered by either faults deep within the ground or Earth's continuous recovery from the ice sheets that covered the UK thousands of years ago."

"Interesting," Lee replied. "Are the quakes major?"

"A major earthquake is seldom felt, sir. Nothing to worry about."

"Thanks, Lewis. By the way, Hayley has found a wedding dress, and it'll be shipped to the house. We'll probably be home before it arrives. Plus, there are a few other items we've purchased that will be delivered. Just a heads-up."

"Thank you, sir. I'll let the staff know. Have a delightful time and a safe trip home."

"Thank you, Lewis," Hayley said.

***

Once their food had been served and they finished their meals, Lee and Hayley relaxed, savoring their drinks while enjoying the heat from the fireplace.

"What should we do next?" Lee asked. "Do you want to drive straight to the bed and breakfast to check in or head to another town and hit a few more shops first?"

"There's an antique store across the street that I'd like to browse."

"Really? I'm surprised you'd want to go into a place like that after all the stories you told me about ghosts attaching themselves to old things."

"It's residual energy that's attached to an object. But I do believe an item can be haunted. I once brought an antique mirror home and wished I hadn't. I don't think the ghost is physically connected but mentally attached instead. For instance, a jockey may be attached to his race car."

Lee chuckled. "Good analogy, sort of, but a jockey races a horse, not a car. Although, I know what you mean. So, wouldn't that worry you a bit to shop in an antique store since you're a magnet for ghosts?"

"It's actually rare that a piece is haunted. It would be interesting seeing what someone from England would consider an antique. This country is so old there would be things displayed that I'd never see in America."

"Okay," Lee said. "I'm ready when you are."

She pushed away her empty wine glass and stood. Lee rose and left the tip. When they walked to the door, they retrieved their coats from the coat tree. Once Lee buttoned his jacket and adjusted his scarf, he grabbed the brass doorknob, held the door open for Hayley, and followed her outside.

Although the rain had stopped, a nip in the air forced Hayley to pull up her coat's hood. They hurried across the dampened road and glanced in the shop's window. She loved the assortment of teacups and teapots. A birdcage held a stuffed bulldog. Stained-glass lamp shades rested on intricately carved brass lamps. *Some of these dolls displayed could give me nightmares.*

Inside, a few feet from the entrance, a dressing table caught Hayley's interest. She wandered over to it and admired a silver box resting on top of a crocheted doily. While Lee glanced over her shoulder, she retrieved the box and lifted its lid. The dressing table began to vibrate, making her second-guess her decision to venture inside.

"Might be one of those rare occasions," he whispered to her.

Hayley quickly closed the lid, and the vibration stopped. She gently set the box back onto the doily. "You were right. Coming here probably wasn't a good idea." She spun around and headed out the door. Without taking the time to pull up her coat's hood, Hayley hurried across the street with Lee at her side. Once inside the rental car, they made new plans.

"To the bed and breakfast, it is, then," Lee said. He started the car and pulled away from the curb. "That could've been an aftershock."

"It could've been. I didn't sense a ghost or spirit."

"We both know that if a ghost or spirit doesn't want to be detected, not even you would be able to sense their presence."

She couldn't dispute his point. Lee had been ghost-hunting from an early age, even before he became one of the owners of Paranormal Search and Analysis, a business designed to hunt ghosts. *He knows from experience that a void of detection proves nothing. A ghost could be sitting beside us, and if he or she doesn't want to be detected, we'd never know.* She nervously glanced at the backseat. "Let's just get to the bed and breakfast."

"I'm on it."

CHAPTER 6

After arriving at the bed and breakfast Lewis had chosen for them, Hayley and Lee found their room on the second floor.

"He calls this a bed and breakfast?" Hayley said, stepping inside a bedroom nearly the size of Lee's at his mansion. "This is almost a castle."

"It's called a manor. It's a little smaller than some. The owners and their ancestors have lived here for generations. Nowadays, the upkeep is so outrageous they rent out their rooms in order to maintain the estate."

The fire in the stone fireplace crackled. They removed their coats, scarves, and gloves and placed them on a rack by the door. Immediately, Hayley felt the winter chill leave her body.

Their shared suitcase had been brought up while they checked in, and now the bag resided by the end of the king-size bed where Hayley stood, scanning their surroundings. A variety of Persian carpets covered the oak floors. The room was decorated in a pale blue. The bedspread with its multitude of pillows, the long velvet curtains, and the floral upholstered chairs arranged near the fireplace seemed to be snapshots out of an unforgettable designer magazine she recalled seeing not long ago.

Before settling in, she crossed the room to one of the many windows looking over a latent garden, and she admired the distant view. "It must look beautiful in the spring. The countryside seems to go on forever without another neighbor in sight."

"It's well worth the drive." Lee placed their suitcase on the tufted bench at the end of the bed.

"I'm surprised," Hayley told him. "I was expecting a quaint little inn or country home."

He joined her. She felt the warmth of his body pressing against her back, his arms wrapping around her waist, his cheek nestling against her long light brown hair. "Lewis doesn't know how to do *little*. Are you disappointed?" he asked.

"Not in the least."

"What do you want to do?" Lee asked. "There's a village not too far from here that we could explore, or we can go downstairs to have tea in the lounge."

"Let's explore."

"Okay. Put your coat back on, and we'll unpack later."

They retraced their steps through the hallways, down the grand staircase, and past the registration counter.

"Hello," Lee said to the woman behind the desk. Hayley waved.

"Good day," the woman replied. "On your way out? Dinner will be served at six, love. Have a nice afternoon."

"Thank you," Hayley told her.

"I'm taking her into town," Lee said.

"Spot on," the woman replied. "Don't forget to stop at the village pub. Ned Baines comes in near this hour to entertain. He's eighty-seven and still sings like an angel."

"We'll be sure to catch him," Lee said.

Lee drove the Land Rover to the carriageway leading into town. Stone walls lining the road gave way to naked hedges as he drove past farmhouses, their fields bare until spring. The closer to town they came, the higher the leafless hedges grew, scarcely giving privacy to Tudor-style homes and stone cottages with thatched roofs.

At the village pub, Lee parked in front and went around to escort Hayley. She walked with him to the entrance. He pulled the door open, allowing her to enter first, and she went in.

Inside, people sang *The Girl I Left Behind,* accompanying a white-haired elderly man. *Must be Ned.* A young woman serving drinks carried a full tray while weaving through the tables. At the bar, two men slid their empty mugs aside, dismounted their barstools, and headed toward the door, tipping their hats to Hayley as they shuffled by.

"Let's take their seats," Hayley said. She hopped onto the stool, and Lee sat next to her.

"Welcome," the bartender told them. "It's not often this time of year that we have the pleasure of greeting strangers. What can I get you to warm your spirit?"

"Guinness?" he asked Hayley.

She nodded. "Two half pints of Guinness, please."

"Straight away."

Hayley turned and surveyed the room. The atmosphere seemed cozy. An array of people sat around the tables, and a couple more besides her and Lee gathered at the bar. From her vantage point, Hayley could see each individual. Ned, holding a microphone, sat on a stool near the fireplace. A mix of ages and genders shared tables.

Hayley closed her eyes, allowing her consciousness to call upon her gift to see auras. Then she opened her eyes. Since Thanksgiving, she'd been learning about auras, the energy field with its layers of colors surrounding each person. Usually, the phenomenon radiated three feet from the human body. Unfortunately, the packed pub forced customers to huddle close to one another, making an individual's aura difficult for Hayley to read. She gazed around. *A crowded room won't do. I need to practice, but this is ridiculous.*

It bothered her to have a talent and know so little about it. Patience never came easy to her when it concerned mastering a new ability. She had been born with the gift to visualize the past, present, and future, plus seeing and speaking to the dead. The ability to use astral projection, allowing her spirit to leave her body and travel to another location; nudging, which lets her send a cognitive message to another; and now the ability to view auras were given to her throughout the past six months.

When Hayley looked toward Ned, his persona caught her attention. Auras surrounded everyone in the room except him. *That's peculiar. Am I blocked for some reason?* She stared at him, blinked, closed her eyes and opened them, then squinted. *Nothing. How strange. There's so much I still have to learn.* She decided to give up and wait for another time and place to make an attempt.

"Learn anything interesting?" Lee asked.

She shook her head. "It's too crowded."

When the bartender placed their beers in front of them, Lee pulled money from his wallet and placed it on the counter.

Across the room, Ned sang *Early One Morning*. Then he joined friends at a table.

Hayley noticed a couple's thick Scottish brogues when they walked past. "Is Scotland far?" she asked Lee.

"Not really. Scotland covers the northern third of the island and borders England to the southeast. It's a separate country but belongs to the United Kingdom of Great Britain. Cool fact—Northern Scotland used to be part of the supercontinent 450 million years ago. It wasn't until hundreds of millions of years later that a crack in the Earth's surface led to a landmass separation. Over time, that landmass collided with this continent and became Northern Scotland, as it is today. While we sit here, a fault line 300 miles long, like the San Andreas on the West Coast back home, is under Loch Ness and runs through the center of Scotland."

The information nudged her psychic instincts, leaving her with a strong feeling that the next earthquake could be more intense. "Do you think that fault line has anything to do with the earthquakes we felt?"

Lee shook his head. "It's been dormant for 60 million

years."

"Maybe it slipped."

"I would think if that were the case, the earthquake would be larger than a 3.0."

"That sounds logical. But my psychic sense is telling me that these minor quakes are leading to something major."

"Hopefully, we'll be back home before that happens." He glanced at his watch. "We have time to kill. We passed an estate management office down the road. Want to stop by and see what's for sale in this area?"

She realized only a few sips of beer remained in her mug. "Sure."

They left the pub, hopped in the Rover, and drove to a row of shops where he had seen the relator's sign on the drive into town. Once they parked and got out of the car, they could see through the window a man at his desk talking on the phone. Lee held the door for Hayley as they entered the office.

The man looked their way. "I'll be right with you. Please have a seat." He ended his conversation, hung up the phone, and invited them to join him at his desk. "I'm Donald Landing." He shook their hands. "You're new to the area. How may I help you?"

"Yes," Lee told him. "From the US. We're shopping around for a vacation home here in England."

"Splendid. What are you looking for?"

"A manor," Lee told him. "Something in the range of two or three million US currency. Five or six bedrooms and around the same number of bathrooms."

He put the information into his computer. "There is a seven-bedroom summer cottage just outside of town that may be appropriate." He turned the computer screen toward Hayley and Lee.

"It's an 18th century neo-classical. Seven bedrooms, five baths, 8,169 square feet. A grand hall, three reception rooms, dining room, billiard room, wine cellar, and two offices." He showed them photos of each room.

"That's exactly what I had in mind," Lee said. "What do you think, Hayley?"

"Does it have a swimming pool?" she asked. "How about stables?"

"Oh yes. It has an inside swimming pool and extensive equestrian facilities. The estate sits on 240 acres."

"The interior of the house is beautiful," Lee said. "But the property is extensive."

"I thought as much when you said it would be a vacation home." He handed them his card. "How long will you be in England?"

"We'll be leaving in a couple of days," Lee told him.

"Give me a call when you get back to the States if you're still looking to buy," he told them, shaking their hand and walking them to the door. "Sorry, I couldn't have been more helpful. Maybe there will be more choices come Spring. Have a safe trip home."

"Thank you very much," Lee said. He took Hayley's hand, and they walked to the Rover.

"I loved the interior," Hayley said. "It reminded me of your home."

"Ours," he told her. "It looked perfect. Too bad, though. We'll keep looking."

***

Hayley and Lee returned to the bed and breakfast, and in the dining room, they found a table near a twelve-pane window, giving them a view of the countryside. The woman they had encountered earlier behind the reception desk handed them a menu.

"Did you come from the pub?" she asked.

"Yes," Lee replied.

"You must have seen what happened," she said.

"What happened?" Hayley asked.

"Poor Ned Baines had a heart attack. Never made it out the door."

"That's crushing news," Lee said. "We must've just left."

"He looked so spry," Hayley said. "Who would've guessed."

"My brother's the bartender," the woman told them. "He belled me up straight away and said nothing could have been done."

"Does he have family nearby?" Lee asked.

"Yes, sir—a son. Plus, the entire town has made Ned part of their family. He'll have a fine send off. God bless Ned's soul."

"If you're sending flowers, would you mind if we contribute?" Hayley asked.

"That's very nice of you," she replied. "Let me get back to you once I get the details."

"Sure," Lee said.

She stepped away, stopping here and there to talk to others.

"I don't know if it was coincidental, but when I was viewing everyone's auras, Ned was the only person in the room who didn't have one."

"That's strange," Lee said. "Do you think there's a connection?"

"I don't know. This seeing auras ability is still new to me."

"Maybe you can search the internet for answers. I left my laptop at the penthouse. You can check it out when we get back." He looked over the menu. "The wild catch salmon topped with lemon caper butter sounds good."

"Great choice. I'll have the same."

A young girl, possibly eighteen, Hayley imagined, took their orders and hurried away.

Once their meals had arrived, between bites, they made plans for the next day.

"I have a couple more villages I'd like to visit," Lee told her. "Both would be amazing places to shop."

"Do you think they'll be open on New Year's Eve?"

"I don't know. I hadn't thought of that."

"It doesn't matter. I'll enjoy the drive nevertheless."

He looked up as the woman they had spoken to approached.

"I have the information you asked for, Miss Johnson. The town is taking up a collection to give to his son tomorrow afternoon."

"Can I give you cash?" Lee asked.

"That would be perfect. And, if I may, I'll need your address or email so the town can thank you properly. I'll carry it into town myself first thing in the morning."

"I'll bring it by the desk after dinner."

"God bless the both of you. Enjoy your meal. Dessert's on me."

"Thank you," Lee said. "Can we have it delivered to our room?"

"Yes, of course. I'll send the waitress over to take your order."

Hayley's thoughts flashed back to a few months ago when Lee had promised to make love with her in every room of his mansion. During one of those occasions, in a room on his list, Lee brought dessert. While they sat in front of the fireplace, eating an array of pastries, somehow the creamy frostings, the sticky fruit fillings, and tasty sauces found their way to the most sensual places on hers and Lee's bodies, creating foreplay she would never forget. The thought of that night made her desire soar. *I'm sure he knows what I'm thinking.*

He smiled, blushing as if reading her mind. He reached across the table and took her hand. "Ready for round two?"

Tingles of anticipation made it hard for her to hold her composure. She scanned a dessert menu as Lee perused his.

"An English trifle made with sponge cake, custard, jelly,

whipped cream, and strawberries sounds delicious," he said.

"And I think I'll have the raspberry crème brulée." She glanced up when the waitress approached.

"Dessert, Miss?"

"Please." Hayley gave her the list. "We'll have them sent to our room if we may."

"Absolutely. I'll have everything sent directly. Cheers." She hurried off.

Lee retrieved his wallet from his coat's inside pocket and left a tip. He strolled with Hayley to the front desk. After taking care of the bill and donation details, they headed to their room.

A fire in the fireplace had again been lit by housekeeping. Hayley hung her coat, walked to the windows, and noticed clouds moving east. "Nice night for hot chocolate."

"Will a glass of Merlot do?"

"That sounds even better."

Lee answered a knock on the door.

A woman carried a round silver tray with their order of desserts under a glass lid. "Where would you like this, sir?"

"On the table by the window," Lee told her. "Thank you." He tipped her, and she left.

"Wine and dessert, perfect," Hayley said.

He uncorked a bottle, poured the wine into two glasses, and passed one to her.

Hayley took three sips and set her glass on the table. She unbuttoned the top buttons on his shirt. As if she had lit a passionate flame, they raced to shed their clothes. When he removed his shirt, she cast off hers. She wiggled out of her jeans and tossed them aside while he stripped down to his boxers.

Lee grabbed a folded blanket from the end of the bed and placed it on the floor in front of the fire. Then he returned and helped her remove her blue lace bra and her matching silk panties. Once he discarded his boxers, with a mischievous grin, he reached over, dipped his fingers into the crème brulée and buttered her lips with raspberry cream.

When his soft lips met hers, she opened her mouth, and their tongues danced together among the savoring sauce. Her pulse quickened as he dabbed the cold dessert on her neck. With heated anticipation, she tilted her head, and he sucked the sticky jelly from her skin. Goose bumps spread across her skin as his tongue traveled upward, and his heated breath inflamed her ear, sending waves of desire through her body. *Best game ever,* she thought.

Lee grabbed the silver tray and led her to the blanket, where they knelt.

Hayley reached for more dessert, dabbed strawberries on his lips, and their heated pleasure continued. As she sucked the vanilla cream from his salty neck, she noticed him dipping his fingers into the sponge cake. She waited for him to make the next move. His eyes twinkled as he looked at her bare breasts. He met her gaze, looked at the cake on his fingers, and a grin lifted his moist lips.

When the food fest ceased, Hayley caught her breath as her pounding heart began to calm, and her sticky body throbbed with satisfaction. "I'll wait," she said. "You take a shower first." She lifted a strand of her cake-covered hair. "Looks like it'll take me a while. I'll need to wash my hair."

"Okay. I'll be out in a minute," he said, heading toward the bathroom.

Once Lee had finished cleaning up, Hayley stepped into the shower. The hot water felt good against her skin as it melted away the evidence of their passion. She stood tranquilly still, letting the water soak her hair and run down her face. After a moment, she reached for the small container of complimentary shampoo, opened it, and smelled the fragrance. *Lavender.* Hayley set out to remove the food from her hair. With that accomplished, she began to rinse away the suds when a noise caught her attention. Through drenched eyes, she glanced at the shower door, and her heart jumped into her throat. A line in the steamy glass shower door, beginning at one side of the door, slowly curved as it moved toward the other side.

Chills shook Hayley when she realized someone she couldn't detect stood in the shower with her. "Lee, come here." She heard the panic in her own voice. "And bring a camera."

Lee dashed into the room, pulled his cell phone from the pocket of his white terry cloth bathrobe, and began taking photos of the snaking imprint.

"She's here." The hairs on Hayley's neck prickled. She pressed against the wall in the corner of the confined space, not wanting to crowd the ghost.

When the phenomenon ended, Hayley scurried out of the shower and wrapped herself in a towel. "That scared the hell out of me. I didn't even sense her presence." She stroked her arms, trying to wipe away the goosebumps and studied the drawing along with Lee. "It's not the same as the others," she said. "The line goes across. It's completely different. What in the world is she trying to tell us?"

"We can't do anything tonight. Tomorrow we need to gather the team."

CHAPTER 7

The next morning on the ride back to London, Hayley yawned again. Night visions of air raid sirens and German planes delivering death in the black of night kept her from sleep last night. While entrenched in her dream, her legs trembled, and the excessive smoke from the city's fires burned her lungs as bombs ravaged London over and over. Gasping for air, she woke in a panic, only to fall asleep once more to relive the nightmares.

"The residual energy from World War II kept me awake all night," she told Lee. "I didn't get much sleep."

He didn't take his eyes off the road. "We'll be returning home tomorrow. The forecast for the next two days shows no threat of delays."

"That's good news. I'm excited to see the New Year's fireworks over the Thames tonight."

"Me too." Lee glanced up at the sky. "All these clouds should be gone within the hour, according to the hotel receptionist's weather report. She said it should be a warm day, somewhere in the high fifties. She said it'll be record breaking temperatures for this time of year. We'll be able to watch the celebration from the balcony."

The word *breaking* echoed in Hayley's mind, and she thought about the little girl. Hayley closed her eyes and rested her head against the leather seat of their rented Land Rover. Looking for answers, she pictured herself sitting on the blue suede couch in Lee's sitting room back home. *Grams, I need you*, she called out in her mind.

She remembered the first time she had seen her grandmother in spirit form. *I owe everything to Grams. She believed in me when everyone else, including my parents, thought I was schizophrenic.* Now since Grams' death, she could speak with Grams anytime she wanted.

In Hayley's mind, she saw Grams manifest herself on the couch across from her. Ever since she had died, Grams had appeared to be no older than thirty, although she had passed at the age of eighty-two. *It had taken me forever to get used to seeing her my own age.*

How can I help you, dear?

I've encountered a ghost, a little girl whose language I don't understand.

Wearing fitted blue jeans and knee-high black boots, Grams had dressed for the winter. Her wavy blonde hair fell over the shoulders of her turtleneck sweater. She nodded. *I'm aware of her.*

Do you know what she's been trying to tell me?

I'm afraid I can't help you this time, dear. You know I can't divulge your future. The Divine rule forbids it.

So, I'll be seeing her again? Is she playing a game?

I've already told you too much, Grams replied in Hayley's mind. *I nearly crossed the line during your last case. There's a lot I still have to learn about being a guardian angel. But I intend to be the best.*

You are the best. I bet you feel like you could explode not being able to tell me everything like you did when you were alive.

What do you mean when you were alive? *I am alive and always here when you need me. And you're right. I could never keep a secret from you. It's the most difficult thing I've ever had to do. But what's the alternative? If I were just a soul who had crossed over and never had this opportunity to be your guardian, I would've had even more limitations. If keeping secrets lets me spend more time with you, it's well worth the agony.*

I hope this little girl has nothing to do with our next case, Hayley said. *We'll be leaving for home tomorrow.*

Grams shook her head. *Sorry. But life always interferes when you have other things planned. There, once more, I said too much.*

Before you go, could you explain why I didn't see Ned's aura at the pub?

You've already guessed why, dear.

Because he was about to die?

I knew you'd figure that out. Now I've got to go. Love you. And Grams vanished.

That told me a lot. I was right about why I didn't see his aura, and from her reaction, I'll be seeing the ghost child again. And that's why she can't tell me what the line on the shower door and the cracks in the glass mean. Hayley opened her eyes again.

"Speak with Grams?" Lee asked.

"Yes, and she won't tell me anything." Hayley smiled. "But she gave me a clue. Seems this little girl has something to do with my future. And there might be a chance we won't be going home tomorrow."

He raised an eyebrow. "Seriously?"

"I suggest we let this play out. I could be wrong."

"I agree. Let's see where it leads. We can take a vote to see if some of us or all of us will stay behind." Lee turned the Land Rover onto the motorway and headed back to London.

***

When Hayley entered the penthouse with Lee behind her, she saw Jim standing at the bar with a Guinness in his hand and Laura and Matilda walking out of the kitchen, each carrying a tray of crackers and cheese.

Roger rose from an overstuffed chair in the living room. "How was your trip? We didn't expect you until later tonight."

"It was great up to a point," Hayley replied.

"Looks like your knickers are in a bunch," Jim said. "What happened?"

"We had two encounters with the ghost girl," Lee told them. "The first time, she was in a mirror at an art gallery, then vanished. The second time, she drew a line in the steam on the inside of Hayley's shower door. I have pictures." He glanced around. "Where's Kathy and Thomas?"

"They went down to the lobby to stretch their legs. We just got back. Lenny took us all on a tour of the city." Roger reached for his cell phone on the end table next to his chair. "Let me give them a call." When Kathy answered, Roger spoke briefly, then returned his phone to the table. "Kathy said they'll be here shortly."

Hayley sat on the couch while Lee, at the bar, filled two glasses with Chateau Le Pin.

"You were in the shower?" Laura asked. "How frightening is that? You must have been scared witless."

Hayley accepted the wine Lee offered, sampled it, and placed the glass on the coffee table in front of her. "Extremely. It was a scene right out of a horror movie." Just remembering the haunting at the manor made her stomach shutter.

"Do you think she was trying to frighten you?" Matilda asked.

"That's what we're going to determine." Lee glanced at the door when Kathy and Thomas walked in. "Glad you guys are here. Kathy, Hayley, and I have photos on our phones of the little girl's drawing. Would it be possible to get them blown up so we can see them clearly?"

"What happened this time?" Kathy asked.

Hayley filled her in on the details of their last ghostly encounter. "I talked to Grams, but she wouldn't tell me what the child wants. But from what she didn't say, I concluded I'm going to see more of this little girl in my future. Plus, there's a chance we won't be leaving tomorrow."

"Let me have your phones," Kathy said. "And I'll need the photo Lenny gave you as well. It shouldn't take long."

She gathered everything and headed to the office to use the complimentary computer and printer the hotel provided.

In a few minutes, Kathy returned with large copies. "Let's go into the dining room." They followed her and spread the photos on the table.

"So, this time, the lines went across instead of upward," Kathy said.

"Yes," Hayley replied. "From left to right."

"Can't get there from here," Jim said.

"What do you mean?" Laura asked.

"We need more information. There's not enough to go on."

Hayley heard a knock on the door. "That's probably Lenny with our bags."

Thomas turned to answer the door.

"Ask him to come in," Lee said.

Thomas let Lenny in. They joined the others around the dining table.

Lenny glanced at the photos. "Another incident?" he asked.

Hayley nodded.

"We're trying to make sense out of all this," Lee told him.

Hayley glanced at the luggage Lenny had set near the doorway. Her thoughts flashed back to the framed map she and Lee had bought in the gallery and the lines she drew with her finger following their journey into the countryside. *Can't get there from here,* she remembered Jim saying. "You could be wrong, Jim. Maybe you can get there from here. Do you think this could be a map?"

"Seems far-fetched to me," Jim said.

"If that were the case," Roger said, "the lines in the cracked mirror should be different from the lines in the car window. They took place in different locations."

Thomas studied the photos. "I think she's right. The

wedding shop is only a mile away. And if you notice the line at the bottom of the image, there's a curve so slight you could almost miss it. But there it is." He pointed, and everyone took turns scrutinizing his find.

"There's only one way to see if Hayley's right," Lee said. "Lenny, you know England better than anyone here. What do you think?"

"I'd have to take a better look at it, sir. If it is a map, these lines could lead near and far. And who is to say if they all lead to the same place? If it pleases you, I can take the photos home and give it a go to see what I can find."

"Thanks. That would be helpful," Lee replied.

"Will this interfere with our flight home?" Roger asked.

"I don't see why we would all have to stay and follow-up on this," Lee replied. "It's up to everyone to decide if they'd like to stay or go."

"I talked to Lewis this afternoon," Laura said. "He's arranged a number of appointments with vendors and needs our decision on flowers, food, kind and type of wedding cake, plus the style of invitations we prefer. Have we determined this is our next case? If we have, this takes priority."

"I still don't have a clue as to what this little girl is doing," Hayley replied. "For all I know, she's just playing games. Why don't you and Roger return home? Whatever decisions Lewis wants you to make, you'll be able to convey the choices to me, and we can make the final decision together. It may take a while to determine what's going on here. Once we find out, we'll let you know."

"Seems like a plan to me," Roger said. "So, talk about staying amongst yourselves, everyone, and give me your decision before tonight's fireworks, and I'll cancel your flights if need be."

"I'd like to stay because Hayley may need an interpreter," Matilda replied.

"If Matdie's stayin', I'm stayin'," Jim told him.

That didn't surprise Hayley. She knew that Jim, now age fifty-two, had waited all his life for the right woman. Yes, he had dated, but not one woman he had dated compared to Matilda. Although Hayley had to admit, Matilda's snobbish attitude when she had first arrived at Roger's home had dismayed everyone. But once she met Grams and became entrenched in the team's ongoing case, she changed her mind about ghosts, spirits, witchcraft, and the paranormal. Once she released her prejudices, she and Jim became friends and now lovers.

Kathy raised her hand. "I'd like to stay too. She may need my expertise." She gave Hayley a wink.

"If it's alright with you, Mr. Franklin," Thomas said. "I'd like to remain with Kathy."

Likewise, Hayley couldn't imagine Kathy staying without Thomas. Although she knew that Kathy had dated from time to time, she had also learned from numerous conversations with her that Kathy had never met a man who hadn't run the other way once he had found that her life revolved around the supernatural — until she met Thomas.

"Understood," Lee said. "You're welcome to join us."

"Thank you, sir."

"You stopped being my security guard the moment you left the US," Lee told him. "And since you decided to stick around, you'll be part of the team. That means no more calling me, sir. Okay?"

"Got it."

Lee gathered the photos and handed them to Lenny.

Lenny glanced at his watch. "I'm finished for the day in ten minutes. I can let you know what I find in the morning."

"We've made our choice to stay, Lenny, so there's no hurry," Lee replied. "If you have plans for tonight, don't let us ruin your evening."

"Thank you, sir. I'll see you in the morning." He turned and left.

Everyone retired to the living room.

Jim circled the room, taking drink orders. He went to the bar and returned with a tray of filled glasses.

While carrying a mug of beer, Roger strolled to the wall of windows and looked toward the Thames. "Can you believe how crowded the streets are already? We still have lots of time. Our dinner reservations aren't until six. The live band starts soon after."

"Hayley, come sit and tell us about your trip," Laura said, sitting on the couch and sipping her wine.

She joined Laura, Kathy, and Matilda while the men, drinks in hand, gathered by the window and pointed to the barges near the banks of the river.

"They're probably set up for ground display, I imagine," Lee said. "I forgot to tell you that Hayley and I are planning to buy a vacation home somewhere in England. We don't know exactly where yet."

"Cool," Roger said. "I know how excited that makes you. And it gives us something else to celebrate tonight." He glanced at his watch. "It's going to be an exciting evening."

***

Later, after an evening of dining and dancing at one of the hotel's restaurants, Hayley strolled with Lee and the others, returning to the penthouse to watch the fireworks. When she entered their hotel room, she noticed that party favors, along with a case of champagne, had been delivered.

"They think of everything," she said to Lee.

"Yes. Very thoughtful of them." He looked toward the river. "We should step out on the balcony before Big Ben strikes midnight."

"At least the sky's clear," she replied. "From the weather we've seen the last couple of days, we seem to be in luck."

"I thought you didn't believe in luck."

"I don't. It's just a figure of speech. I still believe things happen for a reason."

"I do too. But in this case, I think we're damn lucky with the weather," Lee said.

Once they put on their coats, they walked out onto the balcony with their friends. Thomas held the door for Kathy, who carried a tray of glasses filled with champagne and set it on a nearby table.

"I was told that it's only the second year that London's fireworks have been set to music," Lee said. "They'll use satellite technology to synchronize the fireworks with the music, and also the lighting, not to exclude the barges, London Eye and this year Big Ben."

"Big Ben?" Roger asked.

"That's what Lenny told me," Lee replied. "Fireworks are set to explode out of Elizabeth's Tower in unison with Big Ben's 12 bongs count down."

"I expected they'd go all out this year," Jim said. "London's hostin' the Olympics this summer. That's the reason we came this year because we knew they'd be spectacular."

"I thought we were here to celebrate my birthday," Roger said.

"Yeah, that too," Jim said. "What do ya think that dinner, dancin' and drinkin' was 'bout tonight?"

"That was fun," Roger said. "I especially like the birthday cake decorated with Big Ben, and all those sparking candles looked like fireworks lighting the sky around it. Nice touch."

"Kathy thought of that," Thomas told him.

"It didn't take me very long to realize they were trick candles," Roger said, "the kind you can't blow out."

"That was my idea," Jim told him.

"The entire night was amazing," Roger said. "Thanks, guys. It was great."

"I always say, if you're gonna celebrate, go big or go home," Jim said.

"I intend to do both," Roger said. "We're not letting the little flight home stop us from celebrating. When we get home, Laura and I have plans for a romantic evening." A grin crossed his face. "I'm a lucky man."

"Yeah, we're lucky, too," Jim told him. "How many people get to drive all over England chasin' ghosts? Now, that's what I call a good time."

Soon, rockets shot out from the arches above Big Ben as the clock chimed. More people than Hayley had ever seen, except on TV, were in the streets, on bridges, and everywhere in between, counting down.

After Big Ben's last bong, Hayley heard the crowds declare Happy New Year.

Lee turned to Hayley. Their lips met, and their kiss lingered. Her heartbeat quickened with the thought of the coming year. The man who had spent past-life after past-life throughout eternity as her soul mate would soon become her husband.

"Happy New Year, my love," Lee told her.

"Happy New Year, my love," she replied.

He embraced her, and she felt the depth of his love radiate from every cell of his being. When they turned to their friends, they exchanged hugs and kisses. Kathy passed around the champagne. And they toasted each other as the show began.

The theme from *Chariots of Fire* played while an announcement told of the upcoming summer Olympics, proclaiming London as its host. As Hayley watched, streams of pink fire burst from the London Eye's hub.

Three barges anchored in the Themes set off tens-of-thousands projectiles synchronized to *Devil in a Blue Dress* and *Viva La Vida*. Fireworks burst above three barges anchored in the Thames. Pink Olympic pyrotechnic rings and heart shapes hung in the night sky while the music accompanied the display.

Across the Thames, the London Eye glowed under blue floodlights. *You Really Got Me* blared from the speakers while more blue Olympic rings filled the sky. "So cool," she said as glitter stars shot up from the barges.

When an upsurge of projectiles launched simultaneously from the barges and the London Eye, a vision took Hayley away from the dazzling display.

While the explosion of fireworks sounded in her ears, she witnessed bombs dropping from the sky, landing in the fields near a small village. In the aftermath, on the edge of town, a damaged church stood in the dusty debris, its hallowed graveyard desecrated by the blast.

Hayley studied the images. In an instant, the vision ended, and her normal sight returned. *Why now? It must be the explosions from the fireworks that triggered it.* In awe, she continued to watch the extravaganza, while in the back of her mind, she still felt the trepidation from the war's destruction. *Please, no more visions. Just let me enjoy the evening.*

Simultaneously, hundreds of fireworks created the finale, including five colorful Olympic rings crossing the night sky. When the bombardment stopped, blue floodlights lit the London Eye, and the crowd cheered.

"Spectacular," she said to Lee.

"I'll show you spectacular later," he replied as his lips nuzzled her hair.

While the others left the balcony and went back inside the penthouse, Hayley and Lee embraced, and his steamy kiss left her wanting more.

"Should we turn in for the night?" Lee asked.

"I'm looking forward to it," she replied, with a sensuous smile.

He put his arm around her and led her inside. With his free hand, Lee collected two wine glasses while Hayley grabbed a bottle of champagne before heading to their room.

CHAPTER 8

In the morning, Hayley awoke appreciative that dreams and night visions hadn't invaded her sleep. Although she had stayed up later than usual and drunk a lot more than she'd planned, she didn't feel a bit hung-over. *Thank goodness for that,* she thought while dressing. *First things first. Laura and Roger leave soon for the airport. We'll be spending the morning with them before they go. Lenny is taking them. Hopefully, he had time to interpret the child's drawings and come up with a map. I guess the rest of the day depends on his findings.*

After showering, Lee exited the bathroom, wearing a towel around his waist. His damp, dark brown hair hadn't been combed, but he had shaved, Hayley noticed as she wrapped her arms around him. He held her close, then kissed her lips. She couldn't help thinking about how she and Lee had made their own fireworks last night before falling asleep.

"If I had my way, I'd carry you back to bed and give you an encore of last night," Lee said, as if he read her mind. "But the others are already up, and Laura and Roger will leave soon."

"I would've liked that too. But there's no rush. I can wait."

"Until tonight, then." His kiss felt soft.

Hayley saw his love in the depth of his mahogany brown eyes. "Until tonight." She left the comfort of his arms, letting him dress. "I could use some coffee, though."

"Pour yourself a cup. I'll be ready in a minute. Don't forget to wish Roger happy birthday before he goes. I know we celebrated it last night, but tomorrow is his birthday."

She nodded and left the bedroom.

Hayley entered the living room and found Lenny sitting with the other men in front of the fireplace, discussing last night's celebration. She joined them as Kathy, Laura, and Matilda came from the kitchen. "It's too bad you couldn't have stayed a couple more days, so you could enjoy your birthday," Hayley told Roger.

"Being home won't be so bad," he said. "Once we're there, Laura said she has something special planned. I'd say this has been the best birthday ever."

"Or it will be later tonight when we get home," Laura said. "I promise you that." She gave him a kiss. They strolled over to the window and reminisced about the fireworks display.

"Good morning, Lenny," Hayley said. "Happy New Year. Did you find time to assess our situation?"

"Happy New Year, Miss. I gave it a go for a short time last night." He pulled a folded map from inside his uniform jacket and handed it to her. "Plus, I worked on it a tad this morning. It's part of my job to provide mapping and travel information. I came up with a few places you might give a clever going over."

Now all we need is a voice recorder so I can record the little girl's message and Matilda can decipher what she's trying to tell us.

"Lenny also picked up a digital voice recorder with wireless headphones for us," Jim said. "In case ya run into that line-drawin' ghosty girl again, I thought an EVP would help figure out what she's sayin'. Matdie said you'd wished you'd had one at the bridal shop."

Just thought I'd give Matilda a little nudge to remind her of your conversation, Grams whispered in Hayley's mind. *I knew you'd forgotten to get one.*

Hayley remembered when Lee had first told her how to use a recorder to capture an EVP, electric voice phenomenon. *You just have to push this button down and keep the recorder running until the investigation is over. It's a simple voice recorder, but it'll pick up spirit voices and noises we don't hear with the normal ear. You're extra-normal and don't need the recorder at all.* Until now. While in England, her extra-normal hearing, as he had called it, needed a backup. *Perfect.*

She grinned. *Thanks, Grams.* Although Grams had told her she wouldn't be involved in this case, Hayley couldn't imagine her staying completely out of it.

"Good thinking," Lee said, entering the room. "Why don't we all go into the dining room and spread this on the table so everyone can check it out?"

As Lenny placed the photos on the table, Hayley unfolded the map and laid it out for all to see.

"The problem, as you know, is the size of the line in correlation with the map," Lenny said. "The mirror is four times the size of the car door, for instance. Not to mention that the line on the shower door is unique. We would have to be inside the little girl's head to know the specifics, size of map, and length of lines. So, I set about using my best guess."

"I noticed the photo of the crack in the Jaguar's window was taken from inside," Jim said.

"Yes," Lenny replied. "The tinted windows presented a dilemma. We had to open the door and take an interior photo to capture the detail."

"Sounds logical," Jim replied.

"I have an app on my computer that lets me interact with a map of England," Lenny said. "It allowed me to play with the length of each crack or trail as we must imagine them to be. I placed the beginning of the trail cracked in the mirror at its point of conception—the bridal shop. The second trail found in the Jaguar's window, I set forth from this hotel. After playing with each length, I discovered they intersected at a point, then the trails became identical. I varied their length until I came up with several presumptions. It was very flummoxing, to say the least. I marked a few Xs here and about as suggestions to where you might have a go at hunting for answers."

Hayley studied the map with her psychic senses, trying to pinpoint the precise place to start, but failed. She put her finger on the X that seemed the farthest distance from London. "Didn't we just come from somewhere around here, Lee?"

"It's close. The manor is about twenty miles east." He pointed to the manor's nearby village. "This is the location of the manor where we stayed while we shopped," he told the others. "It's the same place where the ghost drew a line in steam on the shower door."

"Ah, yes," Lenny said. "Hayley said it trailed off to the right from that location. So, I began the trail at the manor and directed it eastward, varying the length. Since I have no idea where the little girl is taking you, to a house, a town, or a village, I've marked several Xs in that direction."

"This may take a few days to figure out what the girly-ghost wants," Jim said. "How 'bout we check outta this ritzy penthouse and use the manor as our go between?"

"Sounds like a good idea," Lee said. "I'll call and see if they have rooms available."

"We might have a wee problem gettin' there, though," Jim said. "That Land Rover ya leased won't hold the six of us and all our luggage. We'll need to take two cars."

"I can obtain a Land Rover LR4 if you'd like," Lenny said. "It has three row seating."

"That would work," Hayley said. "We'll load up ours with all the luggage. Once we get to the manor and unload the bags, we won't need two cars any longer. We can take the LR4. It'll be fun."

"How do ya want to go about this, darlin'?" Jim asked Hayley. "You'll be wanderin' 'round like a moose in a corn patch if ya don't have a plan."

Hayley studied the maps and, using her psychic senses, once again tried to find the location where the ghost wanted them to go but couldn't. "According to Grams's vague clues, I'll be seeing the little girl again. The question is, where?"

"Why don't we wait to figure out where to start looking once we get to the manor," Lee said.

Roger glanced at his watch. "We've got to be getting to the airport. When you find your new vacation home, send me photos. I'm happy for you. You've been wanting to buy a place here since you were a boy."

"After we find out what the ghost girl wants, we'll have a chance to look around," Lee said.

"How big of a place are ya lookin' for?" Jim asked.

"A small manor," Lee replied. "No more than six bedrooms and a few bathrooms."

"Well, good luck with that," Roger said.

"Thanks," Lee told him. "It'll be fun checking out what's available."

The women took turns hugging Laura. Roger said his goodbyes. Lenny carried their luggage and followed them out of the penthouse.

As soon as Lenny closed the door behind him, Kathy turned to the others. "We can take one car. The baggage won't be a problem. I can just shrink them."

"Wait just a hair-raisin' minute, Miss Witchypoo," Jim said. "Ya know I love ya, sweet pea, but I'm not comfortable with that witchcraft mumbo jumbo. Ya know you're new at this here spell castin' stuff. Who's to say if ya make our clothes shrink and then return 'em to their normal size that later, once we put 'em on, they won't be shrinkin' again at an inappropriate time?"

Matilda giggled.

"It doesn't work that way," Kathy replied. "Intent creates a spell. Once the intention is fulfilled, and the spell has been cast, it won't recur unless the intent is reestablished."

"Sounds like gibberish to me," he said.

"It's not gibberish," Kathy told him. "Intention comes

from thought, and a spell does not have a mind of its own."

"Stranger things have happened," he said.

Hayley couldn't disagree with that. *Stranger things have happened could be the adage of my entire life.* "Let's just take two cars. Kathy has agreed to keep her talents discreet. If someone were to notice—"

"It would look like we're pullin' out twenty bags from a two-inch trunk, or, as the British call it, the boot," Jim said. "That would be an eye opener."

"It's a plan then," Lee told them. "I'll call the manor, and when Lenny brings us the other Land Rover, we'll be on our way."

***

After they had received the second Land Rover and Lee had reserved three rooms, Hayley and the others started their journey.

At the manor, they gathered in Hayley's and Lee's suite. Lee spread the street map that he and Hayley had used on their trip. Then he studied Lenny's suggestions. "This is strange. Hayley, take a look."

She followed his finger as it slid across their map to a location that surprised her. Recalling the warning vision Hayley had received the other day, *You must hurry,* unsettled her. *The thought of someone in a coma sending me that message still feels eerie.* "We're going back to Harry Tibbs's village. I hope he's recovered and is doing well. I would really like to find out what he was trying to warn me about and if he knows where the little girl wants us to go."

Hayley wished her ability to foresee her own future would help her avoid disturbing him and his family. *But it's forbidden. Although….* "I can view the present and at least see if he's awake." She closed her eyes and cleared her mind. "Mr. Tibbs," she said, concentrating on his whereabouts. A vision in her mind showed the old man, with rumpled white hair and a peaceful expression on his wrinkled face, in bed with his eyes closed. She released the image and opened her eyes. "That didn't tell me anything."

"We can stop by Libby's gift shop while we're hunting for the little girl and ask how he is," Lee said.

Hayley nodded. "Great. Maybe she can find out if we can speak to him."

Jim gave Hayley the box containing the voice recorder and wireless headphones. "It's ready to go. I've set up the wireless connection and made sure everythin' is hunky-dory."

"Thanks. I'll use it to record Mr. Tibbs's conversation if we meet. Hopefully, he can give us another piece of the puzzle."

"Good idea," Lee said.

"Just in case ya get sick of drivin', we can switch off," Jim told Lee. He looked at Matilda. "I'm as used to drivin' England's roads as a one-humped spittin' camel's used to hot sand."

"It's true," Kathy told her. "He's been to England more times than I can remember."

"I can understand why," Matilda said. "He must love the architecture. Some of the manors would probably remind him of Lee's and Roger's estates."

"That's some of it," Jim explained. "I've spent a lot of time visitin' local pubs in 'bout every town I came to. Enjoyin' the British humor and havin' good times was always somethin' to look forward to. But mainly, it was the spine-tinglin', knee-knockin' hauntin's throughout the UK that kept Roger, Lee, and me returnin' over the years. So whatcha say, Lee? Wantta switch off?"

"Sounds like a plan."

"Well then," Jim replied, "let's go ghost huntin'."

While Lee drove to the village, Hayley sat in the passenger seat next to him. Eager to test the voice recorder, she passed the wireless headphones to Matilda, who sat behind her. "Why don't we try the live feed?" Hayley said. "Put the headphones on, and I'll whisper into the recorder."

After Matilda made the headphones fit snuggly, she gave

Hayley a thumbs-up.

Once satisfied the recorder had been turned on, Hayley spoke one word in the softest voice she could manage. "Did you hear me?"

"Just one word. It sounded like *lingering*. What a strange word to choose."

"Right. But not strange at all. Lingering is another name for ghost."

"Yes. I remember you told me that once upon a time. I heard it clearly. But what happens if the lingering or whoever we are talking to is farther away? Why don't I hand the headphones to Kathy? You repeat the whisper, then say the word in different volumes until she gives a thumbs-up?"

Matilda handed the headphones to Kathy, who sat behind her in the third-row seating.

"Ready when you are," Kathy said.

Hayley whispered as she had the first time. No response from Kathy. She spoke a little louder but still in a low voice. Kathy raised her thumb.

"You said *chicken*," Kathy said. "But I could hardly hear it." She passed the headphone to Matilda, who gave them back to Hayley.

"Correct," Hayley replied. "We'll have to at least be that close or closer to make sure we hear what's being said."

"Does a one-legged duck swim in a circle?" Jim chimed in.

"What's that supposed to mean?" Hayley asked.

"Means maybe or maybe not," Jim told her. "From years of experience, Lee and I have discovered that there's nothin' rational 'bout a ghost's behavior, and that includes recordin' or hearin' their voice. There's been plenty of times when Lee and I have been right next to each other when one of us heard somethin' as loud as my Aunt Nelly's yodel, and the other didn't hear a damn thing. It's a tricky situation. Sometimes the conditions are exactly right, and you're able to catch every word. Other times it may be a mumble no matter how near or far you are to 'em. So, don't waste a whole lot of time tryin' to be scientific 'bout it. It's a matter of luck."

"Hayley doesn't believe in luck," Lee said, not taking his eyes off the road.

"I know she believes everythin' has a reason. She has insight, and I only have hindsight. It's damn confusin'. Tryin' to make sense of it all could fry a man's brain."

"I wouldn't want you to hurt yourself," Hayley said. "So, let's go with luck."

The road's gentle slopes and bends straightened up ahead. Wind thrashed the smoke rising from the chimney of a farmhouse. The huge gray barn's doors stood wide open while a man, his coat fluttering in the breeze, led a horse into the barn. They drove past.

"How close are we to the town?" Kathy asked.

"We're a little over two-thirds of the way there," Lee said. "Another twenty-five minutes, I'd say." He stopped at an intersection which gave him two choices, to turn right or to go left. He chose left.

Rock walls lined the carriageway. A little way ahead, two common beech trees stood tall, one on each side of the street. Hayley recalled seeing them on their past trip. They were one of the few trees she had seen that kept their leaves during the winter.

Hayley fidgeted. She glanced at the recorder still in her grasp, turned it on, placed the headphones over her ears, and listened to her whispers, trying to occupy her time.

Lee slammed on the brakes. Hayley's heart leaped into her throat when she looked up and saw why he had stopped. "Do you see her?" she asked Lee, removing the headphones.

"We all see her," Jim said from the backseat.

The ghost girl stood in the middle of the road, her dirty arm stretched out, her palm raised as though shielding herself from the oncoming car. Not a strand of her crusty long hair nor her ragged dress fluttered in the wind, a stark contrast to the shuddering trees above her.

"What should we do?" Matilda asked, panic in her voice.

"I don't want to scare her," Hayley replied, handing Matilda the headphones.

"Scare her?" Lee said. "She almost gave me a heart attack."

"Matilda, you and I will get out and slowly approach her. I want to make sure we record every word she says."

Matilda nodded as she slipped on the device over her ears.

"The headphones are wireless," Jim said. "Do ya really need Matdie to get out? She's shakin' like a shimmy dancer."

"This is important." Hayley turned on the recorder. "I want to make sure we don't lose the connection. Let's go." She opened her door and heard Matilda open hers.

The wind whipping the trees muffled the little girl's words. She seemed to be yelling, but Hayley could hardly hear her and moved closer, holding the recorder in front of her. "What's your name?" she asked. She could see the child's mouth move, but her words were distorted by the wind.

In a moment, the ghost girl's image faded into the breeze, leaving Hayley and Matilda alone in the middle of the road.

Hayley turned to Matilda, who gave her a thumbs-up. They hurried back to the car, climbed inside, and closed the doors.

"I think I heard a whisper," Matilda said. "But it's hard to tell. Too much background noise."

"I have an app on my laptop back at the manor that will fix that," Jim said. "Are we still goin' to the village, or did we get what we came for?"

"I think we should go back to the manor and see what we have," Hayley said. "If we still have to go to the village, we can do it in the morning and get an early start."

"Sounds logical to me," Lee said. He drove down the road until he came to a dirt trail leading into the fields and used it to turn around.

***

At the manor, they gathered in Hayley and Lee's room.

Jim sat at a table in front of the windows and worked on his laptop, separating the background noise from the little girl's words. "I think I've got it," he said.

Everyone moved closer. Matilda looked over his shoulder while he played the edited recording.

Hayley heard a faint voice but still couldn't understand the words.

"Play it again, please," Matilda requested.

Jim did as she asked.

"I've got it," Matilda said. "Her name is Elsie Hudson. She wanted us to go back. She said we were going in the wrong direction."

"Not according to the line she drew on the shower door," Hayley told them.

"Wait," Lee said. "She's right. During all the episodes, Elsie stood on one side of the glass to draw the line, while our photos were taken from the opposite side — with the exception of the shower door drawing. Hayley, you were on the same side of the glass as Elsie when she drew it."

"I told Lenny the line went from left to right," she said. "If I had been standing on the other side with you, it would've gone from right to left."

Lee unfolded the map he had brought from the car and spread it on the bed. He played with the length of both lines, the drawing starting from London, plus the shower door line. He pointed to a village. "They meet here."

Hayley glanced outside. Rain pelted the twelve-pane window. "Let's wait until morning. It'll be dark soon."

***

Before bed, Hayley glanced at the time. *Roger and Laura should be there by now.* Using Skype, Hayley contacted them in Sutterville,

North Carolina. She and Laura chose the style of wedding invitations, decided on the flavors of the two cakes, plus elected to let Lewis select the band for the reception.

When Roger joined the visual chat and waved at Hayley and Lee, Laura turned to him. "They said the ghost child's name is Elsie Hudson."

"It's an old English surname," Roger said. "Maybe we're related. Wouldn't that be a hoot? That could be the reason she's trying to get our attention. Maybe she just wants us to know where she's buried. Could be she was one of the children that were sent away and was separated from the family."

"You know how Kathy enjoys research," Lee said. "I'll ask her to look into it."

"We'll let you know what we find tomorrow," Hayley told them. "I hope we're right about the location."

They said goodnight, and Hayley ended the visual call. She stood and stretched. The ever-present jetlag forced her to retire early, and Lee did the same.

Hayley slept restlessly. Her dreams of combat, death, and destruction filled most of the night. Again, she witnessed bombs dropping, landing in the fields near a small village. On the edge of town, a damaged church stood with its east wall demolished. The blast defiled graves surrounding the ruins. Large trenches revealed caskets. Headstones had been dislodged. When she awoke in the darkness, she gazed through tired eyes at the clock on the nightstand. *Four o'clock.* She moaned, rolled over, and sleep engulfed her again.

CHAPTER 9

Once the team arose, gathered in the dining room, and ate breakfast, they headed out to reach the village circled on the map. After arriving at their destination, Lee drove slowly down what appeared to be the main road while everyone in the backseats of the Land Rover kept an eye open for anything out of the ordinary.

The wind had whipped last night, leaving fallen branches and debris scattered about. In a graveyard on the outskirts of the village, an old man bent over a gravesite, dusting twigs off a plot, his long-handled shovel resting on the headstone beside him.

"Stop," Hayley said.

Lee pulled up and parked a few feet from the groundskeeper.

"I've dreamt about this church and graveyard twice so far," Hayley said. "I'm sensing she's here."

"The rest of us will wait while Lee and ya ask for info," Jim told her, rolling down his window a bit. "We're close enough to hear what he's got to say."

"We won't be long." Lee opened his car door.

Before Lee could shut his door and run around to the other side, Hayley exited the Rover and stood looking at the stone parish. The granite rubble exterior and the slate roof seemed to have been built at different times through the centuries. *Maybe Norman origin with fifteenth-century additions*, Hayley thought.

Their attention turned to the caretaker.

The bent old man straightened. He looked to be about six

feet tall if he were able to iron out the curvature in his spine. His large hand grabbed the shovel, and he leaned on it as if it were a walking stick. A brown beanie covered his scruffy gray hair. His face hid behind a full beard, the wrinkles around his eyes declaring his age. He wore a long-sleeved wool shirt, a down vest, and jeans. "Can I help you?" he asked in an irritated tone.

Hayley stepped forward. "We've been visiting England during New Year's, and while we're here, we thought we'd search for a friend's ancestry."

"What's the surname," he grumbled.

"Hudson," she said.

The old man's face reddened. His glare filled with anger. "Bloody hell!" He seized his shovel, veered away, took a step before he planted the point of his shovel into the ground, turned, and glowered at them. "Tell whoever sent you that I didn't laugh yesterday, and I'm not laughing today." He stomped away.

"But—" Hayley tried to psychically find the reason for his hostility with no success. The Divine rule would not allow it. *Interesting. Apparently, the answer is involved in my future.*

Lee touched her shoulder. "We're not going to get anything out of him. Let's find somewhere to eat. Maybe someone else can help us."

She nodded and walked back to the Rover. Lee opened the passenger door. Once she slid into the seat, he closed the door and went around to the other side to get in.

"Miserly old guy," Jim said, rolling up his window. "Wonder what's got his goat."

Lee started the car and pulled away. "We came all this way. We'll find someone who'll help us. Let's go eat." Down a way and off to the right, Lee parked at a pub.

"Best place 'round to get information," Jim said.

After everyone climbed out of the vehicle and hurried in, they took their seats at a couple of tables near the fireplace. At the bar, two gray-haired men drank beer from thick glass mugs.

A young man wiping down the tables joined them. "Hi, I'm Eddie. Let me be of assistance," he said, pulling the tables together and rearranging the chairs.

All sat while Eddie brought utensils and napkins.

Another man came out from behind the bar. He looked to be in his forties, with his hair neatly cut and combed. An apron covered his plaid long-sleeved shirt and denim pants. "I'll handle this. Go tell your mum we've got guests from across the pond." He glanced around the table, giving each a warm smile. "It would be my pleasure to help you. My name's George. It's a bit unusual this time of year to be greeting travelers, especially those coming from so far away. Can I offer you a pint or two to warm your bones or maybe something to eat?"

Lee introduced everyone. "Do you have a menu?" he asked.

A woman carrying a towel scurried out of the backroom, threw the towel over her shoulder, grabbed a pile of menus, and brought them to the table. She, too, dressed casual in jeans and a shawl-collared green sweater. She passed a one-page menu to each.

"My wife, Eve," George said. He retrieved an order pad and pencil from his apron pocket.

"Good day," Eve said. "I've got a fresh pot of lentil soup simmering. The bangers and mash is always tasty. And I just pulled roasted chickens out of the oven not a moment ago." She took a step back. "I'll let you decide."

Eve strolled behind the counter. The old man with the white beard shoved his empty mug her way. She filled it with beer from the tap and slid it in front of him. "Drink it slowly, Billy. A man your age shouldn't be fallin' off his stool twice in one week."

He chuckled. "'Twas my birthday. A man has a right to celebrate."

"'Twas your birthday," Eve said. "And you're still

celebrating."

The man two seats over raised his mug. "Cheers, Billy. Happy birthday, old friend."

Eve filled glasses with water and brought them to the table while George took everyone's order. Once they finished, Eve took the orders to the kitchen.

"After we eat," Kathy said, "Thomas and I are going to take a walk and check out a few shops up the street."

"Good idea, sweet pea," Jim said. "Hope you find somethin' interestin'."

"We won't come back until we do," Thomas replied.

George went to the bar and returned with their drink orders. "If I may ask, what brings you here?" he said.

Eve joined him from the kitchen.

"A couple of things," Lee said. "We flew over to see the fireworks on the Thames. Since we're here, we've been looking for the ancestry of a friend of ours. We stopped to talk to a man in the cemetery, but when we told him our story, he got madder than hell. He told us to tell whoever had sent us that he wasn't laughing yesterday, and he's not laughing today."

"What surname did you mention, chief?" George asked.

"Hudson," Lee replied.

The men at the bar roared with laughter.

"Of all the names in all the world," George said.

Tears of laughter-soaked Eve's face. "Lord, I would've liked to see the old grump's face."

"We don't get it," Jim said.

"It's a tale to be told," George said. "Seth Crowdus has been grumbling all his life. His father was the cemetery's groundskeeper before him. People remembered his da' as a good, spirited man who'd talk to everyone, himself, and the dead included. But truth be told, the man was as loony as the day is long. In those days, Seth was the center of most fisticuffs nearby, sticking up for his old man. When he was old enough, he worked with his da' in the cemetery, and there he be to this day and as feisty as ever."

"It was hard to believe," Eve added, "that someone would marry the grump, but Robin Lynn did. They had a little girl, Mary. When she grew up, she married a man that drank more than he's worth. Their little boy, Simon, Seth's grandson, spent most of his time keeping to himself, staying away from the yelling and screaming at home. Cute little boy. He played with imaginary friends at the cemetery while his grandda took care of the grounds. But Seth found no peace there. Every time he blinked, that boy was up to something. Simon's excuse was always the same. 'Elsie made me do it,' he'd say. Elsie Hudson."

Not so imaginary, Hayley thought.

"The boy's eleven now," George said, "and yesterday, they arrested him for grand theft. They caught him bang to rights stealing holy property from the church and hiding it in the courthouse basement. How he got into the courthouse is a mystery. And he blamed it all on Elsie Hudson."

"Holy moley," Jim said, glancing at Hayley.

She gave him a stern look to keep him from saying more and glanced around the table, seeing all eyes on her. *They probably think Elsie's playing games. If it weren't for Harry Tibbs's warning, I'd be thinking the same thing.* She turned her attention to George. "Did Simon say why his friend made him rob the church?"

"Said he was saving all the priceless things because the church is going to explode," one of the old men at the bar told them while slapping his hand on the counter and laughing louder.

"Lordy," Jim said under his breath.

Hayley tried to imagine what would cause such a disaster. *I need to talk to Simon. That means I'll have to get on the good side of Seth.* "I see why Mr. Crowdus is so stressed. Is there any way we could apologize to him? We might need to talk to him again about our friend's ancestors since our friend told us the trail leads here."

"You'd need an awfully good peace offering," Eve said. "I've got just the ticket. I have some chicken-and-leek pies in the oven that will be done by the time you finish your meal. It's his favorite. I'll take you over to his cottage and give you a proper introduction."

"That would be grand," Hayley said. "Thanks so much for your help."

"Think nothing of it, Miss. Anyway, Seth deserves a little cheering up."

After the team had finished their lunch, they decided to let Lee and Hayley be the lucky ones to visit the elderly grouch. Kathy and Thomas took a walk to investigate the area while Jim and Matilda had another beer each and asked questions about the history of the village. Hayley knew that history seemed to be one of Matilda's favorite subjects, and drinking happened to be one of Jim's much beloved pastimes. If anyone were to learn what the team needed to know, Hayley knew they were perfect for the job.

The day had turned out better than she expected. Only a few clouds now swept across the sky. Although the weather appeared to mimic spring, the temperature in the low forties reminded them that the warmer days were still months away.

"It's not far," Eve explained, carrying a pie wrapped in a white dishcloth as she led them down the street. "Just around the corner."

When they reached Seth's cottage, Lee and Hayley stayed outside the gate as Eve instructed. "I'll call you inside as soon as I tame the beast."

"We'll be fine," Lee said. "Take all the time you need."

When Eve knocked, Hayley heard a growling voice ask, "Who in the hell is it?"

CHAPTER 10

Eve entered Seth's home, closing the door behind her.

Winter had slain his garden. But in the midst of the desecration, Seth's house and the country-blue front door appeared surprisingly welcoming, Hayley noticed while standing behind the gate with Lee.

A few minutes later, the door reopened, and Eve waved to them. "Come in, come in."

Once inside, Eve introduced them to the old man. He had cleaned up since Hayley last saw him. He now wore a long-sleeved flannel red shirt, jeans, and suspenders.

She surveyed her surroundings. The home's ceiling seemed low. The coziness of the living room and the warmth from the blazing fireplace felt like a hug. Everything looked organized and spotless, each item in its rightful place. From Seth's gruff appearance this morning, Hayley expected to see something quite different. The surprise gave her hope that maybe he had a friendlier side to him.

"I'm going to leave you alone and let you chat. I need to get back to the pub." Eve started toward the door and turned, glowering at Seth.

"You're a hard woman, Eve," he said, showing her out. "I gave you my word, and it stands. I'll be a saint before you know it. Now leave me be, and let me speak with my guests."

"A saint," Eve huffed, while stepping out of the house. "Be civil, Seth Crowdus. The walls have ears."

He closed the door behind her.

"You have a very nice home," Hayley said.

"Thank you," Seth replied, turning to them. "I have my daughter to thank for its cleanliness. If you'd like, you may hang your coats on the rack." Once they did so, he gestured toward the green and blue plaid couch. "Please have a seat."

They sat. A ball of nerves arose in Hayley's throat. She didn't have a clue how to start the conversation, but she knew if she wanted to gain his trust, she had to be honest.

Before Seth could lower himself into his leather recliner by the fireplace, Hayley stopped him. "You might want to answer your phone," she said before it rang. "Officer Bates is calling about Simon."

Seth, halfway into his chair, appeared confused. His brows narrowed, and he straightened when the phone rang. "What game is this?" He hobbled across the room and snatched his cell phone from a small table by the door. "This is Seth." He listened quietly. His eyes widened. "She's here now. I'll get back to you." He ended the call and carried the cell phone back to his chair, easing himself into the seat. "A promise is a promise, Eve," he said softly. Then he crossed his arms, his face hardened, and he glared at Hayley. "Let's start by you telling me how you knew the phone would ring and who'd be on the other end."

"Are you willing to keep an open mind?" Hayley asked.

"I give my word. But I feel I'll regret it."

At that moment, Hayley saw a man's spirit enter the room. She glanced at a framed photo resting on the fireplace mantle. It depicted him and Seth, who appeared to be about six years old. "Is that a picture of you and your father?"

"Yes," Seth said. "Are you avoiding the question?"

"No. It happens that I have the same gifts your father had and your grandson now has."

Seth's face reddened. "How could you know anything about my da'?" he asked.

"People thought he was crazy," she said, "but he was gifted. He could see the past, present, and future, as well as speak to the dead. I have those abilities also."

He leaned forward, his hands gripping the chair's arms. "That doesn't answer my question. How could you know anything about my da'?"

"He's here with us now," she said. "He said his name is Jacob. He's standing by the hearth."

"What malarkey," he replied, falling back into his chair.

"His last words to you were *Tell Simon I'm sorry*. You had no idea what he meant. You never told anyone."

Seth's eyes widened slightly. He studied Hayley and smiled. "I don't know how you knew that, but it's a nice touch."

"He's been moving things around your house."

"Or I could've misplaced a few things." He crossed his arms again. "This is nonsensical."

Seth flinched when the framed photo of him and his dad fell on the mantle. He rose and walked across the room to an ashtray resting on top of a short bookcase. "More games."

"What Jacob meant by *Tell Simon I'm sorry* is that he knew Simon was born with the same gifts he had. He knew how hard it would be for Simon growing up and as an adult. Remember the time your father told your aunt her house was going to catch on fire? When it did, she called the police on him and had him arrested for arson."

"He always said he was innocent," he replied, lighting a cigarette.

"He wants you to sit," Hayley said. "We have serious things to discuss."

Seth extinguished his cigarette and went back to his chair, easing himself into the leather seat while focusing on the air in front of the mantle. "All my life, I thought he was crazy."

"You had no idea."

Seth took a handkerchief from his pants pocket and blew

his nose. "I need a drink. Would either of you care for one?"

"Yes," Lee replied. "Thank you."

"Yes, please," Hayley said.

"Rum and coke okay with you? I'm out of whiskey right now, or anything else for that matter. It's been a rough week."

"Rum and coke will be fine," Lee told him.

Hayley nodded.

Seth stood and wandered into the kitchen as if in a daze.

Hayley glanced at Lee. "I couldn't imagine how this would go."

"Do you think he bought it?"

"I don't know yet. I keep expecting him to explode." She held out her hands. "I'm shaking."

"Is his dad still here?" Lee asked.

She nodded. "He told me that Seth's been carrying this pain from his past since his childhood. He wants me to keep trying."

"Whatever you need to do. I'm finding this very entertaining."

"Feel free to jump in if you want."

Seth returned with two glasses in his hands and passed them their drinks. Then he went back into the kitchen, returning with his own, and reclaimed his seat. "Is he a ghost?" he asked.

"No," Hayley replied. "Everyone who passes and crosses over can come back to visit whenever they wish. He knew we were coming, and so did Elsie Hudson."

He stroked his beard. "So, she's real too."

"Yes," Lee said. "And she's been pestering the hell out of us."

"Simon's as sane as I am," Hayley told Seth.

He chuckled. "Did Eve know how loony you are before she brought you here?"

Hayley sensed a wall rise between them.

"You had me going there for a bit." His face hardened.

"I feel like a damn fool!" He slammed his fist on the arm of his chair. "I'll not be the butt of another joke. Get the hell out of my house."

"This isn't a joke," Lee said, setting his drink on the end table next to him. "How would Hayley know the last words your father spoke to you?"

"It's all a trick," Seth growled. "Get out!"

Hayley stood. "I'm sorry for the misunderstanding, Mr. Crowdus."

Lee rose also. He retrieved his wallet from his pant pocket, rummaged through it, and pulled out a card. "I'll leave my number in case you have a change of mind." He set it by his glass on the end table.

They grabbed their coats and hurried out the door, not slowing until they closed the gate behind them.

"I could have sworn he was coming around," Lee said, staring back at the house.

"We better get to the pub and make sure everyone's there. I'd like to fill them in on what happened before Seth calls us back." She started walking faster.

"Are you sure he'll call?" he asked, keeping up with her. "I know you can't foresee anything that involves your future."

"His dad gave me the thumbs-up as we left. It's a good guess he's up to something."

They entered the pub just as Lee's phone rang. He answered it while Hayley joined the others.

"How was your visit, Miss?" Eve asked.

"Couldn't have gone better," Hayley replied. She glanced at her friends. "We need to go."

"Is everything okay?" Jim asked.

"I'll explain in the car."

Once they piled into the Rover, and Lee, the last one in, closed his door, they began their meeting.

"What happened?" Kathy asked.

"The old man's a stubborn fool," Lee said.

"It started with the spirit of Seth's dad, Jacob, entering the room," Hayley told them. "I tried to explain to Seth that his dad, his grandson, and I have the same abilities. And I told him his father was standing by the fireplace. Seth seemed to go along with it until I told him his dad was expecting me, and so was Elsie Hudson."

"Then he threw us out," Lee added.

"Jacob gave me a sign that it will be okay as we left."

"And that's what the phone call was all about," Lee told them. "Seth wants us to come back. He thinks we're magicians and rigged his house to look like it's possessed."

"Don't just sit there like a frog on a log," Jim said. "Let's get over there."

CHAPTER 11

Lee started the Rover and drove around the corner. Seth leaned on the gate outside his home, shaking his walking stick and cursing at the house. The front door opened and closed over and over, slamming shut. The front windows had shattered. Shards of glass covered the garden. The house shook.

Lee parked, and everyone climbed out.

Kathy glanced at Hayley. "May I?" she whispered.

"Go ahead," Hayley replied. "He'll never guess it's you."

Kathy raised her hand, then made a gesture before faking a cough and covering her mouth. The glass in the garden returned to its rightful windows, each pane repairing itself as if nothing had happened.

Seth's eyes bulged, and his mouth opened. "Bloody hell!"

"Bet that threw your hat in the creek," Jim said.

"Who are these people?" Seth asked Lee.

"They're our friends. Do you want our help or not?"

"I don't know what you and that loony woman did or how you did it. Just make it stop."

"We didn't do a thing," Lee said. "And Hayley's not crazy."

"Your father's doing this," Hayley told him. "He doesn't want you to desert your grandson. It'll stop if you invite us in."

"If that's what it takes, feel free to enter. Just goes to show you're the cause of it all."

Hayley led the way. As she had told him it would, the

slamming of the doors ceased. She entered, and everyone followed her inside.

Seth crept in last, scanning every inch of the cottage. His legs shook. With the aid of his walking stick, he lowered himself into his leather chair. A half glass of rum sat on the table next to him. He snatched it and drank the contents without taking a breath. "Sit," he grumbled. "Sit." He pointed toward the dining room. "There's more chairs over there. Grab a couple if you have a mind to."

The ladies sat on the couch while the men brought three mismatched wooden chairs from the adjoining room and made themselves comfortable, quietly waiting for Seth to start the conversation.

"Who in the hell are you people?" he asked.

"I gave you my business card," Lee said.

Seth pulled it from his shirt pocket and read it. "Paranormal Search and Analysis."

"We're paranormal investigators," Hayley told him.

"This is all your fault." Seth reached for a drink only to notice the empty glass.

"This isn't a good time to get drunk," Lee said. "You need to keep an open mind."

"What do you want from me?" Seth asked. "Why are you doing this? If you're on the fiddle trying to make a buck on my misfortune, you've come to the wrong man. I'm as poor as Kelly's goat."

Grams, I need you, Hayley thought. Even though Grams told her she wouldn't join them in solving this mystery, Hayley knew her grandmother, guardian angel in training, would be wishing she could do something. But guardian angels had rules, and during the team's last case, Grams walked a fine line, and sometimes she overstepped, becoming too involved in Hayley's life by joining the team.

Grams appeared behind Lee's chair, allowing only Hayley

to see her. *Yes, dear.*

Is it possible for you to speak to Seth's dad and find out if he knows how to materialize? Hayley asked.

Certainly.

Hayley watched Grams join Seth's dad by the fireplace. In a moment, Grams nodded to her.

Thank you, Hayley told her.

Anytime, dear. Call me if you need me. Without hesitation, Grams's spirit vanished.

Hayley stood.

"Where are you going?" Seth asked. "I'm not through with you yet."

"I'm giving your father a seat."

"Why do you keep feeding me this malarkey?"

Kathy stood too. Hayley knew her friend had witnessed materialization many times and understood that Kathy wouldn't want to be only inches away when it happened.

Matilda leaped from the couch and dashed behind Jim's chair, watching.

The space on the couch grew frigid as Seth's dad gathered energy from the air. A cloud oscillated into a misty form, then grew in width and height, wavering until his transparent features became detailed, allowing everyone to see him.

Seth covered his face with his hands. "Bloody hell!" He peeked between his fingers. His hands dropped, his mouth gaped, and he stared at his dad.

"He needed to gather a huge amount of energy to show himself," Hayley explained. "I'm sorry he'll only stay a moment."

Before his image faded, Seth's dad made a fist, raised his pinky finger, and wiggled it at his son. In less than a second, he disappeared.

Seth sat speechless with his mouth still agape.

Jim, who had snuck into the kitchen, returned with a full glass of rum and handed it to the old man.

"Bless you," Seth told him. He took a big gulp. "It was really him. He spoke to me with our secret sign language."

"We have a lot to discuss," Hayley said.

"Where do we begin?" Seth asked, looking around the room at all the guests.

Hayley turned to Jacob, who now stood at the end of the plaid couch. "Does Simon know the secret language?"

Jacob nodded.

"He said yes," she told Seth while she reclaimed her seat where a moment ago Jacob had sat. "Before Jacob taught him the secret, Simon spoke to him out loud. Everyone thought he was always talking to himself. That's one of the reasons he was bullied. I can speak to your dad in my mind, but Simon hasn't learned how to do that yet."

Kathy and Matilda returned to the couch.

"Why didn't he tell me he knew the finger talk?" Seth asked.

"He thought it was his and his grandfather's secret. Besides, he never told you much anyway. When he did, you didn't believe him. You called him a liar, a thief, a troublemaker, or crazy."

"How do you know all this?"

"Your dad's been around for years watching Simon grow and seeing all the things that happened to him in his own life now happening to Simon. Remember how your dad was always in trouble? That's what's been going on with Simon. Just as your dad could, Simon can foresee the future. Every time he gave a warning that something would occur, and it did, he was blamed. But the future isn't etched in stone. Sometimes when he gave warning, people inadvertently changed their behavior, becoming more alert and careful. Without realizing it, they changed the future he'd foreseen. So, when the danger didn't happen, they called him a liar."

"One way or another," Jim said, "he was damned if he

told."

Seth lowered his head. "I condemned my father as well as my grandson."

"Don't kick yourself in the ass," Jim told him, leaning forward in his maple spindle-back chair. "Ya didn't know."

"I went through the same thing," Hayley explained. "My parents thought I was schizophrenic." Her childhood's emotional scarring still put a lump in her throat when memories surfaced. The pain she received from strangers and her peers bullying her never compared to the hurtful trauma her parents put her through. She could sympathize with Simon and Jacob. "Simon needs to know you understand now and that we're here to help him get out of the mess he's in."

"What about Simon's parents," Lee asked. "Do they believe him? Do you think they'll stand in our way if we try to help him?"

Seth shook his head. "The courts blamed my daughter and her husband for the lad's behavioral problems. Their nasty fights have brought the police to their door many a night. So, the courts stepped in and removed Simon from their custody. Until he robbed the church, he's been living with me."

"Is he in jail?" Jim asked.

"No, he's too young. The courts are waiting for a mental evaluation before passing judgment on the lad. Meanwhile, they've placed him under Officer Bates's charge."

"It's good he's not behind bars," Jim said. "He doesn't need any more traumatizin', poor kid."

Thank goodness Jacob's been there for him, Hayley thought. *Besides Elsie, he's the only one in Simon's life who has believed in him.* It had been that way in her life as well. Grams believed in her when no one else had.

Seth walloped the arm of his chair. "You're absolutely right. I'll see to it from now on that the lad gets my respect."

Hayley felt chilled and crossed her arms. She glanced at

the fireplace and noticed the fire had died. *No wonder I'm cold.* She flinched when a spark came out of nowhere, and flames danced within the logs. *Was that a spell?* Hayley turned to Kathy, sitting next to her. A smile crossed her friend's face. Hayley arched an eyebrow.

Kathy whispered, "I made sure he didn't notice."

"Oh, by the by," Seth said, turning his attention to Hayley. "Simon's been asking for you. That's what Officer Bates told me when he called. The lad knows you're here and wants to speak to you."

"Elsie must've told him," Hayley said.

"So, you believe she exists?" Seth asked.

"We know she does," Jim said. "She's been scarin' the hell outta us. We finally figured out she wanted us to come here. But we had no idea why."

Hayley visualized the many times Elsie had appeared to her, and she wished more than ever that she could understand the little girl so they could chat.

"We had trouble comprehending her in the beginning," Matilda explained. "Hayley's unfamiliar with the intonations within your country and couldn't understand what the child had said at first. It wasn't until just recently, when we witnessed Elsie materialize, and we heard her speak, that we were able to establish her needs. We assumed Hayley's recurring dreams of the church being destroyed during the war indicated Elsie's burial site to be in the church cemetery."

"I know every name on every gravestone," Seth said. "As I said before, she's not there."

Hayley glanced at Jacob. "Is she buried on the church grounds?" she asked him.

He nodded.

"Your dad says yes," Hayley told Seth.

"Blimey," he replied.

"What's our plan?" Lee asked.

"First, we need to find out why the church is going to explode." Hayley looked at Jacob again. "I guess you were unaware about all this, or you would've stopped Simon from breaking the law?"

She heard his answer in her mind. *You're right. I would've stopped him. But I didn't know. I come and go. I'm not around as much as I used to be while Simon was little when I helped him be less fearful of the dead and taught him the secret language. Now I visit only when he's sad. That's when he needs me the most.*

Hayley knew her relationship with Grams would have been similar if she hadn't become her guardian angel. Grams had mentioned on many occasions that her visits would have been less frequent. To this day, Hayley had never asked her how she finagled her way into becoming her guardian angel. She only knew that she felt blessed that Grams watched over her.

"How many people did he warn about the explosion?" she asked him.

He said he told everyone, but they wouldn't listen. And when he told them why, they didn't believe him. I'm to blame too. I've known about Elsie since Simon was five. I thought this was one of their games.

"Thank you, Jacob." She relayed his answer to the others. "Next, we'll have to convince Elsie to materialize in front of Officer Bates."

"How are you going to talk to her if you can't understand what she's saying?" Seth asked.

"We have no way to contact Elsie other than through Simon," Hayley explained. "Would you consent to be our go-between and talk to him using the secret language? He can ask Elsie for us. And I'm sure you'll have a few questions to ask him."

"I'll do anything you want," Seth said. "Will the charges against Simon be dropped?"

"No," Jim said. "But it'll get our foot in the court's door if we can find some hard evidence. No hearsay or jibber jabber will do. So, once they see she's buried in the church cemetery, we'll have their attention. That's when we'll spring Elsie's ghost on 'em."

"At least then they'll know that Simon's friend isn't imaginary," Lee said.

"Yes," Hayley said. "It's a start."

"Was any of that story that you're trying to find a friend's deceased relative true?" Seth asked.

"Yes," Kathy replied. "Our friend's name is Roger Hudson. We thought maybe Elsie was just trying to get our attention because of the family connection."

"Do you know for sure they're related?" Seth asked.

"Not yet," Kathy said. "We need to do more research. Possibly if we exhume her casket, we may be able to extract a sample of DNA."

"I don't think the church will go for that," Seth told them. "There would have to be a dire need to exhume the coffin. Just to get DNA isn't good enough."

"We'll see where it leads," Hayley said. "For now, I'd like to stick to the ancestral story. I don't believe it would help to tell Officer Bates that we're paranormal investigators, at least not in the beginning. And it would be up to Simon if he wants the entire town to know he's gifted. That would be one of the questions you can ask him."

"Let's just buy time by telling Officer Bates we're here on our friend's behalf," Lee said. "The most important thing you'll need to ask Simon is why the church is going to explode. Is it true, how, and when? And see if he'll ask Elsie to materialize in front of Officer Bates to see how he reacts. We'll need his help. Once we get a few answers from Simon, we can go from there."

"I'll try to research the war's destruction to the church's exterior and to the cemetery," Kathy told them. "If I can find documented evidence of Elsie Hudson's burial, it'll give us some credibility."

"First things first," Lee said. "Officer Bates is expecting

Seth's call."

"I'll ring him up and see what I can do," Seth said, reaching for his cell phone on the table next to him. He dialed and asked for Officer Bates. "This is Seth." He listened. "So, out of all the things, Simon has told you, you choose to believe Miss Johnson has proof of his innocence?" He remained silent for a moment.

"She's here to see me. Her and her friends are looking for one of their ancestors they believe resides in the church's cemetery." He waited to hear the officer's comments. "I know all the names on all the headstones, and the person's name they're looking for is on none of them. I'm going to get them permission to go through the church's burial records. I assure you, Officer Bates, if we dig up any evidence, pun intended, you'll be the first person I'll bring it to." Seth chuckled. "Please tell my grandson I'll be visiting him today. Even after all the trouble he's stirred up, I miss the lad." He listened, said his goodbyes, and ended the call.

"That sounded promising," Hayley said.

"I didn't tell him a single lie."

"That's right, ya didn't," Jim said.

"He thinks Simon is a liar from now 'till Sunday. I'll just leave it to Simon and Elsie to convince him otherwise."

"Good idea," Lee said.

Hayley looked at Jacob. "I'd be grateful if you'd tell Simon to stay silent while we investigate. If he mentions to anyone about what we're doing, he may cause the church and the courts to stop our search. Until we find substantial proof that Elsie's real and why the church will explode, chances are they'll think we're sticking our nose into the town's business. We need time to find evidence. And please, tell him that his grandfather will keep him informed."

Jacob nodded and instantly disappeared.

"Looks like this will take a while," Jim said. "Any hotels around, Seth?"

"A couple. The Night Owl is pleasant. If it pleases you, I'll ring up Mrs. Dickens and let her know you're coming."

"Yes. Thank you for all your help." Hayley stood. Relief washed over her, knowing Seth had become a believer. She knew that convincing others that ghosts and spirits were actually around us more than anyone could imagine becomes an impossible feat in most cases. The majority of people she'd encountered made quick judgement, as Seth had, condemning her of fabricating stories. They resented the fact that she wouldn't admit that she lived in a fantasy world and needed mental help. It took too much of her energy to convince them they were wrong, which led her to keeping her abilities secret, not making friends, and ultimately forcing her to become a recluse. She felt determined not to let Simon live as a condemned lunatic for the rest of his life and, for the first time, she believed, be accepted by those around him.

"Yes, thank you," Lee said, rising from his chair. "We'll head over now. Once we get our rooms, we'll drive back to the manor for our things. Please give me a call after you speak with Simon."

"My pleasure," Seth told him, climbing out of his recliner with the aid of his walking stick. "I'll go see Simon directly."

The men returned their chairs to the other room.

With walking stick in hand, Seth showed them to the door.

***

After they booked their rooms at the Night Owl, a Tutor-style hotel that stood prominently on a corner on High Road, they drove to the manor to retrieve their things. Halfway there, Hayley answered Lee's cell phone for him while he kept his eyes on the road.

She heard Seth's panicked voice. "Simon said there's an unexploded bomb from World War II buried beside the church. He foresees that the next strong tremor will ram it against Elsie's coffin and make it explode."

Hayley gasped. A wave of horror swept over her. "That

changes everything."

"He said Elsie agreed to materialize. She'll do it this evening."

"Thanks, Seth. When we return, we'll need another plan." Once she ended the call, she told the others.

"Holy moley," Jim said. "We need to think of somethin'. We can't just dig up her grave and yank out her coffin. It's too risky. The bomb's too close."

"We'll put our heads together," Lee said.

At the manor, Hayley followed Lee to the reservation desk. "We'll all be checking out," he told a woman behind the desk.

"I hope you had a pleasant stay," the woman said.

"We did, thank you." Lee pulled out his wallet and gave her a credit card. "I'll be paying for my friends as well."

She took the card and completed the transaction.

Once they packed their bags and loaded them into the two Land Rovers, the team went back inside to the dining room and had an early dinner before leaving.

Lee held the passenger door for Hayley as she climbed into the vehicle. When she felt the car tremble, panic enhanced her anxiety to leave. She cursed under her breath. "How much time do we have?"

CHAPTER 12

After the team returned to the Night Owl Inn and took their luggage upstairs to their rooms, they gathered in the lobby and entered a dining room to the right. A stone fireplace on the far wall blazed, making the room toasty warm. Looking out the multipaned window, Hayley noticed an icy rain had begun to fall. She and the others sat at the bar.

People filed in one after another and hung their coats on the coat trees by the door before finding seats. Soon the entire room buzzed with customers.

In the front corner near the window, a small stage appeared deserted. A wooden chair and a microphone waited for someone to perform.

A thin man with wavy light brown hair and carrying a guitar approached the stage. The crowd saluted him, raising their beer mugs high. When he began to sing, the hairs on Hayley's neck stood on end.

"While others slept, Simon crept through the streets of our village."

Even though she detested the lyrics, she listened.

"In the dark, he found his mark and entered the church to pillage."

His voice sounded sweet, but his words struck a brutal chord with Hayley.

"Oh, what will we do with the loony lad? What can we do with Simon McClad? What will we do with the balmy nit when he says Elsie made him do it?"

The audience sang along as he repeated his lyrics.

"Oh, what will we do with the loony lad? What can we do with Simon McClad? What will we do with the balmy nit when he says Elsie made him do it?"

Multiple feelings rocked Hayley to her core, sadness for the innocent boy, contempt for the bully who sang the degrading lyrics, and total disappointment in the people singing along.

The ghastly song ended, the crowd cheered, and the singer moved off the stage, allowing another to take his place. Instead of performing, a hefty bald man taking the microphone began making remarks about Simon and his family.

"Doesn't that rock your boat?" Jim said, sitting next to Lee.

"It's outrageous," Matilda said.

"Don't worry," Jim told her. "We're safe as long as they don't hear what we're thinkin'."

Lee's phone rang. He slipped off his bar stool and strolled into the lobby. After he returned, he whispered to the others. "That was Seth. He wants us to come over. Officer Bates called him and said he needs to urgently speak with him. Seth wants us to be there before he arrives." He glanced at Matilda, Jim, Kathy, and Thomas. "You guys stay here and find out what's going on. Hayley and I can handle this. Call us if there's trouble we should know about."

Hayley and Lee climbed the stairs to their room, and Lee unlocked the door. They hurried in, grabbed what they needed, and threw their coats on while rushing out of their room, closing the door behind them. Without a word, they raced through the narrow hallways and down the stairs to the lobby.

Before stepping into the cold, Hayley raised the hood of her coat. As ice on the ground crunched beneath her feet, she watched her step while following Lee to the Rover. When she pulled open the passenger's door, her shoes lost their grip, and she slipped. Her heart leaped into her throat. Grabbing the door, she saved herself from a fall. *Bloody hell. Hm. England's rubbing off on me.* She hopped in and pulled the door closed.

Once inside the vehicle, not bothering with their seatbelts, they drove off.

The windshield wipers batted away the slushy drops as Lee turned the corner toward Seth's cottage. He parked, they exited the Rover, opened the gate, and made their way to the front door.

Seth opened it. "Come in. Come in. Have a seat on the sofa."

They hung their coats and went around a wooden chair Seth brought from the other room. They sat on the couch across from him.

With the aid of his walking stick, he lowered himself slowly into his recliner. "Now we wait," Seth said.

A knock on the door broke the silence.

"Come in," Seth shouted.

A middle-aged man with red hair, wearing a hooded lambskin coat, jeans, and a sweater, entered, the frigid air rushing in behind him. He shut the door and hesitated before coming into the room. "I see you have company. I can come back later."

"Sit down, Officer Bates," Seth said. "We all know why you're here."

"I doubt that very much." His hands shook as he placed his coat on the rack, causing him to miss the hook. He tried several times to hang it.

"I see you're off duty," Seth said. "Please have a seat."

"What I have to say is a private matter," Officer Bates said, sitting gingerly on the chair.

"Let's not beat around the bush," Seth said. "You're here because you saw Elsie."

Officer Bates's eyes widened. "Did you speak to the lad? He's under the influence of a demon." He stood and paced. Then he stopped, gripped the back of his wooden chair, and glared at

Seth. "Have you seen her? I've never seen anything as frightening in my entire life. What did I let into my house? I feel like I'm in a bloody horror movie."

"Calm down," Seth said. "Sit, sit."

Officer Bates, visibly shaking, sat once more.

"These are my friends, Hayley Johnson and Lee Franklin. They're the folks from across the pond. I spoke about them."

Officer Bates gave them a nod, his eyes still wide. "Have you seen her?" he asked them.

"Yes," Hayley replied. "She led us here. We were in London when she found us."

"Why you?" he asked. "It doesn't make sense."

"Hayley has gifts," Lee told him. "She's able to talk to the dead. Apparently, Elsie was looking for someone who could help save the church, the town, and everyone in it."

"Why? What does the church and town have to do with it?"

"There's a World War II unexploded bomb buried in the cemetery," Hayley told him. "Simon and Elsie were trying to get help before the next significant tremor hits. They said it will ram into her coffin and explode."

"Don't let her fool you," Officer Bates said, raising his shaking fingers. "Demons lie and manipulate to get what they want. She wants Simon to go free so she can use him to create havoc."

"And if you're wrong?" Seth sat forward in his chair. "How will you live with the death toll, knowing you knew of the threat and could have prevented it?"

"Why are you so sure about this, Seth?"

"Hayley has ways of knowing things that we don't. I trust her and her friends. They're professional paranormal investigators."

Cat's out of the bag, Hayley thought.

Officer Bates glared at Hayley and Lee. "So, you perjured

yourselves when you said you're finding your friend's ancestor."

I could see that coming, Hayley thought.

"We told the truth," Lee said. "We're researching Elsie's ties to our friend's family. Until Simon let us know the reason she brought us here, finding the Hudson lineage was our focus."

"She's leading you astray," Officer Bates said, in a tone as cold as the ice hanging from the eves outside. "She's evil. I've seen her."

"How can we convince you she isn't?" Hayley asked.

"You can't."

"Did you know that there's a meeting going on at the Night Owl?" Lee asked. "They sounded like a lynch mob getting ready to go after the boy."

"That's nothing new," Officer Bates said. "The singer presents the same song every Saturday night but changes the lyrics to fit Simon's latest antics." He turned to Seth. "As you know, Simon's in my custody. I'm not permitted to leave him by himself, so he'll be attending church with me and my wife in the morning. It will do him good to get away from that demon. Once he sets foot inside the church, she won't be able to follow him."

"Good idea." Seth gave Hayley a wink. "You should give him the opportunity to apologize to the church and the town."

Simon must have told him something. She looked at her lap, closed her eyes, and used her ability to foresee tomorrow's outcome. She knew the Divine rule that disallowed her to envision her future wouldn't stop her this time since she wouldn't be anywhere near the church. In her mind, she witnessed what would transpire.

Inside the fifteenth-century church, stone columns supported broad arches. The stained-glass windows depicted colorful scenes from the Christian Bible. Above, dark-brown painted ribs crisscrossed the bowed ceiling.

In the front of the church, a priest gave a sermon covering the sins of casting stones based on the meeting held at the Night

Owl. While the parishioners remained silently sitting in the many rows of pews, he called Simon, dressed in a brown suit and scuffed black shoes, to the lectern. He knelt in front of the priest, who dosed him with holy water. The blond-haired boy stood with his hands behind him and looked down as if thinking about how to begin. Then he gazed out into the assembly and spoke softly.

"I've been told that this is a place for forgiveness."

A woman in the back said, "Amen."

Her husband shouted. "Not likely."

She swatted him with her prayer book. "Sorry, Father."

The eleven-year-old continued. "I'd like to tell you about my friend. I've known her since I was five. During World War II, she watched her house being bombed. She was lucky not to be home. But unlucky because her parents and brothers and sisters were, and they died. When children were sent away by their parents to live in the Midlands, the authorities brought her here to stay with a family down the road. A couple of days after that, a bomb hit the field where she played, and she was killed."

No one spoke.

"My friend isn't imaginary. I'm the only family she has. She's buried on the other side of that wall over there." Simon pointed. "When the church was bombed, it messed up the cemetery, and her headstone got lost in the ruins and was hauled away with the other debris. After the cemetery was fixed, no one remembered she was there."

"Where's your apology, lad?" someone asked near the back.

The priest held up his hand. "Now, let him speak his mind. I'm sure it's coming. Continue, Simon."

"I want to apologize if her appearance offends you. When the bomb hit, she got a little messy, and no one bothered to clean her up or dress her nicely before they buried her. But here it goes, like it or not. This is my friend Elsie."

Elsie materialized next to him. The silence broke, and the crowd went wild. Some cried while others prayed. Words not meant to be spoken in church echoed off the walls.

The priest spoke loudly to gain control of the chaos. "Take your seats. Take your seats."

When the upheaval had been suppressed, and all eyes were on her, Elsie vanished.

Another rumble circled the room.

"Now, now," said the priest. "The truth is not always evident. It seems it's time for you to release the hatred in your hearts." He turned to Simon. "Is it true there's a bomb buried next to the church?"

"Yes. Elsie went for help since no one would listen to me. They're here to save everyone. The only problem is we don't know when it'll explode. We only know that the next tremor will set it off."

Gasps spread across the room. Parishioners gathered their belongings.

"We must be calm," Father Farley said. "Please don't run."

Too late, Hayley thought. Her vision ended, and she opened her eyes.

"Let me give you Simon's brown suit," Seth told Officer Bates.

Lee's cell phone rang. He answered. "Thanks," he said and ended the call. "That was Jim. He said the mob's planning to run Simon and his family out of town."

"Over my dead body," Seth said.

"I better get over there," Officer Bates said. "I'll get the lad's suit later." He grabbed his coat and left, not waiting for Seth to show him out.

"Well, that went amiss," Seth said.

"I'm sure Officer Bates will change his mind tomorrow," Hayley told him.

Lee raised a brow.

"I'll tell you about it later," she said. "Let's get back to the others. We need to decide what to do next."

CHAPTER 13

Upstairs in Lee and Hayley's hotel room, each of the team found a place to sit or stand. Kathy and Thomas cozied up on the queen-sized bed, their backs against the high brown tufted headboard and their legs stretched out on the dark brown bedspread. Matilda sat in a yellow-flowered upholstered chair by the small desk while Jim remained standing along with Hayley and Lee. Clouds blanketed the sky, and the wind whipped the trees beyond their window. Lee flipped the switch, illuminating the chandelier that hung in the center of the room.

A tight fit, but everyone's here, Hayley thought. "We met with Officer Bates. About an hour ago, Simon revealed his imaginary friend to him, and it scared Officer Bates so badly he couldn't stop shaking."

"We were hoping," Lee said, "that the reveal would make him realize that Elsie's real and a victim of war. But just the opposite happened. He's totally convinced she's a demon and controlling Simon."

"Betcha it'll be harder than a woodpecker's lips to get 'em to think otherwise," Jim said.

"We won't have to," Hayley replied. "He and his wife are taking Simon to church in the morning. I had a vision of what will happen, and it'll change his mind. He said he's aware that a demon can't enter a church. So, when Simon reveals Elsie to the parishioners while he's standing next to the priest, Officer Bates's assumption will be thrown out the window."

"Well, I'll be…." Jim said. "That kid's gonna shake up the entire town."

"But will everyone be convinced she's not a demon?" Kathy asked. "I've seen Elsie myself, and she looked damn scary to me."

"You're probably right about that," Lee said. "The mob downstairs seems to be a little hardheaded."

"There'll always be haters," Jim replied.

"What matters is it'll change the priest's mind," Hayley added. "We'll need his consent to dig up the grave to uncover the bomb."

"I've researched unexploded bombs in England," Thomas said, "and it seems they're fairly common. It's claimed that they're potentially more dangerous than when they were made. The military bomb-disposal experts are responsible for extricating them. Should we call them?"

"And say what?" Jim said, taking a seat on the arm of Matilda's chair. "They'll ask its location. All we can tell 'em is it's in the cemetery. We're not sure where. They'd probably ask how we know it's there, and when we tell 'em, they'll hang up."

"You're right," Lee replied, rubbing his chin. "It's a dilemma. Maybe when we find evidence of Elsie's burial site in the church's archives, we can give them the location."

"Which still leaves the question," Jim said, "how do we know?"

"Let's talk to the priest after services tomorrow so we can get access to the burial records," Hayley suggested.

"Wish we could be there to see their faces when they see Elsie," Kathy said.

"We have to remember that we're strangers here," Hayley said. "We have to be careful what we say and do. That crowd downstairs could easily turn on us."

"It may be best to take this one step at a time," Lee told them.

"Speakin' of time," Jim said. "Do ya think Simon has any clue 'bout the ETE?"

"What's an ETE?" Matilda asked.

"Estimated time of explosion, of course," Jim replied.

"Time and place would be hard to pin down," Hayley said, knowing what happens in the future is not fixed in stone. *And it's impossible to know when an earthquake will hit.*

"Could be," Jim told her. "Did Simon have a vision, or did Elsie tell him 'bout it? If he had a vision of the future, wouldn't that make the explosion a sure thing?"

"The future isn't fixed," Hayley said. "But you're right. I should talk to Simon and find out how he knows."

"After church services, we'll call on Officer Bates," Lee said. "Then we'll talk to Simon before we head over to the church to get permission to research the archives."

"Do you think we should get ground penetrating radar to scan Elsie's gravesite?" Thomas asked.

Lee nodded. "That's a good idea. It'll show us the angle of the bomb and how close it is to her coffin."

Jim crossed his arms. "Again, there's a little problem. A GPR doesn't give a detailed picture of an object. It only shows wavy lines and a bunch of colors. An expert can't even tell ya what's exactly down there. The question is, who's gonna be brave enough to dig up the grave?"

"We'd better come up with an answer quick," Lee said. "Why don't we go downstairs and see if we can find seating at the bar. We need time to sort things out."

"Good idea," Jim said. "I do my best thinkin' after a few drinks."

They left the hotel room and strolled down the narrow corridor with Lee, Jim, and Thomas in the lead. Hayley walked slowly with Matilda and Kathy.

"I remember seeing that man who spoke in front of the mob earlier," Kathy told Hayley. "When we were in London, the local newspaper was delivered to us while you were away. There was a picture taken in Central London showing demonstrators protesting climate change. It had gotten out of hand, and fights broke out. I'm absolutely positive that one of the men being taken away in handcuffs was the same instigator downstairs tonight."

"I read the same article," Matilda said. "Now that you mention it, he does look familiar."

"How odd," Hayley said.

They followed the men down the stairs and entered the dining room. All had left. The high-backed wooden chairs placed around the round dining tables were empty. Only the bartender wiping down the counter remained. He looked up as they entered. The fire crackled within the large stone fireplace, giving the room the fragrance of hickory. The beamed ceiling made the room feel quaint. *So different from an hour ago when the room was crowded,* Hayley thought.

Lee checked his watch. "It's nearly 8:30. I wonder if Officer Bates cleared everyone out or if people around here turn in early?"

Jim straddled a barstool and sat. "What happened, Henry?" he asked the bartender while everyone pulled out stools and sat. "Where's everyone?"

"The police stopped by," the young man said, "and suggested they'd better call it a night. Seems word got around that they were getting a little rebellious."

"They were a bit," Jim said.

"Yes. In fact, it could have been me who made the call. Can I interest any of you in a mug of brew or something that may lift your spirits?" He placed paper coasters in front of each of them and took their orders. Then he poured beer for the men and wine for the women.

"Cheers, mates," the young man said.

"Cheers," they replied.

"Does this kinda gatherin' happen often?" Jim asked,

lifting his mug.

"The town is normally quiet this time of year. But I'm not insinuating that it's boring. Laughter's the key to getting through winter. There wasn't laughter here tonight. It's been this way for the last three weekends ever since Timothy Dunn rented the McCarthy farmhouse."

"Is that the guy who was excitin' the crowd?" Jim asked him.

"The very same."

"Do you think the mob will cause trouble?" Lee asked.

"I wouldn't count on it," Henry said. "Father Farley stopped by and listened in. I've no doubt tomorrow's sermon will be based on what he witnessed."

"Are ya goin'?" Jim asked.

A smile spread across Henry's face. "I wouldn't miss it, mate. I heard Officer Bates is bringing Simon." He chuckled. "The lad pinched church property and hid it in the courthouse basement."

"Did he?" Jim said. "How old is the boy?"

"Ten or eleven. Tomorrow's services are going to be pretty exciting. I'll be sitting next to the officer and his wife like I usually do. And you know I'm going to eavesdrop."

Kathy leaned and whispered to Hayley, "Coincidence?"

"Not a chance."

"Looks like we'll have our own eyes and ears in the pews," Matilda said, raising her wine glass.

"He appears to be observant," Kathy said, swirling her half empty glass of wine. "I bet we'll get every detail."

"Will ya be workin' tomorrow, Henry?" Jim asked. "We'd like to hear 'bout it."

"Yes. We open at noon," he replied. "I'll be working until closing. More than likely, it'll be fairly slow. After a scolding from the church, most people stay home and repent, or at least make it appear so."

"What kind of things does Simon usually do to cause such an uproar?" Thomas asked.

"It's not just the lad," Henry said. "His da and mum have had bouts with the law as well. His da is a heavy drinker and is known to gamble excessively. Recently he's rattled somebody's cage. Scotland Yard sent someone to question him."

"I would think Scotland Yard would question someone discreetly," Thomas said.

"They did. Simon told someone. A few minutes later, the whole town knew."

"Tough to keep a secret around here," Thomas said.

"It truly is."

"Does anyone know why Simon's parents were questioned?" Thomas sipped his beer.

Henry shook his head. "I'd have heard about it if they did. It's a dysfunctional family. No wonder he's mental. Poor lad goes around talking to himself or," he said, chuckling, "to his imaginary friend."

"So, the kid's a troublemaker?" Jim asked.

"The lad's a bad egg. He likes to excite people by telling them their house is going to catch fire or be robbed or that other sinister things will happen. But, more times than not, nothing happens. The police think it's a bit of a lark to pursue Simon's fabrications."

"What about when something does happen that he predicts?" Hayley asked.

"I wouldn't use the word predicts. Getting people to disbelieve your tales is a creative way to get them miffed enough to look the other way. So, when he's on the rob, they never notice him. And when he's questioned, he always says he didn't have anything to do with it. We all know he's as guilty as sin and maybe not as mental as he appears to be. There just wasn't any proof until a few days ago when he stole from the church and finally got caught, bang to rights."

"Sounds like a clever boy," Jim said.

"That's true, mate," Henry said. "Maybe things aren't what they appear to be."

That's an understatement, Hayley said to herself. *Just wait until he finds out what's really going on. It'll be the talk of the town for generations – if we all live through it.*

"Keeps one guessin'," Jim told him.

"That about sums it up," Henry said. "So, what brings you to our town?"

"We're planning to research the church's archives to find a missing gravesite," Kathy replied.

"That sounds interesting. What's the surname?"

"Hudson," Lee said.

So much for watching what we say to people, Hayley thought.

Henry's eyes widened. He rubbed his arms. "I just got goosebumps. It's a strange coincidence that Simon's imaginary friend's last name is Hudson. I'd keep the name to myself if I were you. Some people will get eggy if you mention it."

"Like ya said," Jim told him, "it's hard to keep a secret 'round here. But we'll try."

"A little excitement never hurt anyone," Lee told him.

Hayley, Matilda, and Kathy finished their wine. Soon afterward, the men took their last sips from their mugs.

"Let's turn in, guys," Lee said. "Who knows what will happen tomorrow?" He winked at Hayley.

"You have that right," Henry said. "Have a good night, mates."

The group rose from their barstools, climbed the stairs, and headed to their rooms.

"I can't wait until tomorrow," Hayley told Lee as they entered their room.

"Don't get too excited," Lee said. "England has an ancient history, and the belief in demons runs deep. Tomorrow might be dangerous."

CHAPTER 14

Hayley's fitful dream jarred her awake. Her nightmare reminded her of an old monster movie she'd watched as a child. The mob had turned violent and marched through town holding up torches, heading to the home of Simon's parents. Outside the gate leading to their front door, the mob threatened to burn down the house and kill the demon child.

Within the darkness of her hotel room, she scrutinized every detail of the horror. *It couldn't have been a foreseeing. People don't do things like that nowadays. This isn't the Middle Ages. Stop this foolishness. Sometimes dreams are just dreams.* She glanced at the clock on her nightstand and sighed. *Three a.m.* Mentally and physically exhausted, Hayley rolled over. The soft bed felt comfortable. Nothing prevented her from falling asleep except her persistent fear-filled thoughts. She closed her eyes and flooded her mind with images of Sutterville, her hometown, in springtime. As she imagined counting pink blossoms covering the apple tree in her, now Kathy's, front yard, and their fragrance filled her senses, she finally drifted to sleep.

In the morning, even though the urge to doze for a few more hours tempted her, Hayley peeked out and watched Lee pull back the curtains. The weather outside looked promising. The dank, misty mornings she had awoken to for days had given way to blue skies. She sat up and yawned. "What time is it?"

"Good morning, love. Nearly ten. We slept in."

Hayley threw the bedcovers off her, sat on the edge of the

bed, and stretched. "Do you think breakfast will be served in the dining room?"

"Jim left me a text. There's a brunch buffet set up. The place looks deserted. Everyone, plus the cook, has gone to church."

"I hope all this hatefulness doesn't traumatize Simon for the rest of his life," Hayley said.

"Services will be over in a half hour," Lee said, looking outside toward the church. "No doubt we'll get a call from Officer Bates shortly after, considering what Simon will do in front of everyone this morning."

"Give me a minute to get ready, and we'll go downstairs to eat," Hayley said. She hurried to her suitcase, extracted undergarments, jeans, and a turtleneck sweater before heading to the bathroom to shower.

***

After brunch, when the hotel staff had returned to work, Hayley sat with her friends, awaiting a call from Officer Bates. The dining room looked empty. Only a few scattered customers wandered in.

Lee glanced at his cell phone. "Finally." He answered the call. "Yes, officer. We'll be right over." He glanced at his companions. "Officer Bates wants all of us to meet him at his house. It's on the edge of town. Shouldn't take us long to get there. We'll take the LR4. I'll drive."

Each of their heads turned toward a curly red-haired man who had raised his voice and slammed his fist on the table.

"The devil will deceive you," the man said.

"The girl looked real to me," the other man replied. "I was only a foot away."

"I'm warning you. Don't be fooled," the red-haired man said firmly. "Timothy Dunn said the devil has ways to trick the eye. How can you doubt that? The lad's the devil's tool. Don't be duped, Dennis."

"Before he faced the congregation, Simon knelt before the

priest and was anointed with holy water. Don't forget that, Zack. If the kid was a demon, we would've known it right there and then. You can agree with Timothy all you want, but I'm standing with the priest. If he believes in Simon, so do I."

"You're a fool," Zack replied.

"Seems like the town's as divided as the gap between Bubba's buckteeth," Jim said in a low tone.

"Let's get going." Lee slid his chair back. "When we get back, we'll talk to Henry and find out what's up." He slid his chair back.

Hayley and the others followed his lead through the lobby and out the door. Above, the promise of blue skies faded as doubtful dark clouds gathered, and the temperature fell. *Looks like it'll snow again.* She wrapped her wool scarf around her neck and stuffed its ends into the neckline of her coat.

When they arrived at the officer's home, Lee parked in front. Ice crunched beneath Hayley's feet as she walked along the winding garden path leading to the dark brown front door. The Tudor-style home had a thatched roof and small windows. Smoke billowed from the chimney, and a dog barked inside as Hayley and the others approached the doorstep.

Lee knocked. Moments after the dog stopped barking, the door opened.

"Please come in," Officer Bates told them.

Kitchen table chairs had been placed near a blue-flowered couch. Simon, still dressed in the suit he wore to church, sat in an overstuffed chair near the brick fireplace. He scanned the guests, and his gaze fixed on her.

"Officer Bates," Hayley said, "would you mind if I had a private talk with Simon before we get started?"

"Not at all." He pointed toward a door across the room. "The kitchen table would be a fine place to chat."

The lanky eleven-year-old, Simon, stood and meekly followed Hayley through the door. A round wooden table left with two chairs took up half of the kitchen. They sat at the table.

"I've been looking forward to meeting you, Simon," Hayley said. "I heard you were asking to see me."

"Elsie told me you were coming."

"I've met Elsie," she told him. "And I've also had visions of you. The last one I had made me proud of you. You stood in front of almost the entire town and politely gave them a piece of your mind."

A grin spread across his face. "That was cool. Now they'll believe me."

"It's not that easy," she explained. "It's almost impossible to convince some people that you're not some kind of demon instead of someone who's gifted. Believe me, I know. My parents went as far as sending me to a shrink, and he diagnosed me as a schizophrenic."

"So, you can see the dead?" he asked.

"Yes, and the past, present, and future. The same as you can. The only thing I'm unable to foresee is my own future. A Divine rule forbids it."

"What's a Divine rule?" Simon asked.

"Divine rules are rules that are made in heaven. There's one that prohibits every psychic from foreseeing their own future. If I had been attending church this morning, yesterday, I wouldn't have been able to foresee your brilliant performance. How about you? Can you foresee your own future?"

"No, and a bunch of what I do envision doesn't happen."

"That usually occurs because you tell what you've seen. People change their actions to avoid the circumstances, like locking doors, going home a different way, and the like. Then when it doesn't happen, they call you a liar. I know about that too."

"But I really do help when I tell."

Hayley nodded. "Yes, but you'd help more if you told Officer Bates and let him handle it if it's an unpleasant situation you foresee. That way, he can prevent it from happening, like catching a thief or stopping an arsonist."

"Have you had dreams about that too? People with torches and setting my parents' house on fire, I mean?"

"So that was a foreseeing," Hayley said. "I didn't think people would do such a hateful thing nowadays. Did you actually see someone setting fire to your parents' home?"

"Yes. It was that troublemaker Timothy Dunn. While everyone was in front of our house raising their torches and yelling, he snuck around back, lit a fire, and then took off running."

"This is something you should tell Officer Bates," Hayley told him. "Tell him exactly what you saw so he can catch Timothy in the act. Let's join the others."

Simon slid his chair back and stood. "Okay, I will."

When they reentered the living room, the conversation stopped.

"We were talking about Timothy Dunn," Lee explained.

"Tell him what you told me," Hayley said to Simon.

"I foresaw a mob carrying torches in front of my parent's house."

"I had the same vision," Hayley added.

"While they were shouting and raising their torches, calling for the demon child," he pointed to himself, "Timothy was around back starting a fire."

"Why would they go there looking for you?" Officer Bates asked, his brow raised. "Everyone knows you're in my custody."

"It's Timothy's idea. He's going to tell them a lie that he overheard the priest say the church dropped the charges, and I was sent back home to live with my parents."

"That wouldn't happen even if that were the case," the officer replied. "You'd go back to your grandda's." He rubbed his chin. "Everyone knows you're not living with your da and mum anymore, and I'm sure he does too."

"He's after my da."

"Why?"

"Remember when investigators came to our house last month?" Simon asked him.

Officer Bates nodded.

"It had to do with my da's car accident in London. I had a vision of it before it happened. My da didn't see the driver's face, but I did. It was Timothy. I'm positive. I wrote down the plate number. When I told my da that I foresaw his accident, he snatched the paper I'd written the plate number on and shoved it in his wallet. He didn't believe me then, and he still says it was just a coincidence."

"So, how did Scotland Yard get involved?" Officer Bates asked. "He must've called the police and reported it."

"No way. My da was as drunk as a hatter. The other car sideswiped his, and da hit a street sign. Da said five cop cars surrounded him. That doesn't make sense. Why so many? Something else must've happened nearby. He gave them the plate number from his wallet while he tried to convince them that the accident wasn't his fault. They took him in, and he spent the night in jail. The car was totaled. Mum was furious."

"So that's the reason she went after him with a meat cleaver," Officer Bates said. "The reports stated it had to do with your da's drinking." He turned to Hayley and the others. "His da dropped the charges against her. That's when the courts stepped in and removed Simon from their custody, giving him over to his grandda."

"But why did Scotland Yard go to his parent's home?" Lee said. "If it was just a fender bender and a case of drunk driving, it wouldn't have been a big deal."

"They told my da the car that hit his was stolen, and it's an ongoing investigation."

Officer Bates's brows furrowed. "Sounds like there's more to the story. I'll check into it when I get back to the station. Tell me more about the arson. When will it take place?"

"Tomorrow night," Simon replied. "Part of what Timothy will tell the mob will be true. The church is going to drop the charges after the priest talks to me in the morning. When they find out he's telling the truth about that, they'll believe his lie about me going back home."

"There's a lot of haters in that bunch," Jim said. "We saw Timothy gettin' their dander up the other night at the inn. He's slicker than snot. He could convince the Pope that the devil's his friend."

Officer Bates glanced at Simon. "Where exactly did Timothy light the match?"

"By the back door."

"From my recollection, there's a tool shed a few feet away."

"Yes, sir," Simon replied.

"Don't worry, lad. I'll have a surprise waiting for him tomorrow night." He leaned forward. "Now, tell us about that bomb."

"What do you want to know?" Simon asked.

"When the bomb will explode," Officer Bates replied.

"The only thing I know is it'll go off when the next strong tremor hits. It could be soon. If we're going to save the church, we need to be quick about it."

"Do you think we'll have at least a week?" Lee asked.

Simon leaned back in the overstuffed chair and closed his eyes. He sat quietly for a few moments before he opened them again and shook his head. "I haven't been able to envision the explosion since all of you came to town." He looked at Hayley. "Why can't I? Can you?"

"Remember you told me that you can't foresee your own future."

"Then why did I see it before?"

"You weren't involved when you foresaw it. The moment you chose to prevent it from happening is when your ability to foresee the explosion ended. You and Elsie have everything to

do with why we're here and what we'll do to stop the disaster."
Hayley, sitting next to Lee on the couch, closed her eyes, relaxed,
and let her mind go in search of answers. No clues, visions, or
knowings came to her. She opened her eyes again. "No. Nothing.
We can't foresee our own futures. It's just the way it is."

"Maybe it's because you changed the outcome," Officer
Bates said. "Maybe you don't foresee it because it's not going to
happen."

"Can't cross the bridge before it's built," Jim said. "Ya
could be right, but ya could be wrong. Won't know for sure until
it happens."

"Too bad it's impossible to pinpoint the exact moment an
earthquake will hit," Hayley said.

"First thing we need to find out is where Elsie's coffin is
buried," Jim said. "Then we'll have to somehow move it, so when
the quake hits, the bomb won't ram it."

"It's better if we go to the cemetery and ask Elsie to show
you where the bomb is," Simon replied. "She's the one who told
me it was there. That's when I envisioned the explosion. I didn't
know what to do. Nobody believes anything I tell them. So, I
tried to save the church's relics by taking them from the church
a little at a time and putting them in the courthouse's basement
for safekeeping."

"As soon as we can prove the bomb exists, I'm sure all
charges against you will be dropped," Officer Bates said. "Go
change your clothes, Simon, and we'll bob over to the cemetery
and talk to your friend."

Simon bounded from the chair, darted out of the room,
and disappeared down the hallway.

"We'll need proof of Elsie's burial," Kathy said. "The
church will need the evidence before we excavate and perhaps
disturb other gravesites. Matilda and I are going to ask permission
to go through the church's archives."

"Good idea," Officer Bates said. "We'll present it to the

court along with evidence that the bomb exists."

"And how do ya plan to prove it's there?" Jim asked. "All ya have is these two's mind-bogglin' insight to offer up."

"I see your point," Officer Bates said. "But finding unexploded bombs in England is a common occurrence. There's a special task force I can contact that will remove the bugger."

"And whatcha gonna tell 'em," Jim asked, "when they ask how ya found it?"

"That's a sticky wicket. They'd definitely think I'm daft if I tell them a psychic told me." He hesitated a moment. "Let's wait until we examine the situation further before we take another step."

"Sounds logical," Lee said.

Simon, his blond hair mussed by the turtleneck sweater he slipped on, came back into the room with jeans tucked into his snow boots. "Ready."

"Simon and I will take my car, and we'll meet you there," Officer Bates told them.

CHAPTER 15

When they entered the church, the priest Hayley recognized from her vision approached.

Officer Bates introduced them, his voice echoing in the empty nave. "And, Father, here we have Kathy Lane and Matilda Rothschild. They'd like to look through your archives to find evidence of Elsie's burial. They're also keen to find a family connection between their friend Roger Hudson and Elsie. They believe the two are related."

"Wouldn't that be remarkable," Father Farley replied. He waved to an altar boy. "David, please, come. I need your assistance."

The young man hurried over. "Yes, Father?"

"Would you please take Miss Lane and Miss Rothschild to Father McShane?"

"Yes, Father. If you'll please follow me." He led them through a door near the altar.

"We've come to speak with Elsie," Simon told the priest. "She knows where the bomb is."

"Why don't we follow you, lad," Father Farley told him, "and see what she has to say?"

He led them past the pillars and pews, out the front entrance, and around the right side of the church to the cemetery. Snow had lightly covered the ground and frosted the top of each headstone. Simon stopped by the corner of the church and called out Elsie's name.

In the distance, Hayley located the little girl dancing by a statue of an angel and saw her turn when Simon called. Once the child joined them, Hayley glanced at her friends and Father Farley. It seemed obvious to her that they didn't detect the little girl's presence.

Simon talked to Elsie. Moments later, everyone looked at the ground and stepped back while Elsie drew lines in the snow. When she had finished, she spoke with Simon, who turned to the observers. "This is where her coffin is. She was buried here a week before the bombs struck the church."

"How far down is her casket?" Lee asked.

"Seven feet. Debris from the church covered it, and her headstone was broken and mixed with the rubble. No one realized she was buried here. When they reconstructed the church, they cleaned up the cemetery, and her coffin was covered over."

"So, where's the bomb?" Jim asked.

"Under her coffin. Just about there." He pointed at a small circle Elsie had drawn in the snow. "The tip's only inches away from her coffin. It's coming up on an angle—the tip's there, and its tail-end angled away." Simon grabbed a twig and drew the shape, explaining as he went along. "The tail of it is facing that way. Elsie says the bomb's as big as she is."

"Holy moley," Jim said. "Do ya think we'll have to dig up the coffin ourselves?"

Chills went up Hayley's spine. She believed Simon had seen the explosion. She had no doubts. The craving to foresee her friends' futures gripped her. Her frustration level peaked, knowing the forbidden knowledge would be denied to her.

Before her birth, Hayley had made a pact with almost all her friends who were with her now and others. They were all reincarnated to this life to become the Saviors of Souls. During the creation of the pact, Divine rules were agreed to—rules that forbid her from foreseeing hers and any of their pasts and futures. *It's our destiny to save souls. If we dig up Elsie's grave, the odds are slim that the bomb will explode and kill us all. Why would our lives be taken from us so soon, ending the mission we were born to do? That wouldn't make sense. But what in life makes sense?*

"We have gravediggers who will assist you," the priest told them.

"This is a tricky situation," Jim said. "If the coffin tips in any direction, it may set off the bomb."

"We can do this," Hayley whispered to Lee. "Kathy wasn't given her gifts to put on the shelf and never use."

"It's witchcraft," Lee said under his breath. "The church would never get involved with the craft."

"We don't have to tell them," she replied.

"We have three able men," Lee said, pointing at Thomas and Jim. "I'd rather not put anyone else's life in danger."

"You have to evacuate the town," Thomas told the officer.

"For how long?"

"Not long, I figure," Jim said. "Seven feet. As easy as catchin' a fat rat in a hat. If everyone could get up and go for a day, they could be home in bed that evenin' if everythin' goes as planned."

"I'll make arrangements." Officer Bates turned to Father Farley. "You know Simon's idea to store the church's artifacts in the court's basement was a brilliant ploy. Maybe you can call on some of the townspeople to help you move the rest of your valuables to the courthouse also. Of course, we'll get the courthouse's approval first to make sure it's okay."

"Brilliant," the priest replied. "I'll ring up Justice Hillard straight away. And there's a couple of other churches on the other side of town that I'll need to speak with so the entire town will get the word to evacuate." He headed back inside the church.

Hayley watched him leave, making sure he would be far enough away not to hear their conversation. "Okay, he's gone."

"All right, Officer Bates," Lee said. "This is going to be a little startling. Our methods are a bit unorthodox, but I can't see any way around it."

"You've blown my mind so far, introducing me to ghosts and the paranormal. What more could you do to flabbergast me?"

"You'd be surprised," Jim said.

Hayley looked at Simon. "Do you know about Kathy?"

He nodded. "Sometimes things just come to me, visions of people I don't know or things that will happen in places I've never seen. I envisioned each of you the moment you decided to come to England. I knew then that you were just like me. And Kathy...." His eyes grew big. "Is she really a witch?"

"You're not bloody serious!" Officer Bates blurted.

"It's goin' to be okay, buddy," Jim said. "All ya need is a good stiff drink."

"Here come your friends and Father Farley," Simon said.

Everyone grew quiet. Officer Bates studied the ground and kicked a rock.

Kathy, Matilda, and Father Farley laughed while they rounded the corner. The priest finished his story as they approached.

"Did you find anything?" Lee asked.

"We have it right here." Kathy held up a leather-bound book, its edges are worn, and its pages yellowed.

"I thought it would take you all day," Thomas said.

"It turns out that I'm gifted." She winked at him.

"We found the date when the church was bombed," Matilda told them, "and backtracked from there. If the church records hadn't been so neatly stored, we would've had a problem."

Nice cover, Hayley thought. *Kathy probably whistled, and the evidence presented itself.*

"I'll make all the arrangements to exhume the body," Father Farley told them. "I'll contact you straight away when matters are complete."

"Thank you, Father," Lee replied.

"Come here, sweet pea," Jim said to Kathy. "I've got

somethin' to tell ya."

She walked with Jim through the snow-covered cemetery. Twenty feet away, she stopped and stared at him. Hayley watched Kathy as he spoke to her and saw the concern on her face. Kathy bit her bottom lip, then nodded.

When they strolled back, Kathy glanced at Officer Bates.

At least he doesn't look as nervous as he did when we first met him after he saw Elsie — just a little twitch in his smile, and his hands are shaking. Hayley whispered to Kathy, "He knows."

"I'll have to give the town time enough to make plans to evacuate." Officer Bates placed his quivering hands into his coat pockets. "Plus, I have to attend to a problem tomorrow night, you may recall." He looked at Simon. "Will I have time?"

Simon closed his eyes. Hayley did the same. In her mind, she could clearly see the mob standing in front of his parents' house. *Are they there because the church exploded, and they blame Simon?*

She envisioned what Father Farley would be doing at that time. In her mind's eye, she witnessed the church filled with people. Father Farley explained about the bomb and the importance of evacuation.

"You're taking the loony lad's word on this?" a man in the pews loudly asked.

Father Farley stood at the head of the aisles in front of the rows of pews. People found standing room only along the walls. When the parishioners grew restless and loud, Father Farley held out his arm, raising his palm in the air to silence the crowd. Many pointed behind him. He looked over his shoulder and jumped.

Elsie stood high on the choir. As if she were an actor on stage, she spoke loudly and directly to everyone.

Hayley paid close attention.

"It's true. I told Simon what I'd found, and he looked into the future and watched it explode. Unless you want to be dead like me, you have to LEAVE." The last word boomed, echoing throughout the church.

Although Hayley had some difficulty, she understood what the little girl said.

People scampered from their seats, pushing and shoving to exit the church.

Elsie smiled and disappeared.

Hayley's foreseeing ended.

"I don't see it exploding anytime tomorrow," Hayley told Officer Bates. "It'll be a good day to move artifacts from the church. And the next day, I believe people will evacuate."

"Good. I'll have time today to do some research on Timothy Dunn," Officer Bates told them.

Lee turned to the priest. "Thank you, Father, for all your help."

"Bless you for saving lives," Father Farley replied.

"Say a prayer for us, Father," Jim told him. "We'll need all the help we can get."

"Absolutely."

Jim turned to the others. "I vote we go have a drink and talk to Henry."

"Sounds like a plan," Lee said.

"I wish I could join you," Officer Bates said. "But I can't drink in public."

"I'd quit the police force," Jim told him. "Socializin' is the key to longevity. I'd be half the man I am today if I didn't have a drink now and then."

Lee laughed.

"What?" Jim asked.

"I was just trying to picture you three feet tall."

"Funny," Jim said. "Let's hit the road."

CHAPTER 16

As Hayley entered the hotel, she retrieved her phone from her purse to answer a call. "It's Laura," she told Lee. "I have to get this." She took the audio and video call.

"Hi," Laura said. "I've been thinking about you."

"What time is it there?"

"Seven in the morning," Laura replied. "What's been going on?"

Hayley looked at Lee. "I'll take this upstairs and meet you guys at the bar."

He nodded. "Tell her and Roger that we may be here awhile. Too bad they returned home. This is something Roger would've found astounding."

"I heard that," Roger said, taking a seat behind Laura. "Lewis was glad we returned. He and Laura have been going over the guest list."

"We've accomplished a lot," Laura told them. "Lewis is the best wedding planner. He knows the food you prefer from past social events and the type of music. He's taken the Christmas guest list, extracted a few names from the charity ball attendees, and has given Grams the pleasure of inviting a number of your spirit friends and family."

"Does that include my mom and dad?" Lee asked.

"It does," Roger replied. "As well as Hayley's, mine, and Laura's."

"Amazing," Lee said.

"How exactly does that work?" Hayley asked. "How do they RSVP?"

"Clint is using his automatic writing ability to allow them to use his hand to give a written reply with their signature. Those who are able to materialize are delivering their RSVPs to Lewis's reply box themselves. Clint helps those who can't."

"I bet Lewis is having the time of his life," Lee said.

"We're videoing his reaction for you," Laura told them. "It's beyond funny."

"We appreciate your thoughtfulness," Lee said. "Can't wait to watch it."

Jim waved at them from the bar.

"Fill them in on what's been going on," Lee said. "I'll call you later, Roger. Bye, Laura. I've got to get back to the others. We're going to have a chat with the bartender."

"I'm sure you are," Roger replied. "Talk to you later."

Lee kissed Hayley's cheek. "See you in a bit."

"Okay." She returned to her conversation. "It's been extremely interesting, to say the least," Hayley said to them. She climbed the stairs and entered her and Lee's hotel room while telling Laura and Roger everything that had happened since they'd left London. She took off her coat, scarf, and boots, propped a pillow against the headboard, and sat on the bed. "Kathy and Matilda found Elsie's burial records. The priest is getting permission to exhume the body. According to Elsie, the casket is resting in a compromising position. Kathy has agreed to help."

"Using witchcraft?" Roger asked. "That sounds like a scandal. How in the world do you plan to pull that off without Kathy being burned at the stake?"

"I really don't think they do that anymore," Hayley replied.

"Use a tent," Roger said. "You can tell everyone it's to protect the dig from the weather. And as long as Kathy's casting spells, see if she knows how to detect anyone who might be hanging around to get a look."

"A couple of good ideas," Hayley told him. "I'll tell the others."

"Exactly when will this take place?" Laura asked.

"In a couple of days. Tomorrow the church will remove its relics and store them for safekeeping."

"Are there any other churches in town?" Laura asked. "Are they moving their artifacts too?"

"There are two other churches on the other side of town. They're storing their valuables in their basements, and they're urging their patrons to evacuate."

"Is the entire town leaving?" Laura asked.

"Yes. The day after tomorrow. Most of the homes are close to this side of town. There's no way we can determine the magnitude of the explosion if something goes wrong. So, the entire town is leaving until we uncover the bomb. Once they've left, we'll begin digging."

"It sounds incredibly dangerous," Laura said.

"It'll be tricky," Hayley replied. "We'll call in a special task force to remove it."

"Who knew the ghost girl's antics would lead to this," Roger said.

"Yes, and of course, I didn't see it coming because we're involved," Hayley said.

"Her DNA will need to be tested," Laura told her. "If you'd like, I can call the morgue and set it up. I'll have the samples sent to a lab in London."

"That's good to hear," Hayley said. "That's a problem I'm glad I won't have to deal with. I'll get the morgue's number from Simon's grandfather and get back to you. Meanwhile, keep me posted on any wedding plans that I need to help you with."

"Will do."

"You're the best," Hayley told her. "I'll talk to you soon."

"Okay," Laura said. "I'm looking forward to it. Bye for now."

Hayley placed her phone into her purse, hurried out of the room, and joined the others at the bar. She sat on the barstool next to Lee and noticed that the dining room and bar would be empty without them.

"Is everything okay back home?" Lee asked her.

"Yes. Lewis and Laura are ironing out the wedding plans. Laura is calling the morgue to arrange the DNA extraction and have them send it to the lab of her choosing."

"Good," Lee said. "The thought of you reaching into that casket and taking the sample is nauseating. I'm just thinking about the condition Elsie's corpse will be in after so many years."

"I know what you mean," Hayley said. "Who would've expected a crack in a window would lead to finding an unexploded bomb that could wipe out the entire town and a possible ancestry connection between the ghost who brought us here and someone on our team?" She began to think of Lenny. "You know who would really like to be here? Lenny. I did promise to call him."

"Flour my behind, stick me in the oven, and call me a biscuit," Jim said. "He has the next two days off. Bet the lad would love to know where that Jaguar's broken window led us. Ask him to join us."

"But I thought you were going to keep this just among our group," Kathy said. "A lot of unforeseen things could happen — if you know what I mean." She glanced at Hayley.

She means she doesn't know how Lenny will take it when he sees her use witchcraft to raise the coffin. "I really think he'd appreciate this opportunity," Hayley replied, "and I totally trust him to be open minded — if you know what *I* mean."

"If Hayley says she trusts him, that's good enough for me," Lee said.

The others nodded.

Thomas turned to Lee. "While you tell Hayley the news

Henry gave us, Kathy and I will track down Officer Bates and let him know about Timothy's plans."

"Good idea," Lee told him.

Kathy and Thomas slid off their stools and left.

"Lenny will need a hotel room when he arrives," Matilda said. "Why don't I find out if there's a room available here?"

"Our small town isn't much of a tourist magnet this time of year," Henry said. "Nearly all the rooms here are empty."

"Sounds perfect," Matilda replied. "If he decides to join us, I'll let the desk know that we'll need another room."

Lee took out his cell phone and called the hotel in London where they had spent New Year's Eve. He rose from his stool and wandered away from the conversation at the bar. When he returned, he reclaimed his seat. "Lenny's excited about being involved with our dig. He wanted to know if he'll be able to see Elsie's ghost. I told him he will. He was thrilled, to say the least."

"This could change his life," Jim said. "Once ya see a ghost, you're either afraid of the dark from then on, or you're yearnin' to see more. Can't tell ya how many haunted houses I took Roger and Lee to. They've never got their fill of chasin' ghosts."

"I know my life was changed," Matilda said. "And I was probably the most stubborn nonbeliever you've ever met."

"Ya can say that again," Jim said.

Matilda gave him a kiss on his cheek and headed for the front desk.

"So, what did I miss while I was talking to Laura and Roger?" Hayley asked.

"Henry told us exactly what your vision foresaw," Lee said. "Outside, though, he heard a few people talking who still think Elsie's a demon."

"Henry said despicable Dunn is gatherin' the haters at his place tomorrow evenin' for a meetin'," Jim told Hayley. "Thomas is on his way to let Officer Bates know."

"I'd like to see Dunn's face when he gets caught," Hayley

said. "I tried looking into the future, but for some reason, I can't envision his arrest."

"Can't you use your gift to see the present," Lee asked, "and envision it while it's happening?"

"Yes," Hayley replied. "That's a good idea. Once we gather the team, I'll see his capture in my mind's eye as if I'm watching a movie, and I'll narrate as the bust is going down."

"Sounds like a winner," Jim said.

"Roger had a suggestion," Hayley said. "He thinks we should get a tent to give us protection and privacy while we dig."

Henry refilled Jim's beer mug and set it in front of him. "The nearest place to find a tent would be at Jill's flower shop up the street. She has a few different sizes she uses for special events. What size do you need? I can ring her up if you'd like."

"Let's see," Jim said, rubbing his chin. "I think twenty-by-thirty feet would be somewhere in the ballpark."

"Don't you think that's a little large?" Lee asked.

"There'll be eleven of us living folk," Jim replied as Matilda returned to her barstool. "And don't forget the number of ghostly lookie-loos that will be there, plus we'll need room for the dirt and casket. Seems right to me."

"Okay," Lee said. "Please give Jill a call to see if one is available for a few days. If she has one, we'll be over to cover the bill."

Henry nodded and retrieved his cell phone. He walked away as he made the call.

"Anythin' else we'll be needin'?" Jim asked. "Even though Kathy will be usin' her witchcraft, we need to make it look like we're diggin' up the grave the normal way."

"I think we need to talk to Seth," Hayley said. "He'll know where to get everything we need."

Henry returned. "All set, governor. She's probably the only person in town that has one left. Everyone's reserved tents for Winter Fest, that's taking place in a few days. I told her you'd be by to dither over details. It's just a short bob up the road."

"Thanks so much." Lee glanced at Jim and Matilda. "Do you want to split up? Hayley and I will talk to Seth, and you two can take care of the tent."

"Good plan," Jim said.

Lee paid the bar tab and placed a hundred-dollar bill on the counter. "Thank you very much, young man."

Henry's eyes widened. "Blimey. Thank you. If you need anything else, let me know."

"Will do, Henry." Jim slid off his barstool and helped Matilda rise.

"We'll drive you to the shop and drop you off if you want," Lee told Jim.

Jim glanced out the window. The sun shone between meandering clouds, and the wind seemed calm. "No need. We should stretch our legs."

They all strolled out to the lobby, took their coats off the rack, bundled up, and headed out of the hotel.

"I'll call Seth and let him know we're coming," Hayley told Lee as they climbed into the Rover.

CHAPTER 17

When Hayley and Lee arrived at Seth's home, they noticed Kathy and Thomas's Rover parked at the curb.

"Guess they tracked down Officer Bates," Lee said. "That's his car in front of theirs, isn't it?"

"Yes. Simon's probably here too."

They climbed out of the vehicle, walked to the gate, and almost made it to the door before Simon opened it. "I knew you were coming."

"Are you psychic?" Lee asked.

Simon laughed. Once they came inside, he shut the door and motioned toward two wooden chairs. "Please join us," the lad said. "We were telling my grandda' what happened in church and what you're planning to do in the cemetery."

"Sit," Seth said.

They took off their coats, hung them by the door, and took their seats while Simon sat on a footstool near Seth's chair.

"So, you'll be digging up Elsie's grave, will you?" Seth said. "I'll ring up my grave diggers and have them there first light Tuesday morning."

"Actually, we won't be needing them," Lee said. "We have enough able-bodied men to get it done. Plus, everyone will be evacuating, and your men should leave with their families. All we'll be needing are a few shovels and whatever you use to raise and lower the coffin."

"If that's what you prefer," Seth replied. "What will you

do about the weather? They say it'll be a blustery day. It may snow."

"We're renting a tent to cover the dig," Lee told him.

You should ask Seth if he'd like to observe, Hayley heard Grams say in her mind. *He won't be able to. But he'd like to be invited.*

Thanks for the info. Hayley glanced at Kathy and knew she'd disapprove of her asking him to attend. Kathy had made clear she wanted to keep her use of witchcraft a secret. But Kathy sat on the couch, too far away for Hayley to whisper that Seth wouldn't go even if asked. "Would you like to join us?" Hayley asked Seth. Glancing out of the corner of her eye, she noticed the sharp turn of Kathy's head and the panicked look on her face, but Hayley ignored her and focused on Seth.

"Thank you, but no. I've already made plans to leave town with my daughter. I can give you all you need, and I'll hear about it when I come home."

Kathy let out a deep breath and now appeared to relax.

"I told Seth about the mob going to his daughter's home tomorrow night," Officer Bates said. "He promised not to say a word to her about it. I want her to act natural so Dunn won't get suspicious, and I can catch him in the act."

"Did you find out if he's wanted for any other crimes?" Lee asked.

Officer Bates shook his head. "Didn't find a bloody thing. Didn't even find his driver's license or school records. It's as if he never existed."

His real name is Rex Wood, Hayley heard Grams say.

Interesting, Hayley replied. *Thanks, Grams.* "His real name is Rex Wood," she said out loud.

"Bloody hell. That's why I couldn't find him," Officer Bates said. "When I get back to the office, I'll have a go at finding the brute. And when I do, I'll ring up Scotland Yard and invite them along." He looked at Simon. "You said he started a fire in the back of your parents' house. What did he use to start it? There may be more unsolved arsons he's committed."

"Hayley had the same dream," Simon replied. "I don't know what he used, but flames engulfed the entire backdoor."

Kathy whispered to Officer Bates. He nodded. "Yes," he replied. "It sounds like the best alternative."

A detonator, Grams told Hayley. *He has a bunch of them hidden in the garage. The oil cans on the shelf have screw-on bottoms and look like normal cans of oil, but they're not. The detonators are hidden inside.*

Hayley repeated what her grandmother had told her.

Officer Bates's eyes widened. "We have him dead to rights. This is incredible. So, you're telling me that your abilities are that precise? Does Simon have that talent too?"

"He's still a boy. If his abilities aren't as defined as mine yet, they soon will be. He just needs practice."

"If he's up for it, I can give him all the practice he needs," Officer Bates said.

"Cool," Simon shouted. "Are you going to make me a policeman?"

"Now calm yourself, lad," Officer Bates told him. "No, you won't be an officer. And it'll be our little secret that you're helping the force. You know how much trouble you've had with nonbelievers. I'd be facing the same treatment if word got out around the station that I'm using a psychic to solve cases. We can start with the cold cases and see how we do."

"I understand," Simon said. "I won't tell anyone." He jumped up, danced his way through the dining room, and, with a grin, returned to the footstool.

"He's never been happier," Seth said.

"His entire life is about to change," Hayley told him.

I have a surprise for Simon, Grams said in Hayley's mind. *He's never met his guardian angel. His name is William, and he wants me to introduce him to Simon before you and your friends leave. Once this is all over, the town will know about Simon's abilities, and he's going to be overwhelmed by everyone's reactions. He needs to know he's not alone and that William will always be there with him.*

That's so cool, Hayley told her.

"We left Jim and Matilda to take care of the tent rental and said we'd be back shortly," Lee said. "We'd better go."

Kathy turned to Thomas. "If you want to go with Officer Bates and investigate Rex Wood, I can go with Hayley and Lee and meet you at the hotel later."

"You really wouldn't mind?" Thomas asked.

"I know you want to. It's okay. You can tell me later what you guys find."

"Thanks, Kat." He looked at Officer Bates. "Do you mind if I tag along?"

"I'd be honored if you would."

Lee, Hayley, and Kathy stood.

"Thanks for letting us visit, Seth," Hayley said.

"My pleasure." He rose and followed them to the door.

They bundled up in their coats and scarves and left.

Seth stood in the doorway waving goodbye as Lee pulled the Rover away from the curb.

"I almost died when you asked Seth if he wanted to join the dig," Kathy said from the backseat. "Good thing he said no. I'm serious about keeping my use of witchcraft a secret."

"I knew he was going to say no before I asked. You were sitting too far away from me, or I would've told you. It was Grams who informed me. And she also gave me Timothy's real name and where he keeps the detonators. On top of that, she made friends with Simon's guardian angel, William, and offered to introduce the two so Simon won't feel alone after we leave."

"That was sweet of her," Lee said.

"What did you whisper to Officer Bates?" Hayley asked Kathy.

"I told him I can prevent the flames from damaging the house. He agreed. I'll make it look natural so the guys from

Scotland Yard won't ask questions."

"That's why I couldn't foresee the arrest because you'll be there," Hayley said. "Officer Bates has become extremely open-minded these days."

"What choice does he have?" Lee said. "He had to become a believer when Elsie appeared in his living room. Then when he met us, his world was turned upside-down. Witchcraft is just the icing on the cake." He pulled up and parked in front of the inn.

They found Jim and Matilda and joined them for dinner and drinks afterwards in front of the fireplace.

"It's a knee-slapper that ya revealed the truth about alias Mr. Dunn," Jim said to Hayley.

"Grams told me."

"Thought she was steppin' back," Jim said, "not wantin' to get so involved in our cases."

Hayley laughed. "Someone would have to tie her to a tree to keep her from coming to our aid."

Jim raised a brow. "I'm sure you've noticed, little lady, that your grandma is in spirit form. Ya can't tie her to a tree any more than ya can tie a ghost to a post."

"Precisely," Hayley said. "No one can stop her, and apparently, she can't stop herself either. I'm sure you've noticed there's more to it than her just being my guardian angel. She's become part of our team."

Grams materialized in an empty chair. "You're very smart, dear. I know you've always wondered how I weaseled my way into being your guardian angel. Once I crossed over and found out you and your friends had made a pact, I signed up too. But to be included, I had to make promises. I had to prove I could stay between the lines. I always told you I had to be careful. Until I pass the test, I'm only an entrant, not a full-fledged member yet. And for now, I'm a desperate want-to-be guardian angel in training."

Lee chuckled. "I know how hard it is for you to keep

secrets from her, Grams. But even though I don't know any other guardian angels, including my own, I'd say you're the best."

"Why, thank you, Lee."

"He's right," Hayley said. "You are."

"To be a pact member, it's necessary that I be included in your life at all times. So, I'm your guardian angel as long as I don't screw up. It's my purpose as part of your team. And I do have rules." She frowned. "You know what I'd like to do with those rules."

"Grams!" Hayley said. "When were you going to tell us?"

"When it's official. I love being your guardian angel. If I can just behave."

"Did you introduce Simon to his guardian?" Hayley asked.

"Yes. I left the two alone so Simon can get to know him. He'll need William once the entire world knows about his gifts."

"I wonder what's keeping Thomas?" Kathy asked.

Grams glanced at the lobby door. "He'll be here in just a second."

A moment later, Thomas entered the hotel and joined them in the dining room.

Grams moved over to sit by Matilda, leaving the seat next to Kathy vacant for Thomas.

"How have you been, Julia?" Matilda asked.

"I miss our talks," Grams said. "Don't you?"

"Very much."

"After you get back to the States, we'll have time to get together," Grams said.

"I'd like that."

Thomas warmed himself in front of the fire before he sat next to Kathy. "Rex Wood has a rap sheet a mile long," he told them. "Most are assaults and robbery. But Scotland Yard's been investigating a number of arsons. Looks like Rex may be a serial arsonist too."

"It was Grams who told me his real name," Hayley said.

"Thanks, Grams," Thomas said. "There's a reward in British pounds that's equivalent to a million dollars US currency for the capture of the arsonist who's responsible for the south side fires in London. Once the bust goes down, and if Dunn's the one they're searching for, Simon will get the reward."

"The lad's a minor," Jim said. "His dad will take all that money, and it'll be gone in no time."

"I'll contact a lawyer I know in London and set things in motion to protect his assets," Lee said.

Hayley closed her eyes, peered into the future, and opened them again. "Officer Bates will tell Scotland Yard that Simon heard Dunn talking about it. After some discussion with Officer Bates, it will be determined that Simon will get the reward. He'll need a bank account."

"When will he receive it?" Lee asked.

She closed her eyes once more and opened them again with the answer. "Friday. Officer Bates will have to drive to London with Simon."

"I'll make an appointment with the lawyer for that afternoon to set up the account for Simon. I'll ask him to become Simon's legal advisor."

"Good idea," Grams told him. "But he'll need more than that, I'm afraid. His granddad will be leaving his home to his daughter, which will put Simon in the hands of the court unless he has a legal guardian."

"That's a problem," Thomas said. "Who can he trust?"

"I have confidence that you'll help him figure it out," Grams said. "Now I have to go."

"Wait," Jim said. "So, you're gonna leave us hangin' there like a hair on a biscuit. Ya expect us to find someone who'll be willin' to raise him? Every crook from miles around will be puttin' his hand up. We don't know squat 'bout who's honest hereabouts."

"Of course, you do. Don't expect me to tell you everything."

She vanished, leaving everyone staring at an empty chair.

"If it has to do with us or someone we know," Lee said, "she can't tell us."

"We're strangers in town," Jim replied. "Who in the hell do we know?"

Kathy took a pad of paper from her purse and began writing.

"Whatcha written, sweet pea?" Jim asked.

"I'm adding a search for a guardian to the list of things we need to do."

"Good girl. It seems it's one thing after another." Lee looked at Jim. "How are things going with the dig?"

"The tent will be erected by the lads from Jill's flower shop first thing in the mornin'."

"We'll have to contact Father Farley concerning the storage of Elsie's remains," Lee said.

Kathy yawned. "I've got it on my list."

Lee glanced at Hayley. "Should we call it a night?"

"Sounds like a plan," Hayley replied.

They all stood in agreement, gathered their winter coats and things, then strolled upstairs.

CHAPTER 18

Turning in early last night gave Hayley and Lee time for intimacy and an evening of passion. When she awoke from a peaceful sleep, Hayley glanced to her right to see the covers thrown back and an empty space where Lee had fallen asleep with her in his arms. The warmth from the fireplace and the smell of coffee filled the air, urging her to crawl out from beneath the down-filled comforter and join her soon-to-be husband by the window.

Hayley rolled out of bed and slid her feet into her fuzzy yellow slippers. She strolled across the room, put her arms around Lee, and gave him a kiss. "You're already dressed. You must've woken early."

"Good morning, love," he said, holding his cup of coffee steady while brushing a wayward hair from her eyes. "About an hour ago. Have some coffee, and we'll go downstairs to join the others for breakfast."

"Have you heard from Lenny?"

"Yes. He's on his way here."

"He's a good young man, polite, and so helpful," Hayley said.

"And unemployed," Lee told her. "After New Year's Eve, the guests become scarce, he told me, and the hotel reduces its staff. He's moved into his brother's house for now. He said he won't have to rush home, and he'll be able to spend time with us if we'd like. I told him he's more than welcome. It was hilarious to hear the excitement in his voice. He was speaking so fast that

I had to listen closely to understand. He reminds me of when Roger and I were young and started ghost hunting."

"Too bad he's going to only get a taste of it and then have to return home," Hayley said. In her mind, she heard Grams clearing her throat. *I know you want to say something. Come on, out with it,* Hayley told her.

I'll give you a hint, dear. What was the last thing I said to you when you saw me last?

I hate guessing games.

Just think about it, dear.

Hayley thought a moment, and her eyes widened. "Are you serious," she said out loud.

"What?" Lee asked.

"Grams just told me who will be Simon's legal guardian."

"Who?"

"Lenny."

Lee blinked. "Are you serious?"

"That's what I said."

"So how are we going to break it to him?" Lee asked.

"You make it sound like a death sentence," Grams said, fully materialized, wearing blue jeans and a white mohair sweater while sitting in the chair by the fireplace.

Lee nearly spilled his coffee. "I didn't mean it that way. It's just that it's such a big commitment for someone his age. Lenny's only twenty-three. He'll be giving up ten years of his life to take care of a teenager. That's a lot to ask of him."

"It's preordained. No one has to ask him. But you can't tell anyone I told you. Someone will innocently bring up the subject, and the seed will be planted in Lenny's mind. The offer will come from him. It will be of his own choosing. All you have to do is sit back and watch it unfold."

"That will be interesting." Hayley snuggled against Lee. "We promise to keep your secret."

"Thank you. Now I must be off." Grams vanished in an

instant.

Lee set his coffee cup on the table and glanced at his watch. "He'll be here soon. Why don't we join the others?"

"I'd better get ready. Can't wait to see this." She left the room to take a shower.

"This is going to be an interesting day," she heard him say.

***

In the dining room, Thomas coupled another table with theirs, and Lenny joined them in front of the fireplace.

"Did I make it in time?" Lenny asked.

"Yes," Lee said.

"So, what happens now?" Lenny asked.

"I've been to the cemetery and met with Seth's groundskeepin' crew," Jim said. "We've got tools and a utility tractor to use to dig up the grave and raise the coffin. All we need to decide is where to set up the tent."

"You'll need to purchase six tarps and duct tape," Matilda said, "in order to construct a containment compartment for the contaminated soil."

"Sounds like you've been to a few casket raisin's, my dear," Jim said.

"I've been to more archeological digs all over the world than I can count," she replied. "My field of linguistics has allowed me to translate words on more crypts than you can imagine. As soon as a body dies, it begins to decompose, and bacteria begin to contaminate its surroundings. Dangerous pathogens, ancient microbes, fungi, and toxic mold could be within the soil, in the casket, and covering debris."

"She's right," Lee said.

"I've read about that too," Kathy replied. "I'll try my best to contain the danger." She pulled out a notepad from her tote bag. She drew a rectangle that represented the church and circled the area where Ellie's coffin rested underground.

All leaned in and watched her draw.

"I've been thinking about this very carefully. During the war, this wall was destroyed." Kathy pointed at the east side of the church. "That means boulders, as well as dirt, cover the coffin. This is going to be tricky. You know I haven't attempted anything like this before. And I haven't had anywhere to practice where I wouldn't be seen. But I'll see what I can do."

"If we erect the tent lengthwise following the line of the church," Jim said, "we can pile the dirt by the backyard."

"Good plan," Lee said.

"What about the coffin?" Matilda asked. "Will you be able to raise it quickly?"

"I believe so," Kathy said. "I'm betting I can easily translocate it."

Lenny's eyes widened. "Blimey! Are you talking about witchcraft?"

Kathy looked at Lee. "You didn't tell him?"

"I wanted to, but.... I wanted to see the look on his face."

"Ya have a warped sense of humor," Jim told him.

"You're a good teacher," Lee replied.

"Did you tell him about the bomb?" Kathy asked him.

"Of course," Lee said. "It's his choice if he's willing to put himself in danger."

"How about the earthquake?" Hayley asked.

"A bloody earthquake?" Lenny blurted. "Are you telling me that a strapping tremor's about to hit, and that's why you mustn't dally to exhume the coffin? I didn't know the casket was sitting right on top of the bomb. I thought it was buried beneath it."

"It is," Jim told him. "Problem is if we don't move the coffin in time, the earthquake will send that bomb sailin' like a shot outta hell into the damn thing and cremate our asses and possibly decimate the entire town." He looked at Lee. "Bet ya didn't tell him that either."

"What are the odds that will happen?" Lenny asked

Hayley. "Is it that precarious?"

She nodded. "There's a chance. Simon foresaw the explosion. That's when Elsie came looking for us so we can stop it from happening. And unfortunately, I can't foresee any of our futures. As long as we're involved, I won't be able to view the outcome."

"Ya mean if we live or die," Jim said.

"Precisely," Hayley told him.

"What about Simon?" Lenny asked. "Does he have the same abilities as you?"

"The same as I had at his age," Hayley replied. "But no one in town, including his parents, believes he's gifted. That's why he and Elsie came to us. The trouble is that he's just as involved in this as we are, and he can't foresee his own future the same as I can't envision mine."

"So, we're workin' in the dark," Jim said.

"What about your ability to see auras?" Lee asked Hayley. "Can that be of help to us?"

She thought for a moment and remembered the old man, Ned, who sang in the pub. "I can tell if someone's about to die because their aura disappears. That could possibly be of help."

"Is that anything like casting a spell?" Kathy asked. "I mean, does the intent of an action have to be decided first in order for you to see or not see the aura?"

"Yes," Hayley said. "So, before you move a rock or shift the casket in any direction, look at me, and I'll let you know if it's safe."

"You should stand across from me then," Kathy said. On the drawing, she drew a *K* on one side of the grave and an *H* on the other. "I'll translocate the rubble and place it into the contamination container the guys will construct with the tarps in the backyard."

"I'm gobsmacked," Lenny said. "This is bloody unbelievable. It's going to be the best day of my entire life if I live through it."

"We don't plan on dyin'," Jim said.

"No, we don't," Kathy said. "I think we've got it."

"Anything else?" Lee asked.

"Father Farley explained it all to me," Jim said. "He's obtained a permit from the courts to proceed. And since this is an emergency and everyone's leavin' town, the health inspector won't be available. Good thing too. Can't imagine what the inspector would say when he sees the casket rise outta the grave with no strings attached. Looks like we've got everythin' covered."

"This is so cool," Lenny said.

"Aren't concrete slabs usually placed around the inside of the grave to keep the walls from collapsing?" Lee asked.

"I've googled the process," Kathy replied. "We've checked off all the rules and regulations except for the health inspector. All I have to do is shield all of you from coming into contact with contaminated dirt and unhealthy air. I can secure the grave's walls as I remove the soil and debris."

"Better not be concrete slabs," Jim told her. "Father Farley will ask where we got 'em. Any other method?"

"I can use an invisible force and cover the inside of the grave with tarps. Would that work?"

Jim nodded. "Buy more tarps. Got it."

"Then, after everything is safe and sound, I'll lift the casket and set it here." She pointed to an area on the drawing a few yards from the gravesite. "Seth said he's made arrangements to have her coffin placed in the morgue until the reburial."

"Sounds like a plan," Hayley said.

"We should buy Elsie a crypt," Lee told them. "She deserves it after saving the town from an explosion. I can ask Father Farley about that too."

"I think that's a great idea," Hayley said. "A monument will take the spotlight off Simon and shine it on Elsie. I'll have a talk with Simon and see what he thinks."

"Can I meet him?" Lenny asked.

"I'd be happy to introduce you," Hayley replied.

"But first, we need to show the crew where to erect the tent," Jim said, "and build the containment unit."

"Let's get going," Lee said.

CHAPTER 19

Hayley watched the pieces of the tent being laid out among the graves. Then skillfully, the crew from Jill's Flower Shop gathered each piece and began erecting it while Jim supervised.

Seth examined the snow-frosted cemetery grounds. "Perfect," Seth told the men who anchored the enclosure's frame. He ambled about double checking the placement. "All graves were respected and uncompromised. I give my approval."

"I give mine, too," Jim said. "Now we can get the roof on and the sidin' up."

The workers tiptoed around headstones and stepped over graves as they rigorously fixed the canvas to the shelter's ribs. Pulling the covering tightly, they tied the fabric down, shielding the coming dig from the weather and securing their privacy.

"Good job, guys," Jim told them.

Lee and Thomas drove up, returning from the hardware store with the much-needed tarps.

"Now, who wants to make some extra cash and duct tape a few tarps together?" Jim
asked.

All the workers raised their hands.

Lenny stood inside the enclosure with Hayley, Kathy, and Matilda near the east wall of the church. "Tell me more about Simon," he asked Hayley. "I'm itching to meet him."

"It hasn't been easy for him," she said. "He comes from a dysfunctional family. His dad is an alcoholic, and his mother is abusive. Neither one believes he's gifted. He's been battered and mentally abused at home as well as at school."

"How old did you say he is?"

"He's eleven now. A couple of months ago, the court stepped in and removed him from his parents' house and gave his grandfather total custody. He didn't believe in his grandson's abilities either. Simon's been basically alone while he's tried to control the voices he hears and visions he sees. I can't imagine how lonely he'd be without Elsie. I know what he's going through. It resembles my past quite a bit. I'm sure he gets overwhelmed with information when he foresees the future and tries to tell someone what he's seen. I imagine that's when the abuse starts all over. People can be so cruel. There's even a sarcastic song written about him and sung over and over at the pub."

"That's the bollocks," Lenny told her.

"Several days ago, he foresaw the bomb exploding, and his first reaction was to move the church relics to a safer place. He was caught and arrested for theft. That's when Elsie came looking for us. The courts placed him into the custody of Officer Bates until Simon's mental evaluation is completed, and his court case is over."

"He's lucky you were in London," Lenny replied.

"Why don't we drive over and see how plans for tonight have worked out?" Kathy said.

"We can take my car," Lenny said.

"Wait a minute." Kathy walked over to Thomas, who stood with Lee by the church's courtyard at the rear of the tent. They talked for a minute before Kathy returned. "We're good to go. He'll meet us at Officer Bates's house in a little while. He's anxious to hear what Scotland Yard said about Rex Wood."

"How are you going to explain why you and Thomas are joining them to catch that troublemaker tonight?" Matilda asked.

"They won't even know we're there," Kathy said. "I intend to cast an invisibility spell on us."

"Blimey!" Lenny said. "You can do that?"

Kathy took a step back and, in an instant, vanished. The next moment she reappeared. "A few months ago, a Viking witch possessed me and took complete control. Her thoughts and memories mingled with mine. But she made one fatal mistake. When she stepped out of my body to possess another's and her butt-ugly ghostly-self stood bodiless, she was whisked away before she reached her next victim and taken to meet her maker. Afterwards, I remembered everything, the hundreds of lives she'd lived and every spell she'd ever cast. I plan to write a book someday."

"I'm gobsmacked."

"Let's go and let the guys take care of the tent," Hayley said. "We can meet them later and figure out our next move."

They piled into Lenny's Cooper, parked next to the rented Rover. Lenny waited for traffic to clear and backed out.

"Looks like some people are leaving town already," Matilda said.

"Lots going on today," Hayley said, glancing at the church parking lot as they drove by. "Some of the congregation is helping Father Farley move the church's belongings to the courthouse basement."

"So that's what this is all about," Lenny said.

"They're following Simon's lead," Kathy told him. "That's where he got caught storing the things they accused him of stealing."

Lenny waited for a truck loaded with items to pull out of the church's driveway. Once traffic cleared, he drove slowly to avoid a crowd of bystanders and turned at the next corner, escaping the mayhem. When he reached Officer Bates's home, he pulled over to the curb.

As Hayley climbed out of the car, she glanced at the house and saw Simon peeking out of the window. She waved, and in an instant, Simon opened the front door.

"I'm glad you're here," he told them as they came inside. "I'm trying to convince Officer Bates to let me go with him tonight."

Officer Bates sat in a chair near the fireplace. "Please come in."

"This is Lenny," Hayley said. 'He's a friend of ours from London."

"Pleased to meet you." Officer Bates rose, and they shook hands. "Have a seat. Simon, go do your schoolwork, and let us chat a bit."

Simon looked down and scuffed the rug with his tennis shoe. "I can't. It's math, and I need help."

"I'm good at math," Lenny said. "Can I help you with it?"

A smile spread across Simon's face. "I would appreciate it. I hate math about as much as I do business and economics." He glanced at Office Bates. "If I'm going to work with the police department for the rest of my life, what do I need school for anyway?"

"Off with you."

Lenny stood and walked over to him. He leaned and placed his hand on Simon's shoulder. "Math is the language of the Universe. And who knows? Someday you might channel Isaac Newton. Everything you learn is important. You want to be smart, don't you?"

"You know I speak to the dead?"

"Yes," Lenny said, taking his hand off the boy's shoulder and standing tall. "I think it's fantastic. I'd like to meet your friend Elsie if I could."

"I think she'd like that," Simon said.

"When did you first discern her?" Lenny asked.

"Discern?"

"It means perceive, become aware of, detect. See how imperative it is to learn as much as you can. When you talk to the dead, it's cracker that you understand what they're saying. You should never stop learning. You could be talking to a scientist, architect, or even someone you'll read about in history books. Do you know how lucky you are to have that opportunity?"

"I never looked at it that way," Simon said.

"Why don't you get set up, and I'll be there in a moment to help you." Lenny reclaimed his seat on the couch.

Simon dashed out of the room.

"Thanks for sharing your wisdom," Officer Bates told him. "He's headstrong. He doesn't listen to anyone. Probably because no one ever listened to him."

"Does the entire town know about his abilities?" Lenny asked.

"No," Officer Bates replied. "And he wants to keep it that way. He's offered to help me investigate unsolved crimes, but he doesn't want any credit."

"He's a good boy," Hayley said. She remembered how spirits came to her when she was his age. It had taken years for her to realize that they only wanted her help. Most asked her to give their loved ones messages, letting them know they were all right and to allow their families to move on with their lives without grief or guilt. Being visited by the deceased day and night without having any control of whom or when it would be was hard enough. If the public knew, she wouldn't have been able to deal with it. *There'd be nowhere to run. I know exactly how he feels.*

"Speaking of Simon…." Officer Bates explained, "we have a little problem. My wife has gone to her mum's. The poor dear took a tumble last night and hurt her shoulder. And as you know, I'll be busy myself this evening. Simon can't be left alone, and he definitely can't come with me."

"I'll stay with him," Lenny said.

And so, it unfolds, Hayley thought.

Officer Bates turned to her. "What do you think?"

"I think he solved your problem."

"That he has. Thank you, lad."

Simon peeked out from behind the kitchen door. "I'm ready."

Lenny stood and started toward the kitchen. He hesitated and looked over his shoulder. "How are you and Matilda getting back to the hotel? If you'd like, you can take my car."

"Thomas will be here any minute," Hayley told him. "We can take the Rover. Thanks anyway."

A few minutes later, Thomas arrived. He sat in a chair across from the couch.

"I haven't decided what to tell Scotland Yard about your involvement tonight," Officer Bates said. "Any ideas?"

"I know how uncomfortable you are when it comes to witchcraft," Kathy said, "but Thomas and I have talked it over, and we both think casting a spell of invisibility would be wise. They'd never notice us. What do you think?"

His eyes opened wide. "I'm sure glad you don't live a life of crime, young lady. How many people in the world do you think have your ability? That could be the reason for so many crimes going unsolved."

"I was given my abilities as a gift, and I gave an oath never to use it for evil. I was born to save souls, and so were my friends. I don't have a trace of evil in me."

True, Hayley thought.

"I can vouch for that," Matilda said. "I've known Kathy for years. You can trust her with your life. And no, there's no one else in the world that can do what she can."

"I'll attest to that," Hayley said.

Officer Bates glanced at Kathy and Thomas. "Well then, what's your plan?"

"Kat will cast the spell before they arrive," Thomas said. "When they come inside, they'll never know we're here. We can ride with you to Simon's parents' house."

"What about the evidence in Rex's garage?" Hayley asked.

"It'll look odd if you tell them the cans have fake bottoms. They'll ask if you've searched the garage already."

"That could be a dicey situation," he said. "Have any suggestions on how I should go about showing them where to look?"

I can take care of that, Grams whispered in Hayley's mind. *I'll just give the Scotland Yard's commander a little nudge. It's the least I can do.*

Are you sure you won't be crossing any lines? Hayley thought.

None whatsoever, Grams told her. *The evidence will be discovered in time anyway. I'll just speed things along.*

Okay then. That solves that. "Yes," Hayley told Officer Bates. "Don't say a word. Let them find it on their own."

"That's a good idea," Officer Bates replied. "They'd never believe a psychic told me anyway." He glanced out the living room window. "They should be here any minute."

"We should go," Hayley said. She and Matilda rose from the couch. "We'll take the Rover."

Thomas handed Hayley the keys.

"Have fun tonight." Hayley and Matilda walked out the door.

"I'm sure we will," Officer Bates said.

After driving away, Hayley looked into the rearview mirror and saw five unmarked cars pull up in front of the officer's house.

"Guess we left just in time," Matilda told her.

"It's times like this that I'm glad I have the gift to see the present," Hayley said. "Let's gather the team and meet in Lee's and my hotel room so I can give a play-by-play of the bust tonight. I expect Rex Wood is going to be incredibly surprised."

CHAPTER 20

The team gathered in the small hotel room. Hayley sat on a chair in front of the desk by the window. She closed her eyes and, using her gift to see the present, watched a vision stream into her mind. As events unfolded, she recounted what she saw.

Twilight cast gray shadows under the bare forest trees behind Simon's parents' home. Kathy, Thomas, and the law enforcement officers, dressed in black, trudged ahead and came to a stacked-stone wall bordering the property. The three-foot-high wall did not impede their progress. In single file, they moved quickly toward the house. Then they spread out, searching for possible places to conceal their presence.

"Officer Bates is heading to a shed about six feet from the backdoor. He's tugging on the padlock. It's unbolted. Another officer has joined him. They disappeared inside." She watched closely. Moments later, they emerged and motioned to others. "Six more men filed inside and closed the door." The rest of the officers disappeared from Hayley's view as they took cover.

Everyone in the hotel room stayed silent, listening to Hayley describe the law officers' step-by-step progress. In her mind, she scanned the backyard. The invisibility spell Kathy had worked to conceal her and Thomas didn't hide them from Hayley's vision.

She watched while Thomas walked to the backdoor, knelt, and inspected the area where Simon's vision had revealed the fire's future point of origin. Then Kathy strolled around the side of the house, looking toward the front yard. Angry shouts came from the street.

"Did Simon say which way Rex will come?" Lee asked Hayley.

"Yes. He's not taking any chances. He's walking from his house and following the creek. He'll be climbing over the same stone wall the others went over. I'm sure Simon told Officer Bates." She concentrated on the vision. "Kathy's hurrying over to Thomas, and they're looking into the woods. I can see a pin light off in the distance. I'm sure it's Rex."

Gray faded into darkness, and Hayley could barely follow Kathy and Thomas's movements. While they watched Rex's approach, the two of them moved about ten feet from the backdoor. Then they waited. Hayley informed the others of Rex's progress.

In the woods alongside of the home, shadows and a gold glow danced on the tall evergreen trees. "It's coming from the torches the mob's carrying," she explained. "It sounds like there's a large crowd. More than I expected.

"The penlight in the backwoods is growing brighter. I see Rex crawling over the stone wall, and I hear heavy breathing as he's hurrying toward the house. He stopped by the backdoor and is kneeling. He set his flashlight down, and it's lighting the small area around him. Melting snow is dripping from the roof and landing on his shoulder. He's snarling and glancing up." Hayley giggled. "A small avalanche walloped his face and is soaring down his arm. He's swearing."

"Did Kathy do that?" Matilda asked.

"I'd bet my mama's teeth that she did," Jim told her.

"Rex is mopping his face with his black scarf. He's grumbling. Now he's rubbing his hands together and blowing on his fingers. He stuck his hands inside his coat and into his armpits. Okay, I guess his hands are warmed. He's yanking off his backpack, rummaging through it, and pulling out a device the size of a cell phone. It looks like he's adjusting the object before setting it against the backdoor. I see sparks. Flames are climbing up the side of the house. But wait. The shed door is opening. Rex is glancing over his shoulder. He's leaping up and turning to run." Hayley laughed. "He darted into the hands of the officers surrounding him. They've got him."

"Cool," Lee said. "What about the fire?"

"Kathy is stepping forward. She's pointing at the fire. It went out."

"That's our witchypoo," Jim said.

"In the distance," Hayley said, "I hear sirens blaring and getting louder as they approach the home. They stopped. I hear car doors opening and closing. Someone with a bullhorn is telling the mob to go home."

"Take the damn fools to the hoosegow," Jim said.

She continued. "Rex is swearing as they're taking him away. Investigators are swarming the area. The lieutenant from Scotland Yard and Officer Bates are stepping aside, letting them secure the area and document the scene. The lieutenant told Officer Bates that he deserves a commendation. He asked Officer Bates if he'd like to go with him to Rex's place to join the search. Officer Bates said he would and that they could take his car."

"Will Kathy and Thomas be okay?" Matilda asked.

"Shouldn't be a problem, little lady," Jim said. "The lieutenant can sit up front with Officer Bates. And as long as Kathy and Thomas keep quiet in the backseat, they'll go unnoticed."

"Exactly," Hayley said. "They're climbing over the wall and heading back to the car now." She released the vision and stood. "That's it for the moment. They're going to Rex's house. It should take them a few minutes to drive there."

"Would anyone like a drink?" Lee knelt in front of a small refrigerator below the coffee machine and looked inside. "We have Guinness and Merlot." He took their orders. Once he gathered glasses, he poured wine for Hayley and Matilda. And he pulled out a couple of beers for Jim and himself.

"Have ya talked to Grams today, darlin'?" Jim asked Hayley. "Do ya think she'll remember to give the lieutenant a nudge?"

"Grams may be dead, but she's not forgetful," Hayley said.

I can hear you, Hayley heard Grams say in her mind.

Where are you? Hayley asked.

In Rex's garage.

Are they there yet? Hayley asked.

Officer Bates and the lieutenant just drove up.

Thanks, Grams. "Okay, everyone." She went back to the chair by the window and sat.

They gathered around, and Hayley closed her eyes. She relaxed and let the vision come to her. In her mind, she saw the checkered chalk-and-flint house with its Flemish bond brick addition that had a thatched roof and a detached wooden slat garage. Officer Bates drove up the driveway and parked. "They're at Rex's house," Hayley told them. "The lieutenant is suggesting they should search the garage while the others take the house."

"Where are Kathy and Thomas?" Matilda asked.

"They're staying silent in the backseat," Hayley said. "Officer Bates is accompanying the lieutenant through the opened garage door. They're surveying the right wall. There are cans of oil, transmission fluid, antifreeze, and brake fluid on a wooden shelf. In the rear of the garage, two men wearing gloves are searching a tool bench. The lieutenant doesn't seem to find anything unusual. Wait. He said something is odd, and he's wandering back to the supply shelf and putting on gloves. He said oil hasn't come in those types of cans for decades."

"Bet that was Grams' nudge," Jim said.

"He took one of the cans down and is examining it," Hayley told the others. "It looks as if it had never been opened. He's shaking it, and something is rattling inside. He said it doesn't sound like oil to him. He's flipping the can over. The bottom seems to be loose. He twisting it off."

"Now the jackass can't pee up their backs and say it's rainin'," Jim said. "They've got his hide for all those arsons in London."

"What did the lieutenant have to say?" Lee asked.

"He said, blimey. The bloody thing screws off. He's carefully removing the bottom and tilting the can, pouring the contents onto a long working table directly below the shelves. He said he's gobsmacked. He's calling over his team to take a look and telling them to gather all the cans and check their contents. Officer Bates and the lieutenant are stepping away and letting the investigators do their job." *Thank you, Grams,* Hayley said in her mind.

You're very welcome, dear.

Hayley opened her eyes. "Thanks to Grams, they found the fake oil cans. That went well."

"I hope tomorrow does, too," Lee said.

"Is the tent secured?" Hayley asked.

"Completely," Lee replied. "Half the town has evacuated. Hopefully, everyone will be gone when we start to dig."

Hopefully? "How will we know if they've all left or if some have stayed behind?" Hayley asked.

"Kathy said she could cast some kind of spell that would pinpoint any stragglers," Lee told her.

"What time do we start the dig?" Jim asked.

"When Kathy gives the okay," Lee replied.

"That might be late in the day," Jim said.

"Let's stop speculating," Lee told them. "We have everything planned. It's in fate's hands now."

"We'd better say a few prayers before bed, then," Jim said. "Let's head down to the bar and have one last drink."

"You make it sound like the world's coming to an end," Hayley said. "Think positive."

"I meant one last drink before the bar closes," he replied.
"Oh."

CHAPTER 21

Hayley awoke early, eager to start the day. The sunrise painted wayward clouds pink and gold. "It's going to be a good day," she said to Lee while looking out the window. A knock on the door surprised her. Lee, still wearing his plaid pajamas, opened it a crack.

"Oh," Kathy said, standing outside their door. "You're up."

"Come in." Lee stepped aside. "Did you get a good night's sleep?"

"Surprisingly, yes. I find meditating before going to bed is a great way to still my mind. I thought I'd let you know that the cook is making breakfast for us, and he'll be leaving us soup and everything we'll need to make sandwiches for lunch. We'll have to put them in the small refrigerators in our rooms until we get hungry, though. He and the hotel owner are leaving by ten. They're locking up before they go and giving the key to Officer Bates. I talked to him when he came in to get it. He's got everything under control."

"Does he know how many are left in town?" Hayley asked. "Did he give them a deadline to evacuate?"

"He thinks a little more than half the residents are still in town. It's going to get crazy when they all try to leave at once. He gave them until noon. I'm hoping everyone will be gone before then. I'd like to get this over with."

"I could hardly sleep last night," Hayley told her. "I keep

reminding myself that everything happens for a reason. But what if we're too late and the earthquake hits? Is there anything you can do to get the people to hurry along?"

"I'll have to think about that," Kathy said. "It might be possible."

"We'll get dressed and meet you downstairs," Lee said.

***

While eating breakfast in the dining room, Hayley gazed out the window, watching a car now and then drive out of town. "At this rate, it'll take another day before everyone's gone."

"I think I know how I can help," Kathy said. "I can literally shake things up. If I cause a quake to give them a scare, it may make them panic and get their tails moving."

"That sounds dangerous," Lee said. "If your little quake triggers the big one, it will set off the bomb prematurely."

"And there'll be no time to kiss your ass goodbye," Jim said.

"It won't be like that," Kathy told them. "Here, let me show you." She closed her eyes, and everything in the hotel began to shake.

"A little harsh, sweet pea," Jim said. "No need to break dishes."

"Oops." She closed her eyes again. This time things moved as if a light breeze circled the room.

"Too unnoticeable, witchypoo," Jim said. "How 'bout somethin' between gut shakin' and whisperin' winds."

"How about this?" She tried again. A subtle vibration ended in an attention-getting jolt.

"That'll do it," Jim said.

"Will the ground move as well?" Matilda asked.

"No. But it will happen so quick that no one will notice."

"It's a go for me," Lee said.

"Me too," Jim told Kathy.

"Okay then. Here it goes." She closed her eyes for a second, then opened them. "It's done. Now we'll see if that works."

In only fifteen minutes, outside the dining room's front window, they saw traffic backed up on the road leading out of town.

Jim took his cloth napkin, wiped the food from his mustache, and patted his stomach. "Good breakfast. That oughta last me awhile."

Matilda dabbed her mouth with her napkin and set her plate aside. "Did the church give instruction on where we should place the casket once it's unearthed?"

"Yes," Hayley said. "After it's exhumed, we're to leave it at the site. The staff at the mortuary have stayed in town to take care of Elsie's remains. They said they would be placing her into a casket worthy of her glory. Officer Bates told them to find a safe place inside the building and wait for our call once we exhume her coffin."

"Speakin' of unearthin' the coffin...." Jim said. "Kathy, can ya use your witchery to see if all the slowpokes have left so we can get our tails in gear?"

Kathy closed her eyes.

Hayley glanced out the window. A patch of fog enveloped the stores and homes across the street, then crept their way. She watched as it invaded the hotel, its feelers billowing under the front door. "Are you doing that?"

"Yes," Kathy replied.

The tentacles of fog prowling the hotel grew and spread as it entered the dining room and carpeted the floor. When it engulfed Hayley's feet, Kathy giggled. "It's telling me about you, and I'm seeing your image in my mind."

"And what exactly did it say about me?" Hayley asked, watching the fog pull away and move on to Lee.

"It said you're a small female with a calm demeanor. You don't intend to leave."

"It's right about that," Hayley said. "Is this fog going into every house?"

"It's covering every inch of the town. I should know in another minute who remains."

When the stream of vapor caressed Lenny's boots, he gasped. "This is freaking cool."

After scanning each of them, the fog evaporated.

Hayley glanced outside. Only the chill filled the air.

Kathy opened her eyes. "Once the cook and the hotel owner leave, there'll be no one left in town except the people at the morgue, Officer Bates, Simon, and us."

Once they finished eating, the cook hurried out to the dining room and collected their dishes. "I've seen photos of towns destroyed by Nazi bombs. Half of our town could be laid to waste and the other half blown off its foundations. Words can't convey our thanks."

"That's mighty nice of ya," Jim said. "But remember, we wouldn't be here if it weren't for Elsie Hudson. She found us in London and brought us here."

"She's not a demon?"

"No," Jim said. "The town owes that little lady an apology. And Simon too."

"I'll see that they get it," the cook said.

"So, what's the weather gonna look like today?" Jim asked him.

"It's calm now, but there's a storm brewing off the coast that'll be hitting us tonight. In an hour or two, the wind will pick up. It will get blustery as the clouds roll in. But the winds should be calm again when the storm hits."

"Thanks," Jim told him. "That's very helpful to know."

"Do you think the wind will pull down the tent?" Hayley asked.

"Spikes are holdin' down the frame," Jim said. "But who knows? It all depends on how hard it blows."

They waited a half an hour until the cook left.

"Let's get this over with," Lee said and rose from the table. Everyone followed his lead.

As they stepped outside, the owner left also, locking up behind her. "May the saints be with you," she called to them and hurried to her car. She waved as she drove off.

A frosty breeze stung Hayley's face when she raised her arm to return the wave. It surprised her when a gust of wind grabbed her scarf and flipped it into her face. She shoved the wrap's knitted ends into the front of her coat and hurried to the Rover.

Lee opened her car door. Hayley slid into the leather passenger seat and shivered while waiting for the others to climb inside. Jim and Lenny sat in the third row. Kathy, Thomas, and Matilda piled into the second-row seating.

After everyone else sat snuggly in the seats behind Lee, he started the engine and pulled away from the curb.

"It's in the mid-twenties, but the wind makes it feel like it's in the teens," Hayley said. "I hope we don't freeze to death before we find the bomb."

"The weather won't bother us once we're inside the tent," Kathy told her.

When they reached the church, Lee stopped in front of the cemetery. They all climbed out of the vehicle and headed into the enclosure.

Inside, the noise from the wind battering the canvas made Hayley raise her voice to be heard. "Where's Officer Bates and Simon?" she asked Lee.

"They're in the church," he said loud enough for her to hear.

"I'll go get them," Lenny told them and dashed outside.

Kathy waved. In a moment, the canvas stopped shuttering, and silence filled the tent. Instantly, Hayley felt a change in the temperature. Frost that had been caked on headstones melted away. The sheets of ice covering the ground cracked, each piece shrinking and changing shape. As the soil warmed, puddles formed.

Jim walked to a toolbox resting by eight sheets of plywood leaning against the side of the tent that hugged the church's stone outer wall. Hayley saw him retrieve a can of spray paint and shove something into his pocket before he hurried back.

Small stones that had apparently outlined the grave had been scattered.

Jim pulled a measuring tape from his pocket and started to find the exact location of the casket. "The head of the coffin is, accordin' to Elsie's guidelines, only three feet from the church's exterior wall," he said. "Right here. Then it goes out in that direction until it ends there." He removed the lid from the can and sprayed a yellow line around the outer edges of the grave. Then he stood back. "Everyone needs to find a place to watch. Wherever Kathy stands, Hayley will stand across from her."

Lenny, followed by Officer Bates and Simon, reentered the tent. "Hold it right there," Jim told them. "You'll have front row seats if ya don't move hide nor hair. Lee, Thomas, and I will stand over yonder so we can all get a gander of witchypoo raisin' the dead."

Kathy glared at him. "I'm not bringing the dead to life. And would you stop calling me that?"

"I certainly hope not. I'm bettin' Elsie wouldn't be caught dead comin' back to life if she'd have worms crawlin' outta her decayin' flesh. Am I right?" Jim glanced at Elsie, who stood next to Simon. She wrinkled her nose and squinted. "And witchypoo's a term of endearment," Jim told Kathy. "Ya know I love ya."

She glanced upward and shook her head.

Everyone got comfortable, shedding coats, hats, and scarves. They took their places. Lee, Jim, Matilda, and Thomas stood at the foot of the grave while Lenny and Officer Bates remained at its head. Simon sat alongside Elsie's ghost on the ground next to Lenny. So far, the paranormal activities hadn't shaken anyone's resolve to witness the bomb's unveiling.

Kathy stood between the grave and the church exterior, her back against the tent's outer canvas.

Hayley took her place on the other side of Jim's diagram in order to see Kathy's aura. "Make sure you picture in your mind what you're about to do before you do it. If your aura disappears, I'll tell you to stop. When I do, clear your mind and don't move. If you don't stop, we'll all die."

CHAPTER 22

While Hayley stood across from Kathy, she glanced at the tent's canvas doorway. Where the door's canvas had flopped aside, she got a glimpse of what they were missing outside. She felt awestruck that Kathy had lifted the cold from the earth and air inside the tent and raised the temperature to a toasty seventy-five. *She's amazing.*

The weather outside the canvas walls grew progressively worse. The icy wind blew, and the clouds thickened in advance of the coming snowstorm. But the tent remained spellbound, its walls shielded from the gusting winds, and the dimness inside replaced by an unseen force that lit the interior.

Memories flooded Hayley's mind. She thought about the Viking witch who had possessed Kathy. When a well-laid plan forced the witch to flee Kathy's body, Kathy had been left with the witch's memories and the powers she now utilized. And for reasons unknown, after the witch's capture, Hayley had received the gift to see auras. She had learned that people about to pass on lose their aura shortly before their death. Only if a colorful aura continued to surround Kathy's body would Hayley allow her to continue.

Kathy studied the gravesite. "I need to take this slowly. I don't know how much debris is covering the coffin." She held out her arm, turned up her palms, and glanced at Hayley.

Convinced it would be safe after she saw the energy field still intact and surrounding Kathy, Hayley gave her a thumbs-up.

When Kathy raised her arms as if lifting something invisible, a chunk of topsoil rose. "Easy enough," she said. Then the hovering grass and dirt vanished. "I'm placing it in the containment compartment."

Translocation, Hayley thought. *How cool is that?*

"Do you think we should be protected from the grave's contamination?" Matilda asked, standing at Jim's side. "Besides harmful bacteria, there may be arsenic in the soil."

"I'll safeguard us just in case." Kathy closed her eyes and reopened them. "Done."

Jim scanned his arms and body. "Are ya sure that worked? I don't feel shielded." His eyes widened when a ball of dirt sailed at him. He raised his hand as the glob of loam clouted an invisible wall inches from his face. He gasped. "No need to give me a heart attack."

"Sorry. I was just making a point. May I continue?"

He nodded.

After checking with Hayley, Kathy began removing more topsoil. About a foot deep, she came to shards of clay tile, wood, and rocks. "This is worse than I thought," Kathy said, her hands on her hips.

"They never noticed this was a gravesite," Lee said, studying the dig. "They just filled in the ditch with rubble and threw dirt on top of it."

"I'll have to take it away layer by layer and support the sides as I go so they won't collapse," she said.

Although Kathy's translocation spell fascinated her, Hayley tried not to let it distract her from watching Kathy's aura. So far, she felt confident that if things were to go wrong, it would happen at a much lower depth. But she never stopped wishing she could rely on more than her gut feeling. Times like this frustrated her because of her limitations to foresee the future. Relying on her gift to see auras had its limits too. There were other things that could potentially set off the bomb. *Totally annoying,* she thought, her stomach in knots. It would take much longer to reach the coffin with each hesitation to confirm the action's safety, but Hayley knew the dangers the dig entailed.

"Once we remove the coffin and we go back to the hotel," Lee asked, "will your spell remain strong enough to shore up the sides?"

"I bought bags of concrete just in case," Jim said. "I didn't know if that would work."

"Good idea," Kathy told him. "I won't be able to leave this invisible support up. It would raise too many eyebrows — especially the church's. We wouldn't be able to explain it. Concrete is something they can see and understand. I'll wait until we lift out the casket so we can support the walls all at once."

"Do ya want me to mix up a bag?" Jim asked. "There's a wheelbarrow over there. All I need is water."

"If you mix the first batch, I can take it from there," Kathy replied. "But we have a way to go before we're ready." She frowned. When she created a hole, the loose rubble from its sides collapsed, filling it again, but that didn't stop her. She kept digging, and to keep the grave's walls from caving in the way each hole had, she cast her spell to shore up the sides as she progressed.

After Kathy had removed the soil and debris to a depth of four feet, Hayley noticed an odd movement underfoot. Her eyes widened, and she looked at Kathy. They locked eyes. Kathy's aura hadn't changed. "Wait," Hayley called out.

The ground movement stopped when Kathy put her arms to her side.

"Did anyone else feel that?" Hayley glanced to her right.

"No," Lenny said.

Officer Bates and Simon shook their heads.

"How about you, Elsie?"

She shook her head.

Hayley glanced to her left at Lee, Jim, Matilda, and Thomas.

They all said no.

"Should I go ahead?" Kathy asked.

Hayley nodded.

Kathy began to dig.

Again, Hayley felt the ground move, but before she could say anything, Kathy stopped. "Something's not right," Hayley said.

"It feels like there's a resistance keeping me from lifting out the next pile," Kathy told her. "Let's see what's causing it."

Hayley, staring into the pit, watched while rocks, soil, clay shards, and wood slivers slid to the side as if an invisible hand pushed them away and revealed a wooden beam—a portion visible, the remainder buried beneath her.

"I can cut it flush with the side of the grave and leave the other end where it is," Kathy said.

"That should work," Hayley told her, seeing no change in Kathy's aura.

When Kathy lifted the next heap of ground, a three-foot section of the beam came with it. She translocated the mass to the containment area.

"Not that I distrust ya, sweet pea," Jim said, "but I'd like to check and see if all you've pulled outta there is goin' where ya think it's goin'." He turned, then hesitated, looking back at her. "If I step away, will that invisible protection 'round me stay in place?"

"Yes. Go ahead." Kathy crossed her arms while he reached the far end of the tent, took a look, and returned.

"Damn good shot," he told her.

"A couple more feet, and we should be there," Kathy said, glancing at Hayley for approval.

After giving her consent, Hayley watched her dig until the coffin became visible. The blast during the war that defiled the cemetery and left the church in ruins had thrust the casket about, pushing it to the side and positioning it at a precarious angle.

"I'm going to lift it out," Kathy said.

Instantly Hayley saw Kathy's aura disappear. "Stop!"

Kathy lowered her arms to her side and looked at Hayley. She saw Kathy's aura return.

Lee and Jim stepped closer to the grave. They knelt on its edge and gazed into the pit.

"If ya can't lift it straight up, sweet pea, try liftin' one of the ends," Jim said.

"Okay. I'm going to lift the end facing you guys."

Again, Kathy's aura disappeared. "Stop," Hayley shouted.

Once more, Kathy placed her hands to her side, and her eyes locked with Hayley's. Her aura returned.

"How about the other end?" Lee said.

Kathy looked at Hayley.

"Is your mind set?" Hayley asked.

Kathy nodded.

"Okay. Go ahead." Even though Hayley saw Kathy's aura unchanged, she felt uneasy. Twice, Kathy's intentions would've killed them all. The direness of the situation struck her hard, tensing her body as Kathy continued.

Kathy reached out and raised her arms, her hands palms up. Nothing happened. She lowered her arms. "Something's holding it. It won't budge."

Lee and Jim hurried around the open grave to the head of the casket and knelt.

"I see the problem," Jim said. "It's wedged between two boulders."

"There's a couple of ways to do this," Hayley said. "You can pull both rocks out at once or remove one rock at a time. Why not think about removing one and tell me which you've chosen. The casket will tip when you eliminate it. So, before you proceed, I'll let you know if it's safe. If it's not, you'll have to rethink your next move."

Kathy nodded. "I'll start with the one on my side." She

closed her eyes and reopened them, gazing at Hayley for direction.

For the third time, Kathy's aura vanished.

"Stop," Hayley said. She felt her heart pound. When the ground started to tremble, she gasped. *Holy....*

Calm yourself, she heard Grams say in her mind. *You have to keep calm.*

Is it the big one? Hayley asked her.

No, dear. Not yet.

Yet? When is yet?

The earth stopped shaking. Hayley felt dizzy and realized she'd been holding her breath. Closing her eyes, she concentrated on her breathing to slow her racing heart.

"I'd say it's less than a 3.0," Officer Bates said, his eyes still wide. The color in his face drained.

Hayley continued to relax by picturing the tension running off her shoulders and leaving her body. She opened her eyes again. "Think strongly about removing the one on the other side," she told Kathy.

After staring at the troublesome area for a moment, Kathy looked at Hayley.

Seeing her unchanged colorful aura, she told her, "Go ahead."

As Kathy pulled the large, jagged rock from the wall of the grave, it scraped the side of the wooden coffin, its loud grating noise filling the tent. Once the rock had been freed from the wall and it had been translocated, the casket tipped. Everyone stepped back.

"It's okay," Hayley told them. She glanced at Jim. "What do you think?"

Without hesitation, Jim sprinted around to the foot of the grave, knelt, and studied the situation. "I can't quite see the problem."

"How can I help?" Kathy asked.

"Got a long stick with a mirror on the end?"

Before Hayley could blink, she saw Kathy handing him exactly what he'd asked for.

Jim's brows raised, and his eyes widened. "I'll be a cross-eyed jackass," he said, taking it from her. He knocked on the long wooden handle and squinted into the mirror attached to its end. "Shove me in the oven and call me a biscuit. The damn thing's real." A wide smile spread across his face. "Cool." He lowered it into the grave and angled it to look under the coffin. "It's gonna be tricky. There's a big loose rock just waitin' to fall. My guess is the bomb is close enough to the surface that the impact will set it off. You'll have to remove this one next whether you want to or not."

"You're right," Lee said, joining him and kneeling. "Can you remove the rock while you hold up the casket? You'll have to do it simultaneously. Is that possible?"

Kathy seemed to think about it and nodded.

"It's okay," Hayley said. "You've got this." But as Kathy held out her hand, Hayley felt a vibration. Then the ground shook. This time the tremor felt stronger. "Hurry!" she shouted. When the casket began to drop, she knew without a doubt that the loose rock had pulled free. "No," she cried out.

CHAPTER 23

Hayley and Lee looked at one another. He started toward her. The last time she died, he had been at her side. Fortunately, it hadn't been her time to pass on, and her soul had been returned to her body. This time the explosion would leave nothing for her soul to return to. She knew Lee wouldn't make it another step. She cringed, waiting for the explosion that would kill them all.

"Got it," Kathy said.

In disbelief, Hayley stared into the open pit. "What happened to the rock?"

"I translocated it. It's gone, and I caught the coffin. There's nothing to worry about. I've got this."

Hayley shuddered, and her stress melted away. Lee stood next to her while she glanced around at the others. No one spoke. They stood like statues, staring into the open grave.

"Come watch, Simon and Elsie," Hayley said, "and stand by Lee. Kathy's about to exhume the coffin."

They hurried over. Simon and Elsie peeked into the pit, then stepped back, moving out of the way.

Kathy, looking as if she conducted a symphony, tilted the coffin with a few waves of her hand until it turned upright and horizontal. Slowly it rose. When it hovered about a foot above the pit, it changed direction and floated to the ground beside Hayley.

A roar of cheers and laughter filled the tent.

Lee and Jim knelt and peered into the pit. Instantly, white light lit the darkness.

"I see it," Jim said, pointing.

Hayley strained to see where he believed the bomb rested. She saw it too. Dirt covered its nose, but its shape distinctly proclaimed its existence.

"Now they'll believe me," Simon said, looking where Jim pointed.

Officer Bates removed his cell phone from his shirt pocket and made a call. When he ended the conversation, he placed another call.

"Ya bet your sweet petunias they'll believe ya," Jim told him. "They'll probably make ya the town hero."

Elsie clapped her hands and danced around while Simon beamed. Hayley knew exactly how he felt since she had also been surrounded with nonbelievers all of her life. She felt the weight of proving his innocence lift from her shoulders and knew from now on, Simon's life would change. *He'll finally have a chance to be happy.*

Officer Bates returned his cell phone to his shirt pocket. "The men from the mortuary are on their way over. And the bomb squad is coming within the hour to evaluate the danger. I told them we've evacuated the town. They thanked us and said because of the evacuation, they'll be able to eliminate the danger by the end of the day."

Everyone put on their coats, hats, and scarves while Kathy changed the temperature of the interior to match the frigid weather outside and also extinguished the mysterious light that illuminated the dig.

Jim glanced at Kathy. "Thanks, little lady. Ya saved our lives. That was mind-blowin'. You're a regular superhero."

"We all are." Kathy grinned.

"We'd better get this hole covered while we wait," Jim said. "Don't want any mishaps."

"First things first," Kathy said. "Before the men from the mortuary get here, I'm going to reinforce my spell that secures the inner walls. I'd better get on it." She slowly walked around the open grave, speaking words Hayley didn't understand. "Now I can cover it."

Kathy joined Thomas, took his hand, and they moved aside. With a gesture of her hand, one by one, the sheets of plywood rose from their resting place against the church wall and glided to their designated place covering the open grave. "Okay, I'm done. I'll wait until the men take the casket before Jim and I secure the sides with concrete."

"I think you'll only need to concrete the areas closest to the bomb," Lee said. "If the other end of the grave's walls crumble, it won't cause an explosion. Plus, it will make it look sloppy like amateurs did it. That'll help keep Kathy's abilities secret. Does everyone agree?"

Everyone replied with either a nod or a verbal yes.

Thomas gave Kathy a kiss and a squeeze. "You're amazing."

Hayley and Lee walked over and hugged her too.

Matilda joined in the congratulating. "It feels like only yesterday when I was absolutely sure ghosts and witchcraft were myths. And now, I've never been so astounded in my life. That was stunning."

"Thank you," Kathy said.

"It's amazing that it only took you a little over a month to learn to do that," Matilda said. "But I always knew you were a fast learner. You seem to have everything under control." She pointed at the boarded-up grave. "And I've no doubt this is why you were given your capabilities."

"I think so, too," Hayley said. She thought about the past, about her gifts and the timing in which they were given. Her ability to astral project had been given to her while thinking of Lee. At that moment, her astral body had left her physical body and soared over parks, homes, forests, and the lake until she found herself a few feet from him in his sitting room. It had shocked her as much as it had frightened him. Soon after, she used that gift to save a soul.

Her ability to store thoughts in an object or to project the thought into someone's mind, nudging, Grams called it, had been given to her to also save a life. *We wouldn't be alive if I hadn't used my newest gift to see auras and Kathy hadn't used her witchcraft.* She knew their abilities were given to them purposely. *I have no doubt.*

Hayley swallowed hard when her mind flashed back to the moment Kathy had caught the rock. *But there are no guarantees our lives will be spared if worse comes to worse. We aren't invincible.*

Outside the tent, a truck pulled up, and four men from the mortuary climbed out.

"How about we grab something to eat before the bomb squad arrives," Lee said.

"You're all welcome to come to my house for lunch," Officer Bates said.

Lenny looked at Lee. "Would you mind if I took him up on his offer, sir?"

"No. Go right ahead. Does anyone else want to join Lenny?" Lee glanced around, but no one stepped forward. "Thanks, Officer Bates, but we have lunch waiting for us at the hotel."

"How about dinner then? Mrs. Bates will make us a grand meal fit for heroes, as you most definitely are. She'd like nothing more than to have all of you grace our humble home."

Hayley glanced around at the others, who all nodded. "We'd be honored," she said. "But if you don't mind, we'd like to wait until the bomb's defused."

"Yes, yes. Of course. Mrs. Bates won't be home until it's safe." Officer Bates reached into his jacket pocket, pulled out a set of keys, and tossed them to Lee. "Make sure you lock up if you leave the hotel."

"Will do," Lee replied.

Lenny hung his arm around Simon's shoulders as they

walked out of the tent. Elsie waved to them, then disappeared.

The four men from the mortuary lifted the casket.

***

After each member of the team ate lunch in their rooms, they came together in the hotel dining room to wait for the bomb squad's arrival. It didn't take much time before Officer Bates came through the hotel's lobby door with Lenny and Simon behind him.

"The bomb crew is here," he told them. "What's your plan?"

"We'll wait in the church while they defuse the bomb," Lee said. "If they have any questions, we'll be close by."

"I plan to take pictures and document this entire affair," Officer Bates said. "The court needs proof that Simon told the truth before they'll drop all charges. The lad and I are headed to the police station to grab forms for the squad to sign and to get my camera. We'll meet you there."

"Cool," Lee replied.

Simon and Officer Bates left, leaving Lenny with the team.

"It's damn cold out there," Jim said. "But it's only three blocks away. We can walk it."

"It may be better to drive," Lee said. "I don't want anyone slipping on the ice and getting hurt."

Once Lee locked the hotel's door behind him, he followed Hayley and the others to the Rover, where all climbed in and filled the vehicle's three rows of seats. He backed out onto the icy street and drove the short distance to the church's parking lot. One by one, they filed out of the Rover.

Hayley noticed the way out of town had been blocked by a slew of massive trucks parked in the street in front of the cemetery. A couple of the trucks appeared to be large containment units. Two men carried a ladder and equipment into the tent. Several voices came from the enclosure. One of the men had a thick Scottish accent, and she couldn't understand a word.

Lee pulled open one of the church's large wooden doors. Inside, Hayley heard laughter and saw Elsie dancing by the altar. The team walked quietly down the main aisle and sat in the first two rows.

Nearly forty-five minutes passed when Hayley had a vision. In her mind, she watched slate tiles on the church's roof shake and come loose. Then she heard Grams's voice say, *Tell them to run*. The vision vanished. Hayley jumped up from her seat. In a panic, she turned to Elsie. "Tell the bomb squad to run, or they'll die." In an instant, Elsie disappeared. Hayley grabbed Kathy's hand as the ground began to tremble. "Hurry," she said, pulling her out of the pew.

They sprinted up the aisle and out the double doors. Steps away, men bolted out of the tent and into the street while the ground shook.

CHAPTER 24

Hayley and Kathy ran to the tent's entrance at the corner of the church. The last man climbing out of the deep pit reached the top of the ladder and raced past them with wide eyes while screaming something in a Scottish brogue.

Still in a panic, Hayley watched as the ladder slipped into the grave and the plywood boards standing against the church took flight. She heard a loud noise coming from the roof and felt the ground shake violently beneath her feet. One by one, the boards slammed to the ground, covering the grave. In that very moment, a deafening noise signaled the avalanche of slate tiles cascading off the church roof. Their sharp edges sliced the top of the tent and shattered on impact against the grave's plywood shield.

The foreman of the bomb squad joined them from the street. "Did you see her?" he asked.

"Her name's Elsie," Hayley told him. "That was her grave. She died during World War II." At the mention of her name, Elsie appeared at Hayley's side. They smiled at one another. Hayley knew Elsie had used a tremendous amount of energy to materialize and shout her warning. In order for her to materialize once again, she would have to gather more energy. She could only be seen by Hayley for the time being.

The foreman glanced upward. The noise ceased, and the earth had stopped trembling. He walked to the grave, squatted, and thrust aside the shards, revealing a sheet of plywood. "My saints," he said. "Elsie saved our lives and possibly the entire town." He walked back to the tent's entrance and waved to his crew.

The men surveyed the damage as Hayley, Elsie, and Kathy stepped outside.

Blue sky peeked between the billowing clouds while rays of sun streamed onto the fields at the edge of town. The cold winds died as the storm traveled east.

"Looks like a beautiful day," Kathy said, gazing up.

"That's an understatement," Hayley said. "Sorry, no one will know you're the real hero. But it is better this way, don't you think?"

"We wouldn't be here if it weren't for Elsie," Kathy said. "The credit should be hers."

Hayley looked to find Elsie had vanished. In the cemetery, she saw the child dancing around the gravestones.

Men from the bomb squad loaded the wheelbarrow with slate shards, clearing off the plywood to continue their mission.

Lee met Hayley and Kathy at the church entrance. "What happened?"

Hayley filled him in.

"Did anyone see Kathy cover the grave?" he asked.

"No," Hayley said. "They think Elsie did it. They said she saved their lives."

"Perfect," Lee said.

After they joined the others, Hayley gave the details.

Jim rose from the pew. "Let's go see how the bomb squad's doin'."

As Hayley strolled out of the church, she noticed Officer Bates's police car pull into the parking lot. He and Simon climbed out of the vehicle and quickly walked over.

"Is everyone all right?" Officer Bates asked, a camera strapped around his neck.

"As fine as pigs in mud," Jim said. "Couldn't be better."

"That was the Earth-shaker we've been waiting for," Officer Bates said. "How can everything be just fine?"

Elsie stood with Simon, and Lenny joined them.

"Have a looksee," Jim said, "and I'll tell ya how our little witchypoo saved the town. Oh, and by the way…we're lettin' Elsie take all the credit. So, if anyone mentions how she covered the grave with plywood, just raise a toast to her. I'm sure ya know that Kathy wants her little secret kept quiet."

Officer Bates, Simon, Elsie, and Lenny wandered with Jim toward the tent's entrance. Hayley and the others followed behind them.

"Yes, of course," Hayley heard Officer Bates reply. "But I thought the bomb squad removed the plywood."

Before entering the tent, Jim told him the entire story.

Hayley laughed as Jim embellished the facts, indicating Elsie had covered the grave. *No one can tell a story the way he can.*

"Elsie deserves a monument," Jim said.

Hayley saw Elsie, wide-eyed, whisper to Simon.

"She wants an angel on her headstone," Simon told them.

"I'm sure the town can do much better than that," Officer Bates said. "For the sake of Simon's integrity and to please the court, I'll ask the bomb squad to submit a detailed report confirming the lad's innocence. Both Elsie and Simon will be looked upon as heroes."

With a pouting grimace, Simon looked up at Lenny. "When this is over, are you leaving?"

"I have to start searching for employment," he said. "But I'll come to visit as much as I can. I promise."

Simon studied the ground. Then he glanced at Hayley. "Why can't I foresee his future?"

"There are times," Hayley said, "when you have to live your life like everyone else and wait to see what will happen. Otherwise, life would be boring."

"Can I have a word with you?" Officer Bates asked Lenny.

They strolled into the church, leaving Simon with Hayley and the others.

When they returned, Lenny said to Simon, "Looks like I'll be staying for your court hearing."

"Cool," Simon replied. "When will that be?"

"Tomorrow at noon," Officer Bates told him. "Now, if you'll excuse me, I need to talk to the squad's foreman to see how things are going and to start the documentation."

"We'll meet you back at the hotel, Jim," Lee said.

"Don't forget to come by for dinner around five," Officer Bates told him. "My wife will be tickled pink. I'll bell her up as soon as the bomb is defused and tell her to get her tail home. I know she'll be sitting by the phone waiting for my call. Don't forget. About five."

"We'll be there," Hayley said. "Please thank your wife for the invitation. We're honored." She walked to the Rover with Lee, Matilda, Kathy, and Thomas.

***

A couple of hours later, the team stopped by the cemetery to check the squad's progress.

Lee and Jim got out of the Rover to talk to the foreman. In a few minutes, they climbed back into the vehicle.

"They've defused the bomb," Lee told them. "Simon was right. The foreman said the explosion would've been massive if we didn't find it in time. I told him Elsie came looking for us in London and brought us here. She said the bomb was only inches away from her coffin and would ram against it when the next strong tremor hit. After I told him we exhumed her coffin and that it's now in the mortuary, he called us heroes."

"The squad can't get over how Elsie warned 'em to leave," Jim said. "And they still think she was the one that covered the grave with the plyboard after they hightailed it outta the tent."

"It's all been nerve-racking," Hayley said. "Especially when we lifted out the casket, and that small tremor hit. I thought it was over then. We can finally relax."

They waited in the hotel lobby until nearly five o'clock.

Jim set his empty beer mug aside. "Whatta we waitin' for, Lee? My whimperin' stomach is lookin' forward to some home cookin'."

The team headed to Officer Bates's home.

Mrs. Bates greeted them at the door when they arrived. "I'm so pleased you could make it. It's an honor to have you in my home. I know you have much to discuss. We'll have time to chat during dinner. I have so many questions."

"Thank you," Hayley told her. "It sounds like a pleasant evening." She smiled at Simon, who sat on an ottoman near the fireplace.

He grinned.

"Please, have a seat," Officer Bates said, gesturing toward the seating in the living room. After everyone got comfortable, he eased himself into a leather recliner. "The bomb squad's foreman just called and said he's on his way over."

"We stopped by the dig," Lee said. "The bomb's been defused. The town's been saved."

"Brilliant," Officer Bates said. "Winter Fest starts in two days. We'll be celebrating for weeks, thanks to Simon, Elsie, and all of you. The town owes you more than their gratitude."

"We were happy to help," Hayley said.

Mrs. Bates dabbed away the tears in her eyes with the hem of her apron. "I don't know what's wrong with me. Every time I think about what happened, I'm overwhelmed with emotion. We have been so blessed." She pulled a tissue from her pants pocket and blew her nose. "I'm so sorry. I'm a blubbering mess. I'll leave you be. I'd better see to supper." She hurried to the kitchen.

Hayley, sitting on the couch next to Lee, glanced out the window and saw the squad's foreman walking to the door.

Officer Bates invited him in.

"As you know, the bomb has been defused, and it's on

its way to disposal," he told them. "We've taken photos as you requested, and we'll make a full report."

"Smashing," Officer Bates said. "We'll be needing the report and photos to present to the court at noon tomorrow in order to prove the lad's innocence."

"I'll have them for you. Does any of this have a connection to the ghost we saw in the cemetery?"

"It has everythin' to do with Elsie." Jim looked at Simon. "I'm sure ya know your entire life is 'bout to change. From here on, everythin' ya say and do will be held under a microscope. Some stuff they'll say 'bout ya will be the truth, but haters will always hate and spread lies. What do ya say to tellin' him the whole truth? I'm sure he can keep whatever ya tell him to himself if that's what ya want. But secrets have a way of being revealed eventually."

"I foresee that happening sooner than you think," Hayley said. "It'll be impossible to contain Simon's and Elsie's story within the town borders. But it's up to you, Simon."

"I'd rather everyone know the truth than to have lies spread about me. I'll tell him."

"If ya don't mind," Jim said, "I'd like to have a crack at it. If I stray from the truth, I expect ya to put me on the right track. Do we have a deal?"

Simon nodded.

"This story started before Simon was born," Jim said. "What his great-grandfather was known for in this town was tellin' stories and talkin' to imaginary people or to himself. The whole town laughed at him and thought he was as mad as a cross-eyed squirrel doin' the jig. But he wasn't crazy. He could see the past, present, and the future. And he wasn't talkin' to himself. He was seein' and talkin' to the dead."

The foreman raised a brow.

"He kept his gift a secret. Until we came to town, his own son never knew the truth. His abilities skipped a few generations.

Simon's grandda didn't inherit a smidgen of it, nor had his daughter, Simon's mother. But Simon did, and up 'til now, he's been the butt of the town's jokes. They even have a song written 'bout him that some barroom bully sings every Saturday night in the pub."

"That will change soon," Lee said.

"When Simon was little, 'bout four or five, he went to work with his grandda, who had followed in his dad's footsteps as the cemetery groundskeeper. That's when the lad first met Elsie. Her parents and siblings had died in London durin' World War II. When other children were bein' evacuated from the city, she was sent inland to live on a farm on the outskirts of this here town. Unfortunately, bombs hit the field where she was playin'. She died and was buried in the cemetery. All these years, Simon and Elsie were best friends. But all the town saw was Simon talkin' to himself when he was actually speakin' to the dead."

"She didn't look dead to me," Simon said.

"Take it from me," Jim said, "when a body's been buried for nearly seventy years, that there person is as dead as a bug on a hot griddle. There's no doubt 'bout it."

"Who found out about the bomb?" the foreman asked. "Did Simon foresee it, or did Elsie tell him about it?"

"Both," Jim said. "Elsie told Simon, and Simon foresaw the bomb explodin'. That's when Elsie came lookin' for us."

"That was my idea," Simon said. "I had a vision of Hayley as soon as she knew she was coming to England. When I wondered who she was, I saw flashes of her past and knew she was just like me. Elsie went looking for her. Because everyone in town thought I was crazy when I told them I saw the bomb explode, I thought they'd listen to her."

"But we didn't know what Elsie wanted at first," Jim said. "Us Americans have a hard time understandin' some of the dialects in the UK, so we did a lot of guessin' to figure out what she wanted."

"Not to be rude, but I thought Hayley's psychic," the foreman said.

"She is. But there's a frustratin' rule people like her and Simon have to live with. They can't foresee their own futures. So, she couldn't foresee comin' here."

"Every time Elsie came to us," Hayley said, "she drew curved lines. One of our far-fetched guesses led us to think it could be a map, and it brought us here. When we finally understood what her name was, we thought she might be related to a member of our group whose surname is also Hudson."

"We thought she was tryin' to tell us how she died," Jim said. "We came to town to find some answers and to look for Elsie Hudson's grave with intentions of gettin' her DNA to find the Hudson ancestral connection."

"Once we talked to the cemetery's groundskeeper, who turned out to be Simon's granddad," Hayley said, "we heard about Simon and the trouble he got into."

"In my vision, I saw the church blow up," Simon said. "I didn't know what to do. So, I snuck into the church and started moving their sacred things to the courthouse basement."

"So, you broke into the courthouse?" the foreman said. "You'll have hell to pay for that."

"That's what we're trying to avoid," Officer Bates said. "The lad had good intentions. And with your report and photos, I'm going to try my hardest to get the charges dropped. Could you possibly have the reports faxed to us by morning?"

"The hearing is tomorrow at noon?" the foreman said. "I'll do you one better, mate. I'll bring it to you personally and give witness to the court if you'd like."

"That would be a blessing," Officer Bates said. "Is there anything we can do for you?"

"I do have a tad of a problem. I could use some advice. My men and I are struggling with our pride. We're not afraid of death. That's obvious by our career choice. The dilemma is we all ran boot over ass out of the tent like a bunch of scaredy cats when we saw Elsie's ghost. If word gets around that we're a group of chicken livers, we'll never hear the end of it."

"Did ya give the order to run?" Jim asked. "Or did they hightail it outta there on their own accord?"

The foreman looked at the floor. "It was me who shouted, run. I'll be laughed out of my job if word gets around."

"Think back," Jim said. "Did ya hear any kind of noise, like tiles rattlin' on the roof?"

"Now that you mention it, I did hear a bit of a rumble."

"So, first ya heard Elsie's warnin', and then there's no doubt that ya felt the tremor and sensed danger," Jim said. "The way I see it, ya did your job by keepin' your men safe. So what if ya agreed with Elsie that if ya stayed, you'd all die? Sounds like ya have good judgment."

"That tremor sent the roof down. If we'd stayed, it's a sure thing we would've died. I did make the right call. We ran because we had to, not because we were scared away by a ghost."

"That's the way I see it," Jim said.

"That's the way we all see it," Officer Bates told him.

The foreman stood. "It's been an eye-opening visit, to be sure. I give you my thanks." He turned to Officer Bates. "We've recovered the grave with the plywood. It's my understanding that the cemetery crew will be filling in the grave. So, we'll be leaving shortly. In the morning, I'll be here at eleven. I won't forget. Good to meet all of you. I'll see you tomorrow, Simon. Keep your chin up, lad." The foreman let himself out.

"That went nicely," Officer Bates said. "Everyone should be arriving back in town soon. In the morning, I'll catch them up on the cemetery's dig and remind them what Simon had told them. I'll make it clear that he and Elsie saved the town. I'll tell them they can start setting up the tents for Winter Fest. You can bet your Aunt Tilly's china there'll be a grand tribute to Simon and Elsie."

Officer Bates turned to Simon. "We have one more thing to discuss. Tomorrow, if all goes as I imagine it will, you won't be in my custody any longer. I understand, since your grandda's health is declining, that the courts are willing to consider someone else as your legal guardian. I've already talked to your grandda about it. He's been worried about his health lately but more concerned that you'd think he didn't want you if he agreed with the court. You know he loves you very much."

Simon nodded. "I love grandda too. I know his legs are hurting him. He's been limping a lot lately. I need to tell him it'll be okay."

"You'll see him tomorrow at the courthouse," Officer Bates told him. "If guardianship becomes the matter at hand, who will you choose?"

With a serious expression on his face, Simon looked across the room at Lenny. "Could you move here? Can't I live with you?"

A big grin crossed Lenny's face. "Yes, of course. I'd be honored to be your guardian. Officer Bates and I have already talked about it. We just wanted to see what you thought."

Simon jumped up and danced around.

"You know, lad, it all depends on what the court decides," Officer Bates said. "Don't get too giddy about it until we talk to the judge."

Simon stopped celebrating. "If they say no, are you still going to move here?"

"Absolutely. I've found a place for sale, a short bob from the police station. I thought you and I could go have a looksee."

"Cool."

"Now you know why you couldn't foresee his future," Hayley said, "because he'll be part of yours."

"I've got so much to learn," Simon told her. "What happens when you leave? Will I ever see you again?"

"Have you ever been to America?" she asked him.

"No."

"Well, that's about to change," Hayley told him. "One way or another, whenever you need me, I'll be there for you."

"Thank you. You don't know how much I need your help."

"I know exactly what you're going through. From now on, your life will be much better."

Mrs. Bates stepped out of the kitchen. "Come eat."

***

After dinner, Hayley made sure she had Mrs. Bates send Lewis the recipe for her lamb stew. Besides the food tasting delicious, Hayley enjoyed learning more about the town. But the day's rollercoaster of emotions had left her looking forward to a good night's sleep. She had only one thing left to do when she and Lee returned to the Night Owl—a call to Sutterville to let Laura and Roger know how things went today.

Lee and Hayley entered the hotel with the others behind them.

"We're going to head upstairs," Lee said, "and call Roger and Laura."

"Give 'em our best," Jim said.

Hayley glanced around the dining room. Only two people sat at the bar, while no one sat at the tables. "Seems pretty quiet. Doesn't look like everyone's back in town yet."

"What do ya say?" Jim asked the others. "Up for sittin' by the fire before we turn in? We have a lot to talk about."

They all agreed.

"We'll join you in a bit," Hayley said, and they started up the stairs.

Once inside their room, Hayley made the call. They chatted for a while. "And that's how it went," she told them.

"I can't believe Kathy's a real witch," Roger said. "She's like our little sister. Thank goodness she's a good person. With talents like that, she could rule the world."

"She's pure of heart," Lee said. "She wouldn't be able to

keep the powers if she wasn't."

"Speaking of the supernatural," Laura said. "As you know, Lewis has asked Grams to invite our deceased friends and family to the wedding. They've been lining up to use Clint's automatic writing ability. Once he's in an altered state, each spirit is able to use his hand to fill out their RSVP cards themselves. Grams has been there to assist if any need her help, such as Abel and his wife." Laura chuckled. "You know how Lewis gets around ghosts and spirits. As a thank you to Lewis for planning the weddings, Grams has asked each spirit, who has the ability to materialize, to drop their cards into a box on Lewis's deck. Each time he detects their presence, he gets giddy. He's loving it."

"That's perfect," Hayley said. "When will he be sending the announcements to our living friends? I have a few more people I'd like to invite."

"He's waiting for your return to get yours and Lee's approval."

"We shouldn't be here much longer. I'm planning to ask Grams to help Elsie crossover. I think it's time for her to be with her family. Simon won't have as much time to spend with her, and she'll be lonely if she stays. I need to talk to her about that. And I also want to know if she would be my flower girl."

Lee gasped. "What a great idea."

"There's a lot going on tomorrow," Hayley said. "I'll have to get back to you and let you know when we'll be arriving home."

They said their goodbyes and ended the video call.

"I think you're going to make Elsie very happy," Lee said.

"I think she will be," Hayley said. "And in the morning, I'd like to find out where her new gravesite will be. I have another idea that I think she'd like."

"Are you going to tell me what it is?"

"I'll give you a hint. It involves the exact location of her grave."

"That's not much to go on."

"Think about it," she said. "I'm sure you'll figure it out." She glanced at the clock on the nightstand. "Let's go down and join the others."

CHAPTER 25

In the morning, Hayley sat with Lee in the dining room. "I need to talk to Father Farley," she said, pushing her empty breakfast plate aside.

"I'll take you," Lee said. "Have you spoken to Officer Bates yet?"

"Yes. He's going to make an announcement on the courthouse steps at nine a.m. and wants all of us to attend."

Lee pulled out his cell phone. "I'll text the others and tell them to meet us there." After sending the text, he placed the phone back into his pocket, left a tip, and they rose from the table.

The air bit Hayley's face as she stepped outside. She pulled her coat snugly around her and went to the Rover with Lee right behind her.

Lee held the passenger door for her, closing it after she hopped inside. "Looks like there's lots of traffic coming from the church," Lee said, sliding into the driver's seat.

"They're probably bringing back the church relics now that the danger's over," Hayley told him. She buckled up.

He waited for traffic to pass before pulling out and drove slowly down the busy main street, following a truck with a tarp over items in the bed. The truck turned into the church parking lot. After avoiding pedestrians crossing the road and going to and from the church, Lee found a place to park in front of the cemetery.

"I saw him by the side entrance." Hayley climbed out, and

they went around to the front of the church.

Father Farley headed toward them. "A blessed morning to you both," he said. "I meant to call you, but I lost track of the time. I was hoping you'd come to church services tonight. The town wishes to give all of you and God our thanks for saving our lives."

"Have you invited Simon as well?" Hayley asked.

"Yes. He seemed shy about accepting our gratitude until Lenny gave him a nudge and told him he'd have to face it sooner or later. Nice boy, Lenny. They'll both be here."

"We'll be here too," she said. "What time?"

"Seven. It will be a late service. People will be setting up for Winter Fest once Officer Bates tells them it's safe, which he said he'd do this morning."

"I see the tent has been taken down, and the grave has been filled," Lee said.

"They've taken the tent to Molly's Meadow and erected it there. And Elsie's gravesite is being moved to the gardens in the churchyard in order to give her a memorial in her honor. We'll do our best to give her the utmost respect she deserves. Would you like to see where her tribute will be placed?"

"I'd like that very much," Hayley said.

They followed a walkway to the back of the church beyond the courtyard to a dormant garden. Boxwood hedges lined a meandering pathway that forked, leaving an island of rosebushes between the trails.

She thought about her English garden in front of her Victorian house back home. When she'd purchased it, she'd realized she knew nothing about the array of beautiful blooms growing on both sides of the walkway in the front yard. The thought of them dying from her ignorance ignited her urge to save them. That's when she began her research on flowers, shrubbery, and trees. *When Lee took me to see the gardens at his mansion, I knew enough to sound intelligent.* She smiled, thinking of their intimate game of hide-and-seek behind the hedges.

"We'll be digging up the roses and replanting them throughout the garden," Father Farley said. "I believe it will be the perfect place for Elsie's new plot. The details haven't been discussed."

Hayley closed her eyes and used her ability to see into the future and envisioned the garden next spring. To her left, beyond the boxwood hedges that curved along the stone pathway, blue English lavender mingled with pink peony, yellow foxgloves, and ice cap phlox. Snowcap Shasta daisy and black-eyed Susan overlapped the boxwood borders. On the right pathway, within the neatly trimmed thigh-high hedges, white daffodils grew in front of purple hollyhocks, blue delphinium, purple irises, and pink roses.

"All I know is an angel will be displayed in some fashion, per Elsie's request," Father Farley said.

Hayley's vision continued, and she saw Elsie's memorial. In the center of the colorful garden, between the pathways, stood an eight-foot statue of an angel with spread wings, her long hair hanging over the shoulders of her flowing garment. She held one hand to her heart while she reached out toward a granite grave ledger. Hayley read Elsie's name and age along with the story of her heroism engraved in the granite slab. Centered under the tribute's last sentence, she read the word *believe* written in capital letters.

"It will be lovely," Hayley told him.

Grams whispered in Hayley's mind, *I have the coordinates for you, dear.*

Thank you. Remember them for me, please. I'll get back to you.

"Father, I have an idea that may be suitable in honoring Elsie and would like your opinion. I know of someone who makes memorial bracelets. He pays tribute to England's World War II heroes by engraving their name and rank into the bracelet's metal face along with the latitude and longitude of each gravesite."

Lee caught her eye and winked.

"That's a brilliant idea," Father Farley said. "Do you think you can contact him and ask if he can honor Elsie? If he's willing and able, I can share a tent with him at Winter Fest, where he can sell them to all who wish to remember her."

Hayley glanced at her watch. "He's probably up now. Lee, do you have his number?" She removed her cell phone from her coat pocket.

Lee pulled out his wallet, thumbed through his business cards, retrieved one from the stack, and handed it to her.

She dialed the number.

"Finley Tibbs speaking."

"Hello. This is Hayley Johnson. I recently visited Libby's shop, where I saw your bracelets and heard about your father's illness. May I ask how he is?"

"Thank you for asking. He's out of the coma and home now. And he seems to be getting on with it nicely."

"That's a blessing to hear," Hayley said. "Would it be an inconvenience at this moment to request a custom order?" She told him about Elsie and the unexploded bomb.

"What a brilliant story. Do you have the longitude and latitude of the gravesite?"

"Yes." She repeated the numbers Grams whispered in her mind. "The town is having Winter Fest starting tomorrow. I know it's short notice, but Father Farley wants to share his tent with you to give you a chance to sell your tribute bracelets that will honor Elsie. How many can you make, and how soon would they be ready?"

"I have a hundred bracelets ready to be engraved. I believe I can have them ready by the end of the day." He cleared his throat. "You don't know how much of a blessing this is. My da's medical bills are more than a man can handle. This is an answer to our prayers. If you please, can you give me Father Farley's number?"

"He's right here." Hayley handed the phone to him. "Mr. Tibbs wishes to speak with you."

Father Farley took the phone while Hayley and Lee stepped to the side to talk privately.

"Finley didn't seem to recognize my name," Hayley said. "More than likely, his father doesn't remember telling me that I must hurry, and I'm not going to bring it up. He'll never know that if he hadn't given me that message, I wouldn't have taken Elsie seriously."

"Like you always say," Lee told her, "there's a reason for everything,"

Father Farley handed Hayley her phone. "Your idea seems to be well-timed," he said. "I'm pleased we'll be able to help Mr. Tibbs in his time of need. And his brilliantly conceived memorial to our heroes will guarantee Elsie will never be forgotten. What a glorious day this is." He checked his watch. "We'd better get to the courthouse to hear Officer Bates."

"If you'd like, you can ride with us," Hayley told him.

"Thank you. I'd be honored."

***

Outside the courthouse, Hayley, Lee, and the others waited off to the side of Officer Bates while he stood behind a lectern and microphone.

He cleared his voice and looked at the crowd. "First of all, I'd like to thank each and every one of you for evacuating the town, even though some of you didn't believe it was necessary. I assure you it was, and we have Simon and Elsie to thank for saving our lives."

The crowd murmured.

"It is true," Officer Bates continued, "that Simon's imaginary friend is real. It's also true that Simon can see the future. When Elsie Hudson told Simon about the bomb buried under her coffin, he foresaw an explosion that would lay waste to our town. By using his gift of insight, he found people who would listen to him," he said, his eyes scanning the audience, his tone a little stronger, "since none of you believed a word he said."

Hayley, Lee, and the others stepped forward.

Officer Bates continued. "Elsie went in search of our guests, and with persistence, she persuaded them to come here. In order for the bomb squad to be called, proof of the bomb's existence had to be found. Our friends risked their lives to uncover the truth. If they hadn't believed in Simon and Elsie, and if you hadn't evacuated yesterday when the tremor hit, our town would have been decimated. Please give them your thanks."

Most clapped and cheered.

"Yes, yes, I know there are a few of you out there that still don't believe. But this afternoon, I will bring you an eyewitness, the foreman of the bomb squad that defused the bomb. Maybe after his testimony, you will release your unfounded resentments of Simon and see the blessing we have in our midst. Believe me when I tell you that without Simon and Elsie, a good portion of you standing here today would be dead or seriously injured." He looked at Father Farley. "Father, would you like to say a few words?"

Father Farley took the lectern. "Bless all of you for being here. I'd just like to remind our parishioners that services will be held at seven tonight. We will have a guest speaker who will be telling the entire story of Elsie Hudson, so don't miss out. Thank you." He stood aside.

Office Bates continued, "Without further ado, I declare our town to be safe and that our Winter Fest will go on as planned."

Everyone cheered.

"And in honor of Elsie Hudson, I will give instructions to our ice sculptors. This year each of you will be sculpting a statue of an angel. Judging the winner will be Elsie Hudson herself. And the winner will be hired by the town to carve the stone angel for Elsie's memorial gravesite."

"Sweet," a man said at the foot of the stairs.

"At one this afternoon, I'll be standing here addressing you once again with an eyewitness who will confirm the heroism of Elsie Hudson. And I will tell you the outcome of Simon's court appearance. The church has dropped all charges, but Simon still faces reprimand for breaking into the courthouse basement. For those who will be getting ready for Winter Fest, plan your day around my midday announcement. And have a good day."

The crowd applauded.

"Who will be your speaker?" Officer Bates asked Father Farley.

He gestured toward the team. "Jim Newton."

Hayley's mouth gaped.

Jim grinned. "I remember you saying a long time ago that you liked surprises."

"I do," Hayley replied. "It makes me feel normal, like everyone else."

"Well, say no more, darlin'," Jim said. "I'm full of surprises."

"You can say that again." Lee looked at Hayley. "Where do we go from here?"

"I want to speak to Simon. I'd like to know how he feels about Elsie crossing over to be with her parents and family."

"We'll take care of this," Lee told Jim. "It shouldn't take long. Simon will have to get ready for his court appearance at noon. Officer Bates doesn't think the hearing should take longer than an hour. We'll meet all of you here at about one."

"Okay, See ya later."

Hayley and Lee strolled over to Officer Bates.

"Do you think Simon will have time to talk to us before his hearing?" Hayley asked him.

"Yes. Lenny took him shopping for a new suit, and after that, they planned to take a look at the house for sale around the corner from the police station. He should be home by now. Come by. I'll be on my way home in just a moment."

"We'll meet you there," Lee said.

CHAPTER 26

Hayley and Lee parked in front of Officer Bates's house. They didn't wait long before he arrived home, and they followed him inside.

They sat on the couch across from Lenny and Simon while Officer Bates eased himself into his recliner.

"What's going on?" Simon asked.

"Things are about to change soon," Hayley said. "Do you have any idea what your life will be like once we leave?"

"If the courts approve, I'll be living with Lenny. And I'm going to be working with Officer Bates."

"That's what I want to discuss with you," Hayley said. "What do you think Elsie will do while you're working? Do you think she'll get lonely?"

"I never thought about that," Simon said. "She can help us if she wants."

Grams, I need you, Hayley called out in her mind.

A veil of mist oscillated two feet above the floor in front of the fireplace.

Simon's and Lenny's eyes widened.

Officer Bates leaped from his chair and backed away. He looked at Hayley. "What's going on?"

"It's okay," Hayley told him. "She's another member of our team."

"Blimey," he said, gawking at the undulating phenomenon.

The wavering vapor streamed to the ground. Starting

at her feet, Grams's image began to take shape. First, her legs, although transparent, formed. As the mist moved upward, her torso became obvious. Then her beclouded arms and head slowly became noticeable. Little by little, the materialization fortified until every detail of Grams' being came into focus. She wore black boots that were tucked inside her blue jeans. Her curly blonde hair draped over the shoulders of her green turtleneck sweater.

"This is Grams, my grandmother," Hayley told them.

"Sorry if I frightened you, Officer Bates," Grams said.

"I'm gobsmacked," he said.

"Good to see you again, Simon. And it's nice to meet you, Lenny."

Lenny's eyes became larger at the mention of his name. He nodded nervously.

"What's with the drama?" Hayley asked.

"It's something Simon will have to get used to. More than likely, if he's visited by anyone who has crossed over, this would be what he'd witness as they appeared."

"That was cool," Simon said. "Were you here all that time? I didn't sense your presence."

"I'm Hayley's guardian angel. I can be anywhere and hear her thoughts. When she calls me in her mind, no matter where I may be, it takes me only a moment to appear. When Elsie crosses over, she'll be able to hear your thoughts as well. And if you miss one another, she can visit anytime, day or night."

"Why would she want to cross over?" Simon asked. "She's always liked being a ghost."

"Doesn't she miss her mom and dad and the rest of her family?" Hayley asked.

He thought for a minute. "She never said so."

"She was alone for about sixty-five years until you found her in the cemetery," Hayley said. "Once your time is occupied by other things, she'll be alone again."

Tears welled in Simon's eyes. "I don't want her to be

unhappy. I'll talk to her and see what she thinks."

"It will be best if we all talk to her," Grams said. "She won't have to cross by herself. I can show her the way."

Simon smiled. "That would be grand. Should we go to the cemetery now?"

"We can talk to her after your hearing," Officer Bates said. "You'll need to wash up."

The Napoleon mantel clock above the fireplace chimed eleven o'clock.

"I'll help you get ready," Lenny said, rising from the chair. "While you're taking a shower, I'll cut off all the tags on your new clothes and make sure your shoes are buffed."

"Thank you, Lenny," Officer Bates told him.

"I'll be going," Grams said. "Nice to meet you, Officer Bates. We'll meet again, I'm sure. Call me when you're ready to speak with Elsie, dear."

"I will." As Grams vanished, a knock on the door surprised Hayley. She glanced out the window and saw the bomb squad's foreman.

Officer Bates went to the door and opened it. "Come on in."

The foreman stepped inside. He wore a suit and tie, and his hair looked freshly cut. "Hope I'm not late."

"No. You're right on time," Officer Bates told him.

Lee stood. "We'd better get going and let you get on with the matters at hand."

Hayley rose also. "We'll get back with you this afternoon."

"Yes," Officer Bates said as he showed them to the door.

***

After Hayley and Lee had lunch at the hotel, they went to the courthouse. Only a handful of people gathered in front of the steps.

Lee checked his watch. "It's early yet."

Hayley looked toward Molly's Meadow, where a crowd

of people about four blocks down headed their way. She turned abruptly when she heard arguing nearby.

"She's not real," an old man shouted at a younger man standing next to him.

"She is so," the younger man told him. "There are witnesses."

"It's bunk," the old man said.

A few more people joined their discussion, and voices rose.

"I saw her myself in church," a woman said.

"The lad's a trickster," someone said. "She was a trick of the eye."

"He's only eleven," the young man said. "He's not smart enough to create a hologram."

"Who said anything about a hologram," someone said. "She looked real to me. Maybe she was someone trying to con us into believing she was a ghost."

"Spot on," someone else said. "If she was a ghost, we would've seen right through her."

The coming crowd, only a minute away, moved silently toward the courthouse. Hayley, Lee, Matilda, Jim, Kathy, and Thomas decided to find a place to wait away from the multitude. They sat on the wall boarding the steps, giving them a clear view of the speakers and a chance to catch any words spoken away from the microphone and the lectern a few feet away. If Officer Bates needed any of them, they'd be right there.

When the town clock struck one, the courthouse doors swung open. Office Bates walked with the foreman at his side, Lenny and Simon following behind them. When they reached the top of the stairs, they waited while Officer Bates proceeded to the lectern.

He spoke into the mic, addressing the people filling the streets. "Thank you for coming. I'd like to start by telling you what the court has decided. As you know, Simon was accused of stealing from the church and breaking into the courthouse basement, where he stored the church's property. The court has dropped all charges pertaining to the incident at the church, but the basement break-in had to be resolved. After examining all the evidence, the photos showing the unexploded bomb buried in the cemetery, and hearing the witnesses—the foremen of the bomb squad and Elsie—the court found Simon McClad not guilty. The guilty party turned out to be Elsie, who gave testimony that she was the one who broke into the basement by unlocking the door from the inside."

Officer Bates chuckled. "If charges were to be brought against a ghost, the entire court system would be laughed out of existence." Most of the crowd laughed with him. "Now, I'd like to present the foreman of the bomb squad, Foster Eastland." He moved aside as the foreman stepped forward.

Mr. Eastland cleared his throat and removed a sheet of folded paper from the inside pocket of his suit. He unfolded it and studied it for a moment before reading it out loud. "It has been over seventy years since the Blitz in 1940. Overall, 30,000 tons of bombs were dropped throughout England. Since then, it's been common to find many that did not explode. They are unpredictable, inherently unstable, and contain explosives with the ability to do vast damage.

"My team and I are the army's bomb disposal experts. We are called upon to defuse or detonate unexploded bombs throughout our homeland. Yesterday we responded to a call concerning a bomb discovered in a cemetery on church grounds. When we arrived, we found a coffin had been exhumed from its grave. At the bottom of the open grave, we saw the tip of the bomb. If the coffin had remained in its grave, the next strong tremor would have pushed the bomb against it, and an explosion would have occurred. The 500 kilograms bomb we found had the ability to successfully destroy and seriously damage approximately 1,200 homes and businesses. Thankfully, the town had been evacuated, and we were able to defuse the bomb without delay."

A loud mumble came from the onlookers.

He peered into the crowd as if searching for everyone's attention. As the rumble quieted, he continued. "When we arrived in your town, we knew nothing of Simon or his vision foreseeing the bomb's explosion. I have no doubts that if we had not been called, his foreseeing would have been correct. Likewise, we had no knowledge of Elsie, the ghost whose coffin had been exhumed. When we entered the tent beside the church, we found plyboard covering the empty grave. After we removed the boards, we started to work to accomplish our objective."

He cleared his throat before continuing.

"While my men were inside the grave, we felt a strong tremor. We were warned by Elsie that we should run or we would die. In that instant, I heard the distinct sound of slate tiles sliding down from the church roof and realized she was right. I ordered my men to run. As we cleared the tent, the sharp edges of slate sliced the tent's canopy, and an avalanche of slate tiles poured directly onto the grave. We ran into the street, expecting the bomb to explode. If it hadn't been for Elsie, who had thrown the plyboards back over the open grave, we, and anyone remaining in town, as well as this town itself, would have been obliterated."

Hayley gave Kathy a wink and a smile.

Again, a roar of conversation came from the crowd.

"I am here representing myself and the men Elsie saved and give an oath to the fact that the bomb was real as Simon had warned. In good conscience, I could not stand by and watch this innocent boy, who was only trying to save the church, its artifacts, and the town from destruction, get jailed for his heroics. And it is my honest opinion that Elsie should have a monument built to honor her for saving your town. I thank you for listening."

Everyone applauded.

"I told you so," the young man said to the old man. "She's as real as you are."

"Bullocks. When I'm a ghost, I'm coming back to scare the arrogance out of you, lad."

"Does that mean you believe in ghosts now?"

"I'll let you know when I'm dead," the old man told him.

Officer Bates returned to the lectern. "Thank you for your understanding. Now I'll let you get back to preparing for Winter Fest. Good day, and thanks again." He stepped away from the mic and walked over to Hayley and Lee.

"Good news," he told them. "Lenny has obtained custody of Simon under the conditions that he establishes permanent residency and finds employment suitable to managing a household."

"Are there any job opportunities available in town?" Hayley asked.

"There's one that I think he'd be perfect for," Officer Bates said. "I need someone to oversee unsolved cases. He has a sharp mind and a curiosity for detail. He'd be perfect. And, of course, there's no one else I'd allow to work with Simon."

"Well, that solves that problem," Jim said.

"What does Lenny think about working with the department?" Lee asked

"I haven't mentioned it yet. I'll discuss it with him when we get home. It shouldn't take long. We'll meet you at the cemetery after I talk him into it."

"See you then," Lee said, as Officer Bates headed to his car.

"Looks like Grams was right," Hayley said to Lee. "Lenny will be Simon's guardian."

"I can't remember a time when Grams was wrong," he said. "Can you?"

"Never."

"We'll meet you in a while for dinner at the hotel," Lee told the others. "Then we'll head over to the church to hear the story of Elsie." He raised an eyebrow. "Try your damndest to stick to the facts, Jim. Don't adlib and exaggerate."

"Would I do that?"

"In a heartbeat," Lee said. "And whatever you do, don't change the subject and start talking about all our past ghost hunting cases. No telling them how Hayley wrapped two ghosts around her finger on the first day of her job. Say nothing about the ghostship that healed itself. And whatever you do, don't start talking about witches or spirits that turn into birds."

"You're taking all the fun outta my story tellin'."

"It's important," Lee told him. "The people in this town have a hard enough time believing Elsie's real. If you start telling them about our past cases, they'll be convinced that Elsie is just one of your Grimm's Fairytales."

"Grimm's Fairytales, ha," Jim replied. "Our cases are scientifically proven as factual and as real as my Aunt Mannie's buckteeth."

"See, it's things like that that sound farfetched," Lee said. "Who would know if your aunt has buckteeth or if you're just making it up like all the rest of your stories."

"Okay. Okay. I'll stick to the facts."

"Thanks." Lee looked at the others. "See you all later." He took Hayley's hand. They walked to the Rover and drove to the cemetery.

***

Hayley and Lee sat in their vehicle in front of the graveyard, waiting for Officer Bates, Simon, and Lenny. Through the windshield, Hayley saw Elsie playing amongst the headstones. When the police car pulled in and parked, Hayley and Lee got out of their car.

The five of them gathered in the area where Elsie's grave had been filled and covered with paving stones that created a pathway leading to her new gravesite. When Grams appeared next to Officer Bates, he leaped behind Hayley.

Hayley noticed his hands were shaking.

He cleared his throat and shoved his hands into his pant pockets.

When Elsie saw them, she came running.

"Can you see her?" Hayley asked Lee, Lenny, and Officer Bates.

"No," Lee said.

"Can you gather enough energy to materialize?" she asked Elsie.

In a moment, everyone nodded.

"We came to ask you something," Simon told her. "Have you ever thought about going to see your parents and brothers and sisters?"

She answered, but Hayley couldn't understand her.

"She said she didn't know she could," Simon said.

"Would you like to?" Hayley asked her.

"She wants to know where they are," Simon said.

"Let me show you," Grams told her. She held out her hand, and Elsie took it. They walked down the pathway toward the gardens. Everyone followed. When they stopped, Grams turned to the others. "I know some of you can't see this. There's a white light streaming down from above." She leaned in to speak to Elsie. "This is like a stairway. It will lead you to your family and others who have crossed over. If you want, I can take you to them. They're in heaven. It's beautiful there. You'll never be alone. And whenever you miss Simon, you can visit him. Would you like to go?"

She nodded.

"Wait," Officer Bates said. "What about tomorrow? She's supposed to judge the ice carvings. I promised everyone."

"Can she wait one more day?" Simon asked. "Anyway, I'd like to say goodbye to her before she goes."

"Is that alright with you?" Grams asked her.

She nodded again.

"Well, in that case...." Grams told her, "Let me see what

I can do to get you cleaned up. Do you know anything about thought creation?"

Elsie shook her head.

"That's okay," Grams said as she knelt in front of the little girl. She ran her fingers through Elsie's dirty hair. As she combed through the kinks and knots, Elsie's hair became clean, and her long messy locks became untangled and filled with waves that loosely hung down her back.

Everyone gasped.

Then Grams ran her finger across Elsie's muddy cheek and touched the tip of her dirty nose. The mud on her entire body vanished, and Elsie's face lit up. When Grams lifted the edge of Elsie's ragged clothing, it turned into a dress covered with flowers and butterflies. Her crusty shoes became pink sparkly sneakers.

Elsie held out her arms, touched the butterflies on her dress, and examined her new shoes, then gave Grams a hug.

Tears welled in Hayley's eyes.

"Now go with Simon, and we'll see you tomorrow after the contest," Grams told her.

Simon followed Elsie through the cemetery as she ran among the headstones.

"Well, that was something else," Officer Bates said, pulling a handkerchief from his pocket and blowing his nose.

"I'm gobsmacked," Lenny said.

"Looks like we'll get together tomorrow," Office Bates said.

"Yes," Hayley replied. "And we'll see you in church tonight."

"I'll be leaving then," Grams said and vanished.

Officer Bates, who stood next to her, jumped again. "Bloody hell."

"Give it time," Hayley said. "You're not just working with Simon from now on. You'll be working with the dead too. You'll have to get used to spirits popping in and out."

"Now that's a scary thought. I never looked at it that way."

"Once you solve your first cold case," Hayley said, "a little scare isn't going to bother you."

He smiled. "You're right. It will be brilliant."

"I'm looking forward to it," Lenny said.

"We'll be going now," Lee told them. "We're joining our friends for dinner. We'll see you later."

"I'll save all of you a seat in the pews," Officer Bates said.

CHAPTER 27

The parishioners were jammed into the church. Not an inch of standing room remained vacant. The front doors were wide open, allowing those outside to hear Jim's story of Elsie.

In the front row, Lee sat on Hayley's right and Lenny on her left. Next to him, Simon sat with Elsie, although no one but Hayley and Simon could see her.

Father Farley started the services with a prayer which led to a short sermon on casting stones and loving thy neighbor. "I know you didn't come to hear me. So let me introduce tonight's speaker, Jim Newton."

Jim walked up to the lectern and gazed at the crowd. "My friends and I are from a small town in America called Sutterville, North Carolina. We're a team of paranormal investigators who have spent most of our lives researchin' ghosts and paranormal activity. Simon told me that as soon as we decided to come to England, he received a vision of us and knew we could help." He glanced around the audience. "We all know what he needed help with. It seemed no one in town would listen to him, so he had to look for someone who would. That's where Elsie comes in. She came lookin' for us in London. Ya probably know all 'bout that too. So let me tell ya 'bout Elsie."

As if a magnet grabbed hold of Hayley's attentiveness, her interest turned to Lenny as a vision took her sight. She no longer heard Jim's raised voice addressing the congregation. Gone were the stone columns supporting broad arches that ran one after another along both sides of the interior, the arched stained-glass windows depicting colorful scenes from the Christian Bible, and the painted ribs crisscrossing the bowed ceiling.

Instead, her foreseeing showed her cars backed up on the road coming into town. All parking along High Street had been taken by visitors. People strolled the streets, entering gift shops, pubs, eateries, and other businesses near the church. They walked through the cemetery, in and out of the church, and paid a visit to Elsie's memorial.

On the other side of the street, a stream of pedestrians wandered past the police station and trailed around the corner. Hayley's vision followed them to Lenny's house, where he and Simon lived like prisoners while a crowd of people camped outside, waiting to get a glimpse of the psychic medium. Most were respectful and remained quiet, while others called out to the boy to bless them with a reading, to tell them the future, to connect them with loved ones, or to prove the stories about him were true.

Hayley could feel the fear and frustration coming from inside the house. Simon had nowhere to run. While Hayley watched, a deep sadness overwhelmed her. She knew she'd be a thousand miles away when this would occur. But the necessity to do something to change the future needed to happen now while she, Lee, and the others were still here.

Her vision ended when she felt Lee's hand in hers.

"Are you alright?" he asked. "You're crying." He reached into his suit coat pocket, retrieved a handkerchief, and passed it to her.

She dabbed away the moist trails streaming down her cheeks. "I'll tell you later," she whispered. The wait for Jim to finish his story tested her patience. When he ended his tale, she wanted nothing more than to grab Lee's hand and take him outside to reveal her foreseeing. But Father Farley stepped behind the lectern, and a few more words of wisdom were given to the congregation. Prayers were said before people gathered their belongings and began to file out of the church.

Once outside, Hayley waited until Father Farley had thanked them again for saving the town and gave praise to Jim for his presentation.

"If you will excuse me," Father Farley told them after a lengthy accolade. "A few of my parishioners want to speak with me. I'll see you at Winter Fest tomorrow."

"We'll be there," Jim said.

The priest wandered away and joined others nearby.

"We need to speak with Lenny and Simon," Hayley told Lee and Jim. "Lenny must've made up his mind to buy the house around the corner from the police station. His decision triggered a foreseeing, and it wasn't pleasant."

"What did you envision?" Lee asked.

"The town is going to become a tourist attraction. There'll be flocks of people coming to see Elsie's monument, but worse, to gather in front of the house Lenny intends to buy and make him and Simon prisoners in their own home."

"He can't buy that house," Lee said.

"No, he can't," Hayley said. "But what can he do? He's going to have to buy a gated house, and that's something I'm sure he can't afford."

"What 'bout Simon's reward money?" Jim asked. "That should take care of it."

"I'd hate to see Simon spend all his money on property," Hayley said. "But how else can they finance such a home?"

"How about us?" Lee said. "Our vacation home. We can see if there's something we'd like to purchase around here. Maybe we'll get lucky and find what we want."

"Let's check it out," Hayley said.

"First, we have to talk to Lenny and stop him from purchasin' a nightmare," Jim said.

Lenny walked out of the church with Simon, Officer Bates,

and Mrs. Bates.

"Lenny, come here a minute," Jim called to him.

"We have to find a place to talk," Hayley told him once he joined them. "It will only take a minute. How about inside the church? Everyone has left, and it's quiet."

"Sure," Lenny said, following them inside.

When they sat in the first pews they came to, Hayley told him about her foreseeing.

"I can't afford a bigger place," Lenny said. "What should I do?"

"Hayley and I plan on visiting England a number of times," Lee said. "We thought if we purchased a vacation home, we would need someone to look after it while we're back in the States. I'm not talking about upkeep. I can hire people to do that. But we don't want to keep the place empty for extended periods of time. Would you and Simon consider living there?"

"Blimey, Mr. Franklin. I'm gobsmacked. I don't even know how to act."

"Is that a yes?" Lee asked.

"Yes. I mean, yes."

"Okay," Lee said. "I'll talk to Officer Bates. I'll tell him what I'm looking for. He would be the one who'd know if it exists." He kissed Hayley on the cheek. "I'll be right back."

She watched Lee walk away. When she turned back to Lenny, she almost laughed at the expression on his face.

"Is all this really happening?" Lenny asked her. "It's mind-boggling. I've seen a ghost and a witch, I meet Simon who blows me away, became his legal guardian, and now this."

"I guess things are moving a little fast for you," Hayley said. "Your entire world has been turned upside down. This next phase of your life is going to be just as crazy. Are you up for it?"

"Is that a foreseeing?" he asked.

"No," Hayley replied. "I just know that living with a psychic medium will be very…interesting."

"The way I see it, I'm a lucky man," Lenny said.

Lee returned. "Officer Bates said he'd meet us at the hotel."

***

It didn't take long before Officer Bates entered the hotel dining room. "What's up?" he asked Lee.

"Hayley and I were hoping you could help us find a vacation home somewhere nearby," Lee told him. "Five to seven bedrooms and a few bathrooms would be ideal. Something in the range of two or three million US dollars."

Officer Bates scratched his head. "There's a place on the other side of Molly's Meadow about ten minutes from here. But I'm afraid it's in a bit of a mess. The outside is in need of repair. Shrubs are overgrown, hiding a good portion of the house. And the inside needs some work. It's not a bad place, really. Renovations were made on a portion of the inside. But repairs were stopped when the owner ran out of money. It's been abandoned for years."

"It's worth a look," Lee told him.

"I can't wait to see this," Jim said.

"It may need more work than you'd like," Officer Bates said to them.

"It's a dream come true if ya ask me," Jim said.

Hayley knew that Jim had helped restore downtown Sutterville and a number of historical homes built in their hometown. His interest in restoration led him to become friends with Lee's parents while he worked on their eighteenth-century mansion. "Jim's a fanatic about restoration," Hayley explained. "It's been his lifelong obsession."

"Well then," Officer Bates told them. "I'll fetch the key from the property manager. Then, if you'd like, you can follow me out there."

Lee and Hayley, along with the others, followed Officer Bates a couple of miles out of town to a long drive leading to a wrought iron security gate. He came to a stop and waited while

Officer Bates got out to unlock the padlock and pull the gates back against the red-brick columns.

"Gated," Lee said. "That's a plus."

"The brick walls are in good shape," Jim said.

A graveled drive led them to a round turnabout in the front yard. Lee parked, and everyone got out. They stood looking at an Elizabethan red-brick manor. Shrubs and vines blocked sixty percent of the exterior.

"The main house needs major work," Officer Bates said.

"I can fix everything," Kathy whispered to Jim.

"Don't even try it," Jim said. "This is my baby."

"How about the yard?" she asked. "I can have lots of fun out here."

"The yard's all yours, witchypoo."

"Cool. Thomas and I are going to have a look around."

"Don't twitch a finger unless we buy it," Jim told her.

"I can wait," Kathy said. "We'll just stay out of the way and let you have a little fun checking it out."

"Good girl." Jim surveyed the exterior. "Stone mullioned windows."

"Most of the windows in the main house were replaced, as you can see," Officer Bates said, standing next to Lee."

"What year was it built?" Jim asked.

"The main house was built in the fifteen-hundreds by the father of the British Secret Service during the reign of Queen Elizabeth I. It has been rumored that he hired witches and psychics to help the throne spy on France. As you can see by the property's condition, he spared no expense to construct his residence. The foundation is solid, and the masonry work is exemplary. Over the centuries, wings were added. There are eight bedrooms and six bathrooms. That doesn't include the two bedrooms and two baths in the guesthouse, which had been fully renovated and lived in during the most recent construction done on the main house."

Hayley searched the windows. "Is it haunted?"

"There have been rumors. But the owner never mentioned anything out of the ordinary. He seemed to be saddened that he could no longer afford the repairs. Let me unlock the door."

The thick wooden door opened easily when he turned the key.

Hayley walked into the reception hall. The walls were painted a pale green. *The same color as Lee's ballroom.* She looked up at the white coffered ceilings. *Nice touch.*

"Some rooms have been totally finished, while other rooms look untouched," Officer Bates said. "Seems odd that he didn't work on the entire home at the same time."

"What's odd is he painted over the entire staircase with the same paint as the walls," Jim said. "I'd like to remove it and see what kinda wood's underneath." He looked at Matilda. "Would you mind very much if we stayed for a few months, my love?"

How can she say no to that look on his face? Hayley thought.

"Only if I get to help," she replied.

Jim's face lit up. "You're makin' my heart do summersaults."

"Do you really want to take this on?" Lee asked.

"Darn, tootin'."

Hayley wandered with Lee into the great room. "I like the stone fireplace," she said. "It should heat this room nicely."

"I wouldn't change anythin' in this room," Jim said. "Well, maybe the windows, the floorin', strippin' the wallpaper, and addin' a few new light fixtures."

Hayley entered the library down the hall. *This feels cozy even without furniture.* Maple wood paneling covered the walls. Floor to ceiling dark oak bookshelves wrapped around the room and on each side of the carved wood fireplace. *I like this.*

She strolled with Lee into the dining room. A sizable chandelier hanging in the center of the room had the capabilities to illuminate a grand table.

"Let me take you into a few of the rooms that haven't been

worked on," Officer Bates said.

They followed him through a butler's pantry to the kitchen.

"I noticed that most of the rooms that aren't complete happen to be where plumbing is needed," Officer Bates said.

"Plumbin' doesn't scare me." Jim looked around at the walls. "That and electrical work are my favorite hobbies."

"I can't count the number of homes Jim has restored in our town," Lee told Officer Bates. "This is his heaven. I know he'd do an excellent job."

"Does that mean you'll buy it?" Officer Bates asked.

"Let's see the rest of the place," Jim said.

They continued perusing a morning room, sitting room, breakfast room, kitchen, and conservatory, among others, on the first floor.

"How big is the lot?" Lee asked, following Officer Bates upstairs. "How much are they asking?"

"The home has 6,000 square feet of floor space and now sits on eight acres," Officer Bates replied. "There had been much more land at one time. Through the decades, most of the acreage has been sold off and is being used as farmland." He took out his cell phone. "Let me convert the price to US currency." He entered the data into his phone. "Got it. They're asking 2.2 million American currency. Trouble is, since you're not a citizen of England, they'll want all cash."

"Not a problem." At the top of the stairs, Lee took Hayley's hand. They strolled into a spacious room with a fireplace and looked out the window at a partly frozen river while Jim and Matilda inspected a room across the hallway. "What do you think?" Lee asked her.

"I think you should ask Jim if it's doable," she told him.

"Precisely what I was thinking," he said. "let's go upstairs."

Continuing on, Hayley strolled through bedrooms that looked move-in ready. "I love the detailed ceilings in each room," she told Lee.

"So do I," he agreed as Jim and Matilda came through the door and rejoined them.

"If it wasn't for the plumbing and the electrical, everything else is almost cosmetic," Hayley said.

"Don't forget the age of the foundation, darlin'," Jim told her. "We need to hire a constructional engineer."

"Does that mean it's fixable?" Lee asked him.

"Ya know I love a challenge," Jim said. "It's fixable. I can't wait to see what's inside these walls. In my mind, I can picture how it'll look. I say buy it."

"I agree," Hayley said.

Lee gave Hayley a hug. "This is so cool," he said as he left her embrace. "I can't stop grinning."

"Let's take a look at the guesthouse," Officer Bates said.

They followed him outside, where they caught up with Kathy, Thomas, Simon, and Lenny in the courtyard.

Officer Bates unlocked the guesthouse door and stood aside. "I'll let you give it a looksee."

Jim, Lee, and Hayley went inside.

"They did a damn good job in here," Jim said. "Can't find anythin' I'd change."

The details in the guesthouse were as ornate as the main home's finished areas in its interior. Crown molding framed the architectural ceilings, the oak wood flooring had been laid in a herringbone pattern, a small chandelier hung in the dining room, and the kitchen's dark oak cabinets hugged two walls.

"Come in and take a look," Lee called to Lenny and Simon from the doorway.

They entered and wandered through each room.

"It might be called a guesthouse," Simon said to Lenny, "but it's bigger than the house around the corner from the police station."

"You're right about that." Lenny turned to Lee. "You're really going to buy this place?"

"Yes. Do you think this guesthouse is suitable for you and Simon?"

"It's grand," Lenny said.

"We'll make the spare bedroom an office, and I'll have a security system set up in there," Lee said.

"I can give you the name of someone who can help you with that," Officer Bates said.

"That would be great," he replied. "I just want to make sure you guys will be safe. There's a lot of nuts in the world."

"Whatever you say, Mr. Franklin," Lenny said.

"There'll be no more formalities from here on," Lee said. "Call me Lee. I'm not your landlord. You're not renting from me. You and Simon are doing me a big favor." He looked toward the gate. "If I were you, I'd let the town know that you'll want your privacy. And I'd advise them not to tell the tourists your address. All I ask in return is keeping an eye on the place. There's a lot of land surrounding the manor. The security system will let you know if someone's trespassing. Other than that, the property manager has agreed, if we purchase the place, to handle all financial matters, including all utilities and staffing. If you or Simon notice anything that needs repair, you can contact him, and he'll see to it that everything is taken care of."

"Should I contact the property manager and get things started?" Officer Bates asked.

"Yes," Lee replied.

"I'm ecstatic that you like the place," Officer Bates said. "When are you planning to return to the States?"

"Once I hear from the property manager and complete the transaction, I'll let you know." Lee reached into his pocket and pulled out a folded piece of paper. "By the way, I have the name, number, and address of the lawyer Simon will be needing. He'd like you to stop by his office Friday morning at ten." He handed it to him.

"Thanks for all your help." Officer Bates placed the

information into his wallet. "I, the town, and Simon bless all of you." He looked up at the sky. "It's getting late. We should leave before sunset. It gets bloody dark hereabouts."

Everyone piled into the vehicles, and they drove off to town.

When they arrived at the hotel, Lee and Hayley ate a late dinner and sat in front of the fireplace drinking Merlot.

"Tomorrow should be interesting," Hayley said. "Elsie will pick the winner of the sculpting competition. I'm going to ask her if she wants to be my flower girl at our wedding. And Grams is going to take her to see her parents."

"Don't forget, I have to talk to the property manager," Lee said. "As soon as I transfer the money and sign a few things, that should be it. We'll be on our way home soon."

They set their empty glasses on the bar.

"Good night, Henry," Lee said.

"Good night, mates."

CHAPTER 28

In the crowded dining room, Lee set aside his morning cup of coffee to answer a call. He rose from his seat and left the noisy room while Hayley remained at the table with Jim, Matilda, Kathy, and Thomas. When he returned, he grabbed the car keys. "I'll be back shortly. I have to sign a few papers and see how soon we'll get the manor." He kissed Hayley's cheek. "It shouldn't take long."

"See you in a bit," Hayley told him. She took a sip as she looked out of the window and watched Lee drive off.

A young man rolled out a cart loaded with fresh pastries and stopped at their table.

Hayley and the others browsed the goodies. Once they made their choices, the waiter dished up their selections and served them.

"A new grave has been dug for Elsie's casket," Kathy said, sitting in front of a couple of hot cross buns. "The reburial should be done by the end of the day. Do you think we'll still be here to see the entire monument completed?"

"No," Hayley said, as the waiter placed a pecan and maple pinwheel by her empty coffee cup. "It'll probably take a while to inscribe the granite grave ledger. And who knows how long it will be before the angel is carved and put into place at the head of her grave."

"Whatta ya mean, who knows?" Jim said to Hayley as he eyed the plate stacked with pastries in front of him. "You'd know.

If you're no longer in England, you should be able to foresee it happenin'."

The waiter went to the bar, retrieved a fresh pot of coffee, returned, and refilled their cups.

"Will you be there?" Hayley asked.

"Does a rabbit's farts smell like carrots?"

Matilda and Kathy giggled.

"How would I know?" Hayley asked. "The reason I can't foresee it is because you'll be there, and I can't foresee your future."

"I clearly forgot 'bout that," Jim said. "That means ya can't foresee when Lee will get the key to the manor."

"You also forgot that I can see the present with no restraints. But give me a chance to eat first." She took her time savoring every bit of the tasty pinwheel before trying a cream-filled horn and finishing her coffee. Once everyone had eaten their sweets, Hayley closed her eyes to use her gift to see the present and focused on Lee. In her mind, she saw Lee shaking hands with a tall thin man dressed in a suit, and she listened to their conversation.

When Hayley's vision ended, she opened her eyes. "He's got the key."

"Well, I'll be a cross-eyed dodo bird. When can I start work?"

"Right away," Hayley said.

Jim rubbed his hand together and looked a Matilda. "Where should we begin?"

"We'll need furniture in the bedroom if you plan to live here while we renovate," she told him. "I think Hayley, Kathy, and I should shop on the internet while you do whatever you need to do."

"Ya hit the nail on the head, my love," Jim said.

Hayley saw the gleam in Kathy's eye. *She can't wait to use her witchcraft. And I have all afternoon before the sculpting contest declares a winner.* "As soon as Lee gets back, we'll go." Hayley looked out the window. "He's here."

Lee came inside, hung his coat on the coat tree by the hotel's entrance door, and walked toward them. He dangled the house key in front of Hayley. "It's ours," he told her. "Hold out your hand."

A grin spread across her face as she held out her palm. "We decided to have another girls' day out," she told him. "Matilda had the best idea. We're going to look for furniture on the Internet."

"Okay. Are you ordering from somewhere in England?"

"We're not ordering from anywhere," Kathy told him and gave him a sly smile. "We're going to have fun."

"I bet you are." Lee looked at Jim. "I called a structural engineer and told him we'd meet him at the manor."

They piled into the Rover. When they arrived at the manor, Hayley, Kathy, and Matilda went straight to the guesthouse while the men proceeded to the main house.

Kathy sat in the middle of the living room floor with the laptop. "All set. What should we shop for first?"

"Since we're in the living room, let's start here," Hayley said, joining her on the hardwood floor and sitting cross-legged. "How's this going to work?"

"The problem is," Kathy replied, "that I don't want a copy of a photo. I want a solid piece of furniture. I'm guessing I'm going to have to get creative."

"Creative how?" Hayley asked.

"It's kind of like letting my mind travel, enabling my subconscious to find what I'm looking for. Since I have the name of each store, that will make it easier. It'll allow me to envision the actual piece in order to manifest a replica."

"Go for it," Matilda said, looking over her shoulder. "I'd like to see that."

Kathy scrolled through the websites until she came to a

piece of furniture they agreed on. They continued the process until all the furniture, artwork, and decorative pieces had magically appeared. Then they moved things around a bit until they were satisfied with the placement and moved to the next room.

Hayley pulled out her cell phone and looked at the time. "We decorated this entire guesthouse in an hour and a half."

"We're not done yet," Matilda said. "I know Jim said the work inside the manor is off-limits to Kathy's witchcraft, but he and I will be staying in one of the bedrooms."

"Okay," Hayley said. "Let's go find a room you guys will occupy." When she entered the main house, she heard men's voices echoing from somewhere in the back.

"I'll ask Jim," Matilda said. "He'll know which room will be the best."

They found him in the kitchen with the structural engineer.

"We'll be going upstairs in just a minute," Jim told Matilda. "I'll check it out when I'm up there."

"We'll meet you upstairs." Hayley headed for the servant's stairs around the corner from the kitchen. The narrow stairway curved as they ascended. Halfway to the second floor, as she watched her step, her eye caught a glimpse of something wedged in a crack in the wall. Hayley reached down. "It's something shiny." Her fingers couldn't grasp it.

"Let me try," Kathy said.

Hayley saw the piece move, lift out of the thin crevice, and float in the air for a moment.

Before it could fall back into its hiding place, Kathy seized it. Although dirt and lint covered the trinket, the underlying metal appeared to be gold. "It looks like a brooch." Kathy rubbed it against her coat. "This is old."

They took a closer look. Intricate looping filigree along its edges framed yellow and red flowers within white-enameled gold. In its center, a twisted gold rope encircled a red stone.

"Do you think that's a ruby?" Matilda asked.

"We'll have to have it appraised," Kathy said, and passed it to Hayley.

As soon as the piece of jewelry rested in Hayley's palm, a vision came to her.

In her mind's eye, she saw a woman sitting on a stool, pinning up her long braided golden hair. When she turned around, Hayley saw her face and the same piece of jewelry Hayley held in her hand dangled on a ribbon around her neck. Her vision ended, and she opened her eyes. "It was worn as a necklace." She flipped the piece over to inspect the clasp. "It looks like it could've been used as a brooch too. Clever."

"Now you have something old to wear at your wedding," Matilda said. "Something new, something borrowed, and something blue should be easy to find."

Hayley placed it into her coat pocket and looked into the crack in the wall. "It's a strange place to find a piece of jewelry."

"Maybe that's why it was never found," Matilda said.

They climbed the stairs to the second floor and wandered into a spacious bedroom. An eight-pane window gave a view of Molly's Meadow. A river flowed across the vast field and snaked its way across the manor's backyard until it disappeared into the woods.

To judge the property's distance from town, Hayley looked to the south across the meadow, searching for Winter Fest and spotted it far off in the distance. *We'll have plenty of privacy. This is perfect.* She turned her attention to the interior. "Looks like these windows were replaced," she said.

"One less thing to worry about," Kathy told her.

"I love the fireplace." Matilda peeked into an adjoining room. "This looks like a sitting room, and the fireplace is double-sided. Cool."

"Yes. It's perfect." Hayley strolled across the bedroom and walked into a recess that led to a door on the left and a door on the right. She opened both. "There's a huge walk-in closet. But the bathroom's unfinished."

Jim joined them. "This would've been my choice too. But we can't live here without a bathroom."

"I can help with that," Kathy said.

Jim scratched his chin and thought a moment. "Gettin' our bedroom and bath finished is number one on my priority list. Otherwise, we'd have to remain at the hotel, and that dog don't hunt. I'll take ya up on your offer this one time, witchypoo. We can start tomorrow. Are ya up for it?"

"You bet." Kathy looked at Thomas as he entered the room with Lee. "This is a game changer. Would you mind if we stay for maybe another month?"

"It's up to the boss," Thomas told her.

"It works for me," Lee said. "You're just the man I need to set up a security system. Stay as long as you'd like."

"But make sure all of you are home in time for the wedding rehearsal," Hayley told them.

"Time to book a flight home," Lee said. "If that's all right with you, Hayley."

"Tonight, Grams will help Elsie cross over. After that, we're good to go."

"I'll make our reservations for tomorrow afternoon," Lee told her.

"Looks like we're finished here today," Jim said.

Lee checked his watch. "Good timing. We can grab a late lunch or early dinner and head over to Winter Fest."

CHAPTER 29

The mild forty-degree weather allowed the first day of Winter Fest to be enjoyable. Even though a few clouds drifted overhead, the day looked much like spring. But the frozen ground felt hard beneath Hayley's feet. And the piles of snow that had been plowed and stacked beyond the multitude of tents reminded her that she'd be back in the States by the time the temperatures woke the dormant grass covering Molly's Meadow.

Hayley spotted Father Farley and Harry Tibbs's son, Finley, sharing a blue tent next to a vendor selling knitted hats, scarves, vests, sweaters, and other apparel. Finley's bracelets were displayed next to an array of candles, hand-carved wooden crosses, ceramic plaques, and other items Father Farley planned to sell.

She and Lee stopped at their booth first and introduced themselves to Finley.

"It's truly a pleasure to meet you," Finley told them. "I can't thank you enough for this opportunity."

"We're glad it worked out, and you're able to make some money," Hayley told him. "You have a unique product. I'd like to purchase one myself."

"Hayley's gifted," Lee said. "She's a psychic medium. Each time she touches one of your bracelets, she envisions the hero's gravesite and sees the last moments of their life."

"Blimey," Finley said. "That must be overwhelming."

Lee tried to pay Finley for the bracelet, but he refused to

take it. Not giving up, Lee left the money on the counter and stepped back.

"You can see how it surprised me when I picked up one of your bracelets at Libby's Gift Shop," Hayley said. "Each hero you've honored knows about the tribute you've given. You may have provided the latitude and longitude of their gravesite, but each hero has placed the vision of their headstone and the circumstance of their death within the metal. Your homage is appreciated."

He smiled. "We will never forget."

Hayley glanced around. As if walking through an invisible vale, the spirits of military men and women appeared. She giggled. "They're here," she told Finley. "I know you can't see them, but they're here to thank you."

Finley looked around.

"We'll take it from here," a soldier told Hayley. "Ask him to clear a spot. We won't leave until we show our gratitude."

"You need to clear the counter," Hayley told Finley. "It's important to them to personally show their thanks." She took Lee's arm, and they stepped away.

Finley moved things aside and gasped when one of his World War II bracelets appeared in front of him. Then one after another, solidified as those he couldn't see placed their bracelets on the table. Finley swallowed hard.

"These are the heroes who stand before you," Hayley told him.

Finley squinted through his tear-filled eyes as he searched for their presence. His hands shook. "You will not be forgotten," he repeated as each bracelet appeared.

A heaping pile lay before him as he met Hayley's gaze. Father Farley shoved a chair behind him, and Finley sat.

"They've left," Hayley said. "Are you all right?"

"I can't thank you enough for this," he told her.

"I deserve no thanks," she replied. "This wasn't my idea.

It was as much of a surprise to me as it was to you."

He stood and began placing the honoring bracelets into a box. "I'll treasure these."

"I'm sure this isn't the end of it," Lee said. "There's no doubt that Elsie will be by to thank you also."

Finley's eyes widened. "Unbelievable."

"Good luck with your sales." Lee gave him a firm handshake. "Have a blessed day."

"You as well, my friends," he replied.

"We'll see you again before we go, Father Farley," Hayley said. "Elsie's crossing over to be with her family later. I'll remind her to tell you goodbye before she leaves."

Father Farley nodded. "I would appreciate that very much."

"Well, that was amazing," Lee said to Hayley as they walked away. "How do you think they obtained the bracelets?"

"Grams calls it thought creation. She does it all the time."

"Like when she gave Elsie her new clothes and shoes?" he said.

"Exactly."

"Thought creation," Lee said. "I've heard plenty of stories while being a ghost hunter about how things appear or disappear just out of the blue in people's homes. Or how something will move from one spot to another. It's a mystery."

"Even for me," Hayley said. "I bet Finley will be talking about today for the rest of his life."

They strolled about, stopping now and again to purchase handcrafted items to take back to the States.

"Am I losing my memory?" Hayley asked Lee. "I don't remember meeting half the people that have said hello to us."

"I'm pretty sure we haven't," he said.

"The chaos is beginning," Hayley said. "The town's starting to focus on Simon, Elsie, the bomb, and us. Soon their lives will be turned upside down when all the tourist pour in.

Thank goodness Simon and Lenny will have a safe place to live."

"Are you ready to go home?" Lee asked. "I've made reservations for noon tomorrow. If you change your mind about leaving, let me know."

"I'm ready. After Elsie picks a winner, Grams is going to take her to see her family. Once they leave, we can wrap things up here and be on our way."

They stopped to watch a wood-splitting contest. As they stood among the crowd, Lenny and Simon joined them. Elsie and Grams stayed undetectable to the multitude.

"There's only fifteen minutes left on the clock before the contestants lower their sculpting tools," Lenny said.

"Elsie will pick the winner and tell me her choice," Simon said. "We all agreed she should stay indiscernible."

"Good word, indiscernible," Lenny told him.

Simon nodded. "I'm trying to learn a new word every day."

"The way to success begins with a single step," Lenny said. "And education is the key."

"We'd better get over there then," Lee said.

They wove their way through the crowd and walked toward the clearing at the end of the festival grounds. Hayley looked over her shoulder and realized almost the entire town followed behind them.

Ten sculptors from all over England put the finishing touches on their masterpieces. When the whistle blew, all set their tools aside and stood by their work.

Hayley, Lee, and the others followed Elsie, who stopped at each six-foot sculpture of the artist's interpretation of an angel. She examined each thoroughly before she told Simon who she chose to be the winner. Then he whispered Elsie's first-place choice to Officer Bates.

"Seems we have ourselves a winner," Officer Bates said, standing at the microphone with Simon by his side. "And the trophy goes to Oliver Andrews. Please come up and claim your prize."

When a rugged, bearded man walked forward, he came to a halt in front of Officer Bates. A woman dressed in a white furry jacket, white jeans, and a furry white hat presented him with a silver-wing trophy and the prize money, then gave him a kiss on the cheek.

"And as you know," Officer Bates said to him, "the prize comes with an added bonus. You have also been chosen to carve the angel that will be placed at the head of Elsie Hudson's grave. And, of course, we will discuss the payment in private. Do you agree to this?"

"Yes, sir. I'm honored."

The crowd rumbled with applause. Simon joined the winner, and they started chatting while the crowd dispersed.

"I knew it would be him," Hayley told Lee.

"Is that supposed to surprise me?"

"Ha, ha."

Grams and Elsie materialized. "That was fun," Grams said, holding the child's hand. "Such a talented young man. So, are we about ready to go?"

"We're waiting for Officer Bates," Lee said.

"While we're waiting," Grams said. "We're going to pop over and say goodbye to Finley and Farther Farley."

"Okay," Hayley said. "Don't be long."

It only took a couple of minutes before they returned.

When Simon walked over, Hayley asked him, "Isn't Officer Bates coming with us?"

"Yes. He'll be here in a minute. Are we going to the cemetery?"

Hayley looked at Grams. "Do you have a chosen place for Elsie's departure?"

"I thought we should go to your new manor where Lenny and Simon will be staying. The courtyard in front of the guesthouse will be ideal. Then whenever she wants to see him, she can think of the courtyard, and she'll be there."

"That's perfect," Lee said.

"Will we need light?" Kathy asked.

"Preferably dim," Grams said.

"I can do that," Kathy told her. "How about candles?"

"That's perfect, too," Grams said.

When Officer Bates joined them, Lee told him the location. "I'll take Simon and Lenny with me."

"Okay," Lee said. "We'll meet you there."

***

Twilight announced the coming of nightfall. With a wave of her hand, Kathy lit the white candles she had placed around the guesthouse courtyard. Although the wind blew enough to be annoying, the candle wicks did not stir in the least. "Ready when you are," she told Grams.

Everyone spread out.

Grams knelt, and took Elsie's hands. "There's a stream of light off to the right," she told her. "Can you see it?"

Elsie nodded.

"After we enter the light, it will only take a moment before you'll be with your parents again. It's as easy as blinking. You have nothing to be nervous about. I'll hold your hand the entire time. First, you must say your goodbyes. But remember that once you cross over, you'll still be able to return and visit Simon. If you prefer, you can just say you'll see him later. It may be easier for both of you if you do."

Elsie walked over to Hayley. "I'm sorry I scared you when I tried to get you to come."

This time Hayley had very little trouble understanding her. "It's okay. You did a good job bringing us here. I'm very happy I met you. But most of all, I'm thrilled you'll be my flower girl at my wedding."

Elsie smiled and giggled. "That's going to be fun. Now I

won't have to miss you because I'll see you again. I guess I'll see you later."

"Yes, you will," Hayley said.

Elsie turned away and stopped in front of each of the others. She saved her goodbye to Simon for last.

Simon appeared to be very happy for her. But tears still filled his eyes. "I'll see you soon," he told her. "Grams told me that if I ever want to see you, all I have to do is think about you, and you'll hear my thoughts."

"When I do, I'll be here lickety-split."

They both laughed.

"Grams said you can visit me in dreams, too," Simon told her.

"She said she'd show me how. She told me too that I'll be able to grow up. Someday, I'll be as big as you."

"Wow," Simon said. "That's cool."

"I'll come back to visit you as soon as I can."

"Bye, Elsie," Simon said. "I'll see you later. Have lots of fun."

Grams reached out, took her hand and walked to the edge of the beam of light. Elsie turned to wave before she and Grams stepped into the white light and vanished. It took a moment before anyone spoke or moved.

Twilight had faded into darkness. Only the candlelight remained. Lenny walked over, opened the guesthouse door, and turned on the porch light.

"I'm gobsmacked," Officer Bates said. "Never in my life did I think I'd witness something like this. Or anything else that has happened since all of you arrived. Mind-blowing, I must say. I'd better be getting home. Are you boys staying?"

"Yes," Lenny said.

"I think I've thought of everything they'll need," Kathy said. "If not, we'll be close by." With a flick of her finger, she snuffed out the candle flames, then the candles themselves disappeared.

"We'll see you in the morning, Officer Bates," Lee said.

"You can count on it." He walked to his car and drove off. His car headlights illuminated the darkness that shrouded the long driveway that led to the main road.

"You should be all set," Lee told Lenny and Simon. "The electric's on, there's food and water, and plenty of heat. See you in the morning."

"We'll be fine," Lenny told him. "Have a good night."

Lee took Hayley's hand and followed Kathy, Thomas, Jim, and Matilda to the Rover and headed back to the hotel.

CHAPTER 30

It seemed like weeks instead of months to Hayley since she and Lee had arrived home from England. All of her things had been moved out of the Victorian home she had given Kathy and brought to Lee's mansion. The wedding plans were agreed to within the first few days after their arrival. Just yesterday, Lee's ballroom received a polish. Finishing touches and replanting within the garden, which extended from the back of his mansion to the riverbank, had been completed this morning. Hayley kept herself busy collaborating long-distance with Kathy and Matilda to decide how to furnish her and Lee's new vacation home in England. And she made sure they would arrive back in Sutterville in time for the next major event in her life—her and Lee's wedding. *Tomorrow. Unbelievable.*

Hayley placed the painting she had bought in England on the mantle above the white marble fireplace and stepped back. The summer's morning sunlight flowing in through the tower's tall multipaned windows illuminated the sitting room. The room's apple-green colored walls complimented the painting's rolling hills and the forest at the edge of a river. The blue carpet and blue suede couch enhanced the painting's sky. And the espresso cream drapes highlighted the colors of the thatched-roof cottage along the masterpiece's country road.

"How does it look?" Hayley asked.

"Splendid," Grams replied. Her blonde curls hung over the straps of her yellow-flowered sundress.

"The manor is fully furnished now. Kathy said I have good taste in design. After Lee and I return from our honeymoon, little-by-little, I'll redecorate this one." Hayley looked around the room. "It's going to take me years." She sighed.

"So, what's really bothering you?" Grams asked.

"I thought you could read my mind."

"I can, dear. But sometimes, it's good to talk about it."

"I'm worried about the wedding guests," Hayley told her. "How will the living react to the spirits who may sit among them? As far as I know, only you and Elsie will be seen. Anyone else?" She knew her parents, who had died when she was fourteen, would be there, but she doubted they would materialize. When they were alive, they had called her a liar and a mental case. It had taken Divine knowledge given to them after their death to enlighten them about her gifts and her preordained destiny. This would be the only time in Hayley's life when she'd be certain they understood her and would look at her with love in their eyes instead of chagrin.

She felt a lump in her throat.

"Let it go," Grams told her. "Don't hold on to the negativity."

The word negativity reminded her of a case she'd been involved in as a member of the Saviors of Souls. Able had been murdered during the mid-eighteen-hundreds. After his death, his soul had been invaded by a negative entity. "Did you invite Abel and his wife, Emma?" Hayley asked Grams.

"Yes, dear."

"Did they say they'd be here?"

Grams chuckled. "You should have seen Lewis's reaction when Abel materialized next to him. Lewis was as giddy as a little girl. Abel couldn't stop laughing as he placed the RSVP in the reply box on Lewis's desk."

"He remembered how to materialize?"

"It's not something that one forgets how to do," Grams

said.

"Do you think Lee's parents will be able to materialize so Lee can see them?"

"I've already spoken to them about that. We're working on it."

"I asked you to walk me down the aisle instead of my dad," Hayley said. "Do you think I hurt his feelings?"

"He understands why. Anyway, it would be impossible. He'd never be able to gather enough energy to remain solid for that amount of time."

"I'm glad he understands," Hayley said. "It's not that I don't love my dad, but you've been more of a parent to me than my dad has ever been."

"He regrets that, you know."

"He was in my dreams and tried to explain."

"Forgiveness will remove the negativity," Grams said.

"I know you're right."

"Elsie is excited to be your flower girl," Grams said.

"Will she be able to carry a basket of flower petals, so she can toss the petals as she walks down the aisle?"

"Yes," Grams said. "I can share my energy with her. She's small and won't require much help from me. The basket, on the other hand, may be tricky. She has to keep her solidity intact, or the basket will fall to the ground. Don't worry. I'll take care of everything."

"Thanks, Grams," Hayley said. "I thought rehearsal went well. Jim seemed to enjoy being both Roger's and Lee's best man."

"I thought it was cute the way he danced his way from Roger's and Laura's wedding rehearsal to yours and Lee's," Grams said. "He's unpredictable but fun."

"True. And Admiral Wayne was there to rehearse walking Laura down the aisle. It's so good to see him again." She recalled the first case she had taken part in after being hired by Paranormal Search and Analysis. Admiral Wayne had led her and the team halfway around the world to a remote island to speak to the dead onboard a World War II ghostship. On the way, when they stopped in Oahu, he had introduced them to Laura. She had been his daughter's best friend and became part of his family. "And his daughter is Laura's maid of honor. Laura's so happy."

"Yes, she is."

"I almost forgot," Hayley said. "I hope Admiral Wayne remembered to bring the envelope to give to Laura after the wedding." It had been a year since she had made the prediction that Laura and Roger would marry. Roger had only met Laura an hour before Hayley wrote her prediction on the hotel letterhead, placed it into an envelope, and gave it to Admiral Wayne to give to Laura on her wedding day. *Tomorrow. Who knew that time could fly by so fast?*

"That was one of the few times that you were able to foresee any of the team's future," Grams said. "Sometimes rules are allowed to be broken. Oh, Captain Jordan will be attending tomorrow too. Admiral Wayne will be happy to see him again."

Captain Jordan. The captain of the ghost ship. I have him to thank for telling us that we had been reincarnated into this life to become the Saviors of Souls. "It will be good to see him, too," Hayley said. "How about Ben Franklin? Will he be attending?"

"Of course, he is, dear. He's Lee's family. Although the ancestral connection is a bit confusing, without doubt, he's Lee's grandfather many times removed." Grams laughed. "He's an interesting man."

"I enjoyed talking to him the short time we were around each other," Hayley said. "The audience is going to be surprised when the minister says Lee's name since no one knows him as Benjamin Lee Franklin."

"What were his parents thinking?"

Hayley counted on her fingers how many of her spirit guests would be materializing. *Grams, Elsie, Captain Jordan, probably Abel and Emma from my second case will want to say hi to everyone on the team, and Ben Franklin, of course.* "I'd rather not have them scare our other guests. What should I do to make sure I don't hurt anyone's feelings?"

"It's already been taken care of," Grams said. "We put on the invitations that they should expect your previous clients, who are deceased, to be at the church and also the reception."

Hayley thought a moment. "What if we have all of our spirit friends sit together. They can have the entire row upfront to themselves."

"It would solve a number of problems, such as people screaming and running out of the church because one of our transparent friends sat next to them. I'll give Lewis a little nudge to include the front row seating in the wedding plans." She closed her eyes a moment. "Done. He's changing the seating as we speak."

"Great," Hayley said. "I can stop worrying about that now."

"It's not your job. It's Lewis's. The bride is not supposed to worry about anything but marrying the love of her life. Or, in your case, the love of your many lives. Sit for a moment. I want you to see something."

Hayley sat on the blue suede couch. She felt a light breeze on the back of her neck coming from the sitting room's opened windows. Taking a deep relaxing breath, she put aside all her elations concerning tomorrow and focused on what Grams wanted to show her.

"Close your eyes and use your gift to foresee the future. Place yourself in the spot where you and Lee will say your vows and turn toward your wedding guests seated in the pews."

"Isn't that considered to be my future? Is it allowed?"

"Yes, dear. But it's on the edge of breaking the rules. None of the reincarnated will be in the room at the time. Now relax and focus on the moment when everyone has taken their seat. A bell will chime to catch everyone's attention."

Hayley's foreseeing placed her in front of the gathering. She gazed up the aisle where large vases filled with purple, yellow, and white bouquets rested on pedestals flanking each side of the garland-framed main entrance. Along the wide aisle, attached to the side of each pew, small sprays of white, yellow, and lavender roses were wrapped within draped satin bows. *It's beautiful.*

Her attention focused on the main entrance. When the bell sounded, and the doors opened, the crowd quieted. Whispers arose as the spirit guests began walking down the aisle to the front row seats assigned to them. Captain Jordan, completely materialized and wearing his dress whites, led the procession. Lee's parents followed with their ghostly persona, barely noticeable. Abel, dressed in a brown suit, and Emma, wearing a simple but elegant blue dress, came next. Hayley's parents, also hardly detected, trailed. At the end of the line, Ben Franklin, dressed in a light brown suit with a white laced shirt under a paisley vest, appeared as real as anyone else in the audience. They strolled down the main aisle while the living marveled at their presence. As they walked, they began to lose their solidity. People gasped, murmurs spread, a few applauded while others giggled. By the time the transparent guests reached the front of the church, they filed into the front row without detection. Hayley's vision ended. "That was very theatrical," she said. "How brilliant."

"It was your idea."

"This still seems like a dream to me," Hayley said. "All through my school years, I saw how boys would walk the other way whenever they saw me. So, I never dated. Why waste the time when heartbreak was inevitable."

"And that's exactly why you tried so hard not to like Lee," Grams said.

"Everyone knows it's disastrous to fall for the boss. I was sure it would end badly. I was only being logical until destiny stepped in."

"Lee was your one and only. Without your knowledge, you had been waiting for him since birth."

"And look at me now. I'm happier than I've ever been."

Lewis entered the room. "Miss Lane is here to see you, Miss."

Kathy, wearing pink shorts and a pink halter top, carrying a magazine and a makeup case, skirted by him. "It's girls' fun day. Oh, hi, Grams."

"Good morning, dear," Grams replied.

"I brought a bridal book with me so we can decide what hairstyle you'd like. And we can paint your nails while we're at it. Matilda is downstairs talking to Jim before he takes Lee and Roger to their bachelor party. She'll be up in a minute."

"I'm so glad all of you made it back for the rehearsal this morning," Hayley told her. "I was biting my nails."

"Here, let me see," Kathy said, taking Hayley's hands in hers and inspecting them. "Fixable, thank goodness."

Hayley drew back her hands. "Who's going to notice?"

"I hate to miss all the fun," Grams said, "but I must go. I have to save my energy for tomorrow in order to stay presentable."

"We understand," Kathy told her.

"I love you, Grams," Hayley said. "See you in the morning."

"Have a good time." Grams slowly faded away until not a trace of her remained.

"I like it better when she gradually leaves instead of disappearing in a blink," Kathy said. "Don't you? I always jump when she instantly vanishes."

"There are times she makes me jump, too," Hayley said.

Kathy reached into her pants pocket and pulled out the brooch Hayley had found at the manor in England. "I had it cleaned for you. The stone in the center is a ruby, and the metal, as we expected, is gold. Someone very wealthy must've owned this." She handed it to Hayley. "Something old to wear at your wedding. How old is undetermined. More tests will have to be made to establish the age."

As the brooch touched her palm, Hayley received the same vision she had seen on the staircase where she had first held the pin. This time she studied the seeing closely. The woman she had seen once before in a vision raised her arms and wound her golden braid into a bun. She used a silver comb to keep it in place. Then she fastened the ribbon strung through the jeweled gold piece around her neck. Before Hayley could examine more of the image's details, the vision ended. *That didn't tell me anything. The hairstyle and the comb seemed timeless.* "I don't have a clue about its age either."

"It would be interesting to find out," Kathy told her. She glanced around the room and held up the carrying case she had with her. "Where should we go to get you glamorous? We'll need a mirror."

"I know just the place."

"Lead the way." Kathy took Matilda's hand as she came through the door. "We're following Hayley."

"When Laura gets here," Hayley told Lewis, who stood in the doorway, "show her to Lee's dressing room, please."

"Yes, Miss." He turned and headed down the hallway.

"We'll take a shortcut." Hayley opened a door that led to the bathroom. The spacious room had three vanities with Brazilian-gold marble countertops, one off the sitting room and two by the entrance to the bedroom. The cabinets resembled fine rosewood furniture. The glass-enclosed shower in the center of the bathroom could hold nine or ten people. Their footsteps echoed as they strolled across the marble tiled floor.

"Cool," Kathy said.

"For the longest time," Hayley confessed, "I thought the bathtub was a Jacuzzi."

"No doubt," Matilda said.

"Right this way." Hayley escorted them into the dressing

room. "I've already unpacked all the clothes that I brought from the other house, and as you can see, my part of the closet still looks empty."

"There's a reason to shop." Kathy looked around. "This is huge. There's enough room to have a fashion show in here. Look at the size of that mirror."

Two wingback chairs rested in front of a multipaned window that brightened the room with afternoon sunlight. A chandelier dangled from a coffered ceiling. Plush light-blue carpet silenced their steps. Motion detecting lights illuminated their intended working area as they approached the vanity.

Kathy set her case on the tabletop in front of a gold-framed mirror, unlatched it, and opened it, revealing more makeup and beautifying tools than Hayley had ever seen.

"I want to still look like myself after you finish," Hayley said.

"You're going to look beautiful." Kathy turned Hayley's chair around to face her while she worked.

"It's too bad that the DNA test didn't result in an ancestry connection between Roger and Elsie," Matilda said.

Kathy ran lipstick across Hayley's lips.

"Once Grams took Elsie to see her parents, it took a couple of months before she returned to see Simon again," Matilda told her. "He said he's never seen her so happy. It would've been nice if she and Roger were related, but she has her family again, and that's what's important."

A light knock on the door caught their attention. "Come," Hayley said.

Laura entered. "Hi. Did I miss anything?"

Lewis followed behind her, pushing a cart carrying crackers and cheese, dips and chips, and a few other snacks to go along with the bottles of wine he had on ice.

"You're just in time to see how beautiful Hayley looks," Kathy told her. She stepped aside to let the others see. "What do you think?"

"You look gorgeous, Hayley," Laura said.

Matilda nodded. "Perfect."

"Turn me around so I can see," Hayley told Kathy.

Kathy rotated the chair to face the mirror.

"Is that really me?" Hayley asked. Her lips were a soft peach. The foundation made her complexion appear flawless. Blush brought out her cheekbones. "My eyes are amazing. And look at my eyebrows." Black eyeliner accentuated golden eyeshadow tones, while mascara made her lashes appear long. *I never would have thought about putting a touch of color under the lower lashes.* She felt astounded.

"Do you like it?" Kathy asked.

"I love it. Thank you."

"Roger couldn't understand why we didn't hire a stylist for the occasion," Laura said.

"What?" Kathy said. "And miss out on having fun." She handed the bridal book to Hayley. "What kind of hairstyle would you like?"

"I don't have a clue."

"We have all evening to play," Kathy said. "The guys are staying at Roger's tonight. We won't see them again until tomorrow. All right, Hayley, go sit over there and look through the pages while I do Laura's makeup."

Hayley rose and let Laura sit. Before perusing through the magazine, she filled a few glasses with wine for her guests. She sipped her drink while she sat and searched for a hairdo she'd like. A few pages in, a braided hairstyle reminded her of the brooch Kathy had given her. She stood and retrieved it from her pants pocket. As always, the vision of the woman pinning her braided hair into a bun and fastening the necklace around her neck played like a movie in her mind. When it ended, Hayley reached around Laura and placed the jeweled brooch into the small jewelry box on the makeup table. *Braids*, Hayley thought.

That would look perfect.

***

Hayley could hardly remember changing clothes and falling into bed. But after a moment to get all the swirling fog out of her head, she threw her robe on and gazed into the mirror before going in search of her friends. She gasped. Her hair stood on end, and her pillow had left a crease across her face. *I hope Kathy can fix this.* She recalled that she'd told them to meet her in Lee's sitting room for breakfast and headed in that direction.

When she entered the sitting room, she noticed that Matilda, Laura, and Kathy looked a bit disheveled themselves. "Will it take long to make us look presentable?" she asked Kathy.

"No time at all," Kathy said. "I promise. We saved ourselves a ton of time experimenting last night. I know exactly what you want done. We'll all be beautiful in about two hours. We'll start getting ready after lunch."

"It's only seven a.m.," Matilda said. "There's no rush."

"Hayley and Lee are going back to England for their honeymoon," Kathy said. "Laura, where are you and Roger going?"

"Paris."

"Maybe we should check out the sights and restaurants on the Internet," Matilda said. "You won't be spending the entire time making mad passionate love."

Hayley giggled. "If I know Lee, I'll be lucky to see the daylight." *Not that I'd mind.*

***

After lunch, while Hayley dressed for the wedding, the fluttering in her stomach surprised her. *Why am I so nervous? All I have to do is walk down the aisle, repeat after the minister, and then I'll be Mrs. Hayley Franklin.* But her pep talk did nothing to settle her anxiety. Hayley stood still as Kathy zipped the back of her gown and adjusted her wedding veil. She joined Laura, who stood in front of a huge mirror in the dressing room. Behind them, Kathy slipped into her yellow bridesmaid dress, and Matilda wore a teal-colored pantsuit that accentuated her long auburn hair. They filed out of the dressing room and into the sitting room to wait until their ride arrived.

Grams materialized along with Hayley's and Laura's parents.

"What happens if I cry," Laura asked Kathy as her eyes began to water.

"Not a problem," Kathy said, tearing up.

Hayley knew her parents couldn't hold their solidity for long. She didn't want her joy of seeing them again cause her to ruin the moment. She held back her tears and let them do most of the talking. As their parents gave their love and wished them well, they slowly faded and disappeared. *A bittersweet moment.*

Grams, wearing a yellow full-length dress, remained until Hayley received a text that a limo would be waiting for them by the front door. "I'll meet you at the church," she told Hayley.

"See you there."

CHAPTER 31

Out of view of the wedding guests, Hayley stood in the vestibule between the outer door and the interior double doors leading into the church and held her bridal bouquet in trembling hands. Her gown's long lace sleeves hugged her arm, leaving the round of her shoulders bare. The lace-over-white satin sweetheart bodice embellished with pearls and diamonds snuggly fit her body to the waistline, then flowed into an A-line skirt that brushed against her white satin heels. A train cascaded from the waist and trailed three feet behind her. She stood with Grams, waiting for the wedding march to begin.

Everyone in her procession took their positions. Kathy, Hayley's bridesmaid, would go first. Elsie, her flower girl, would go next. Then Grams would take Hayley's arm and walk her down the aisle.

The double doors opened.

Kathy glanced at Hayley and smiled.

Elsie, in a frilly yellow dress, peeked around the corner at the crowd.

"Any moment, dear," Grams told Elsie. "Let me give you a little more of my energy." She placed her hand on her shoulder. "You'll follow Kathy. Remember to walk slowly and throw the petals as you go along. We'll be right behind you."

When the procession music began, Kathy, holding a bouquet of yellow, white, and lavender roses in hands, stepped through the double doors and proceeded to the head of the aisle.

She walked forward, taking measured steps down the aisle.

Seconds later, Elsie followed at a steady slow pace, tossing the petals in front of her as she strolled.

Grams hooked her arm around Hayley's, and they moved into position at the head of the aisle between two pillars amassed with three-foot bouquets. White gladiolas, arranged with white and yellow calla lilies, surrounded by lavender sprigs, green orchids, and among other flowers, filled the room with fragrance. Hayley breathed in the aroma, filling her lungs with soothing tranquility, calming her racing heart.

The afternoon sun flowed in through the Gothic arched stained-glass windows, shedding light on the two hundred people who came to witness the happiest day of Hayley's life.

Without turning around, she sensed Matilda arranging the three-foot train trailing down Hayley's back and onto the gold-carpeted runway. Then the wedding march began to play. As she walked forward, Hayley's heart pounded loudly in her ears. She concentrated on each step, trying not to trip or miss a beat. All heads turned toward her.

In front of the pews to her left, Roger and Laura stood watching. Admiral Wayne's daughter, wearing a full-length purple satin bridesmaid dress, stood behind Laura. Jim, Roger's best man, glanced across the aisle to the right at Lee, who waited. When Hayley's and Lee's eyes met, she felt the magic, the invisible pull that made her want to walk faster. Since the moment she had met him, an unyielding bond drew them together. But why the infatuation gripped her so completely evaded her when they'd first met. Once she learned that Lee had been her love throughout lifetime after lifetime, it finally made sense. The magnetism grew stronger the farther she walked. She looked down and focused again on her steps. *Are we there yet*, she asked Grams in her mind. The impatience to be at his side intensified.

Just a little farther, Grams told her. She led Hayley to the right, rounding the last row of pews. Once she released Hayley's arm, relinquishing her to Lee, Grams and Elsie strolled to the center aisle, waved at the guests, and vanished. The crowd gasped, and applause filled the church.

The minister, who stood between the two couples, walked over to Roger and Laura and took his place in front of them. A hush spread throughout the pews.

As her friends spoke their vows, Hayley waited for the right moment. "Watch, Lee." When Roger and Laura sealed their vows with a kiss, Hayley whispered, "That's the kiss I envisioned when I foresaw their future a year ago."

"You amaze me," Lee said.

After the completion of Roger and Laura's wedding ceremony, the minister took leave and joined Hayley and Lee. Jim waltzed his way from Roger's side to Lee's.

When all whispers in the pews ceased, the minister began. "We are gathered here today to celebrate the blessing of eternal love bestowed upon this couple. Let us rejoice and give our best wishes as they are united in marriage." He paused for a moment, then continued. "Should there be anyone who has cause why this couple should not be united in marriage? Let them speak now."

Not a sound came from the guests.

"It is not by coincidence but by the hand of God that has brought our couple here today. Life is filled with the unexpected, even when fate is leading the way. It has led them here today to declare in front of man and God their love for one another. For them, love's journey will go on and on. Time has no meaning. Their love for each other is endless." He asked Lee, "Do you wish to speak your vows?"

Lee took Hayley's hand in his. "I give my oath to be by your side as life's destiny lays its path. From this day until evermore, you will always be the air I breathe and the reason my heart beats. My love for you is endless."

Hayley swallowed her emotions, blinked back the tears that filled her eyes, and said, "Nothing can compare to the immense joy I feel knowing you are my soul mate. My love for you is immeasurable throughout time and space. I will love you for eternity and beyond."

"Benjamin Lee Franklin, do you take Hayley Elizabeth Johnson to be your wife? Do you promise to love, cherish and protect her from this day forward?"

"I do," Lee said.

"Do you, Hayley Elizabeth Johnson take Benjamin Lee Franklin to be your husband? Do you promise to love, cherish, and protect him from this day forward?"

"I do," Hayley said.

Jim handed the ring to Lee.

"With this ring, I thee wed," Lee told her, slipping the ring on her finger.

Kathy handed a ring to Hayley.

"With this ring, I thee wed," she said, and placed the ring on his finger.

"By the power vested in me," the minister said, "I now pronounce you man and wife. You may kiss your bride."

When Lee's lips met hers, Hayley felt her soul fill with more joy than the universe could hold.

"Excuse me," the minister told them. He took his place once more between the two couples. "Ladies and gentlemen, I present to you — "

The wedding march began to play, cutting off the minister's words.

The guests' attention turned toward the head of the aisle. A woman in a wedding gown, standing alone, holding a bouquet of white flowers, and a veil covering her face, stood silently. A rumble of whispers spread within the pews.

"Is she alive or dead?" Lee asked Hayley.

"I can't tell from this far away," she replied. "What's happening? Who is she?"

Jim glanced at the veiled woman. "I'll take care of this."

He strolled over to the minister, who looked confused.

An array of emotions threatened to pierce Hayley's happiness. She forced herself to be calm during this apparent misunderstanding.

The woman walked forward down the aisle as the wedding march continued to play. The guests remained quiet.

"No one knows what to think," Lee whispered to Hayley.

"Someone needs to stop her," she said.

The music played on, and the woman, looking straight ahead, came toward the minister, who continued discussing the predicament with Jim. When she reached the middle of the aisle and appeared to be unbothered by her intrusion, Kathy walked over to Jim and joined his and the minister's conversation.

Lewis sprang from his seat at the end of the pew and also joined him.

"Lewis is probably furious," Hayley said.

"I bet," Lee said. "His plans for our wedding were perfect. Now this."

As the woman reached the end of the aisle, she slowed.

Kathy backed away. Jim retreated a few feet, while Lewis stood behind him.

The woman came to a halt in front of the minister. The music stopped.

Silence filled the room.

Jim lifted her veil.

"Holy moley," Hayley said.

CHAPTER 32

About to enter their reception, Hayley stood with Lee outside the doors leading into the ballroom at their mansion. They waited until the applause died after Roger and Laura had been introduced as newlyweds and received congratulations from the nearly two hundred guests.

The double doors opened wide for them as they heard their introduction. Hayley, in a scooped-neck, short white dress, and Lee, wearing a white shirt, gray vest, and black dress pants, entered. Friends and family seated at their round, white linen-covered dining tables gave them a standing ovation. Everyone they had invited to their small weddings attended, including Frank Thompson, the owner of the town's largest newspaper, the *Sutterville Times,* who took photos for the society page. And a photographer Lewis had hired also circled the room.

Lee led Hayley onto the dance floor, where Roger, Laura, Jim, and Matilda waited during the soft introduction to the *Blue Danube.*

Once Lee put his hand on Hayley's back and took her other hand in his, the three couples simultaneously twirled around the edges of the dance floor, waltzing to music composed by Strauss. Above them, a fresco depicting the gardens of Florence covered the ceiling. Five chandeliers spanned the vast ballroom, the largest in the middle of the room, illuminating their first dance. Under its twinkling glow, in the center of the floor, the translucent spirits of the newlywed's parents also waltzed in time to the opus.

The urge to glance at their deceased parents tugged at Hayley, but she knew she had to concentrate on every move Lee made. As they twirled, the celery-green walls with elaborate gold trim spun around them. When the music ceased, they came to a halt, and the wedding guests applauded once more before taking to the dance floor themselves.

"Best wedding ever," Frank Thompson said, snapping another shot of the spirits as they faded.

"Glad ya approve, Frank," Jim said, escorting Matilda, who wore an off-the-shoulder blue dress, away from the dance floor.

"I concur," Roger said, taking Laura's hand. She wore wide-legged yellow pants with a diamond and pearl-adorned halter top.

Lee led Hayley to a long linen-covered table the three couples shared in front of a twelve-pane window. Before taking her seat, she gazed outside at the garden below, dotted with topiaries scattered among the boxwood hedges that framed a multitude of colorful flowers. *Beautiful.*

And look at that. One by one, the round, coned, cubed, and spiraled, along with a lion, tiger, and bear topiaries, lit as the sun set, their lights twinkling throughout the garden. Pastel-colored florescent floodlights washed over the flora within the multitude of perfectly trimmed boxwood and English holly hedged planters. She knew from Lee's previous costume ball that speakers had been placed inside each illuminated bed, which allowed guests to dance down the carpets of grass pathways crisscrossing between the geometric designed garden that extended all the way to the river bank.

Below, round tables had been covered with white linen clothes and candlelit, awaiting guests to come out to the veranda. Along the terrace's travertine stone walls, urns planted with azaleas added to the floral fragrance filling the twilight's soft, pleasant breeze. Hayley looked forward to a stroll with Lee after the reception, taking the veranda steps to the manicured lawn, through the scented garden, and down the hedged trail leading to the arched bridge overlooking a tranquil pond. She turned away and took her seat next to Lee. On her left, Jim pulled his chair in next to Matilda.

Once Roger and Laura settled in next to Lee, Lewis stepped up to the microphone. "Ladies and gentlemen, let's raise our glasses and toast the newlyweds, Mr. and Mrs. Lee Franklin, Mr. and Mrs. Roger Hudson, and Mr. and Mrs. Jim Newton."

All wedding guests rose and raised their glasses of Champagne.

"May their love last throughout eternity and beyond," Lewis proclaimed, raising his own glass. "To the brides and grooms."

"To the brides and grooms," the guests echoed.

Lewis took a sip and turned to the wedding table. "Congratulations."

A stream of waiters and waitresses entered through the double doors, pushing carts carrying gold-rimmed dinner plates ladened with the meals of each guest's choosing from the wedding invitation menu. Once they parked the carts against the wall, the servers went to work delivering the meals to each table.

Hayley ordered the prime rib covered with horseradish, mushrooms, and onions, alongside mixed vegetables and mashed sweet potatoes. Lee preferred the steak, mashed potatoes and gravy next to steamed cauliflower.

"Were ya surprised?" Jim asked Hayley and Lee.

"Yes," Hayley replied as the waiter filled her glass with red wine.

"How long did it take ya to figure out who she was?"

"I didn't know if she was alive or dead, if she made a dreadful mistake, or if she deliberately set out to upend our wedding," Hayley said before lifting her glass to take a sip.

"It was my idea to walk down the aisle by myself," Matilda

said. "I wanted it to look like a scene out of a spooky movie."

"It definitely was," Lee said, cutting his steak. "Like us, the wedding guests were totally confused."

"Kathy helped plan it," Matilda told them. "After Jim proposed to me, she had a slew of ideas. I think this one was the best."

"How did Jim propose?" Hayley asked. "Did it happen before we left or after?"

"After," she replied. "He drove me to London. We had dinner at an elegant restaurant, and after the first dance, he got down on one knee and asked me to marry him."

"I must've done it right 'cause she said yes," Jim told them.

"I didn't know you had a romantic bone in your body," Lee said, taking a bite of steak.

"I've never had a reason to, until now." He gave Matilda a kiss on her lips.

"Control yourselves down there," Roger said from the other end of the table. "Save the little you have left for your honeymoon."

"Are ya insinuating I'm old? I've got more energy than a whale's got blubber."

"I know you're old, and I've heard you blubber a number of times," Lee said.

"Speaking of blubbering...." Jim said. "That's why we stayed in England for so long. If we'd returned sooner, Matdie would've let the blubbering cat outta the bag."

Matilda nodded. "He knows me so well."

"I'm glad your psychic senses didn't give away our little secret," Jim said.

"We didn't know who she was until you lifted her veil," Lee told him.

"At least you got to see her face, so you knew what was happening," Laura said, sitting on the other side of Lee. "All we saw was the back of her head. But we figured it out after she turned toward Jim to take the vows. We were dumbfounded."

Admiral Wayne, wearing his dress whites, approached their table. "Congratulations, all of you." He turned to Laura and presented her with a sealed white envelope. "As I pledged."

She took it from him. "I forgot all about this. The prediction that Hayley made that would happen in a year." She hurried to open it and read. "You foresaw our wedding. How amazing."

"Thank you, Admiral Wayne," Hayley told him. She looked at Laura. "I'm sure the prediction has lost its wonder after you've gotten to know me this past year. It was supposed to prove to you that psychic abilities really do exist."

"That cat's been outta the bag since the cows came home," Jim said.

"In any case, it's still amazing," Roger told him.

"I can't believe you kept the secret from me all this time," Laura said.

"You told me once that you liked surprises," Hayley said.

"Indeed, I do," Laura replied. "I will cherish this always. Thank you."

"Well, my mission is accomplished," Admiral Wayne said. "If you'll excuse me...I promised to dance with a very remarkable woman."

"Thank you so much, Admiral," Laura said.

"Have fun," Hayley told him as he turned and walked away. She took another sip of wine and finished her meal.

"There's something you should know about the manor," Matilda said to Hayley and Lee.

Jim cleared his throat. "We found vermin in the attic. I had a long talk with 'em, and they decided to live somewhere else." He rose. "Care to dance, my love?" he asked Matilda.

She gave him her hand, and they walked out to the floor.

"Would you like to dance?" Lee asked Hayley.

"I'd rather mingle. There are people here that I may not see again."

"Good idea." Lee stood. "Look who's dancing with Admiral Wayne."

"Our good friend, Annie. She's a remarkable woman. They'll be talking about us all night."

Hayley glanced at Jim and Matilda as they danced. "Matilda gave Jim an odd look when he started talking about vermin. Do you think there's something else wrong at the manor?"

"No," Lee said. "Jim would've told me if there was."

They wandered toward their guests. Hayley noticed the chairs where Kathy and Thomas had been seated were empty. She glanced at the dance floor and found them slow dancing to Elton John's *Your Song*.

"They'll be married next," Hayley told Lee. She pointed to a table to their left. "Isn't that Brea? It seems like forever since our haunted plantation case in Georgia. It's good to see her again."

The twenty-year-old waved.

Hayley approached her and gave her a hug. "I'm happy that you made it. Whenever I see spirits materializing, I think of you, your mom, and your dad. How are they doing?"

"They're great. No more yelling." She grinned. "Your wedding was spooktacular."

"I knew you'd love the theatrics," Hayley told her. She remembered a couple of months ago when Brea, her dad, and her mom stayed a few days at Lee's mansion. Brea's dad didn't believe in ghosts or spirits. He complained about everything and treated his family badly. Grams changed all that by reacquainting him with his deceased mother during dinner. After that, he became a believer and under a threat that she would return and haunt him, he became a nicer person. "I'm sorry your mom and dad didn't come."

"Mom wanted to," Brea said, "but my dad was afraid he'd see his mother again." She laughed.

"Poor guy," Lee said.

"I liked your parade of ghosts when they took their seats,"

Brea said.

"Spirits," Hayley reminded her.

"Yeah, that's what I meant."

"I was on my way to the church when our guests took their seats," Hayley said. "But I did get to see their parade in a vision, and you're right. It was spooktacular. What did you think about the ceremony? It was meant to be a double wedding. We had no idea who the third bride was until the very last minute."

"That was cool too. Everyone around me thought it was supernatural."

"Why don't you come with us and meet some of our friends," Lee said.

Lenny and Simon stopped their conversation with Roger's nephews, Clint and John, as Hayley and Lee walked up.

"Hi, guys," Hayley said.

"Congratulations," they all said.

"Thank you," Lee replied.

Hayley introduced Brea to them.

"Sit with us, Brea," Clint said. "I'm sure Lenny and Simon would like to hear about the plantation you and your family inherited. That ghost that lived there was evil."

Lee pulled out a chair for her, and she sat. "We'll be back around after we mingle awhile." He took Hayley's hand.

As they greeted their guests, Hayley remembered meeting most of them at Lee's costume ball last Halloween. In this very room, they had witnessed Lee ask for her hand in marriage. That night of happiness would have to take second place in her heart after today. At the costume ball, after some guests had their fill of dining and dancing, they seemed to have left. She and Lee had found many of them in the gardens, a few on the veranda, while others inside roamed the hallways looking at art and décor. Hers and Lee's wedding reception guests would be doing the same, she surmised. For years the parties at Lee's mansion had become an open house, and guests were allowed to peek into rooms if they pleased. *That's what I wanted to do the first time I entered his home a year ago.* She had walked these halls with wide eyes, totally dazed that he actually owned the home and amazed at its grandeur. Even his choice in décor and design had made her jaw drop. She remembered thinking *Beauty surrounds him. What good taste he has.*

Lewis approached her and Lee. "There will be fireworks in your honor over the lake tonight, Mr. and Mrs. Franklin. You'll have a nice view from the window or, better yet, the garden."

"You outdid yourself, Lewis," Lee said.

"My pleasure, sir," Lewis replied. "I'll make the announcement."

While waiting for the firelight display to begin, all of the guests slowly made their way outside. Lee led Hayley down the veranda steps to the garden and strolled along the pathways lined with English holly and boxwood hedges. While many danced around the flower beds, Hayley and Lee casually walked to the pond on the north side of the estate. They stood on the top of the arched bridge by the keystone. The evening held on to the warmth, making it an enjoyable summer night.

"I won't be able to thank Lewis enough for planning all this," Hayley said. "It's fabulous."

Lee offered her a handkerchief to wipe her misty eyes.

The pink, gray, and golden sunset announced the coming of nightfall. She glanced at the pond. Along its banks grew azaleas, copper beech, cherry trees, and weeping willows. "I know why this is your favorite spot. It's mine now too."

Lee lifted her chin and placed his lips on hers.

Her entire body and soul wanted nothing more than to follow her husband to their chambers and make love with him for days, only coming up for air if need be. "When do we leave for England?" she asked.

"I booked a flight for tomorrow morning."

She kissed him passionately. "We're not going to get any

sleep tonight."

He smiled. "You can sleep on the plane." He put his arm around her as the night sky over Lake Tales lit with dazzling light. "Lewis went all out."

After the display, once the guests had a few more drinks and said their goodbyes, the gardens appeared empty and peaceful. Arm-and-arm, she walked with Lee toward the house.

As she took a step up to the veranda, Hayley looked up at the ballroom windows. The lights were out on the second floor. But the twinkling lights and colored floodlights adorning the garden were still lit, and the candles on each table on the veranda burned dimly.

Lewis met them as they entered the double doors. "The guests have all left, sir."

"Thank you, Lewis," Lee said. "What time do you have?"

"Not quite ten p.m., sir."

"That late, huh?" Lee yawned. "I think we'll turn in now."

A slew of images of the wedding and reception played like snapshots in Hayley's mind. She couldn't walk away without giving Lewis a huge hug. "You gave us the best day of our lives. Thank you, Lewis." The grin on her face persisted as she returned to Lee's side.

"My pleasure, Mrs. Franklin." He clapped his white-gloved hands together.

Hayley knew without looking back that Lewis's appropriate butler-style straight-face had been brightened by a smile. She gloated. *Mrs. Franklin. I'll never get tired of being called that.*

"You're the best, Lewis," Lee said. "Goodnight."

They walked down a black and white marble-tiled hallway. Above, honeycomb pattern plaster bas-reliefs blanketed the ceiling. At the hallway intersection, she and Lee, walking hand-in-hand, turned down the main hall. A tapestry depicting a similar garden to the garden in their backyard hung on the gold-tone Venetian-plastered wall. A French-style console accommodated the cobalt-blue vase she and Lee had bought in England. The beautiful glass-blown piece now displayed a colorful floral arrangement beneath a portrait of a young woman by Rembrandt. In the center of the main hall, a chandelier dangled in front of the elevator they intended to take to their bedroom on the third floor.

Lee called for the elevator. When they stepped inside, and the doors closed, Lee took Hayley in his arms. She felt the heat of his kiss all the way to her toes. His hands surveyed her body while his heated breath on her neck filled her with anticipation. She tilted her head in offering. Then the elevator stopped, and the door opened. On the champagne-colored carpet, red rose petals led the way to the north hallway.

"Too corny?" Lee asked.

"No. Very romantic." The smile on her face seemed unrelenting. She had seen rose petals scattered around in movies and had read about them in starry-eyed novels describing sensuous senses. But she had to admit that not one romance in any book or movie had ever been as breathtaking as her and Lee's passionate love story. Her smile remained fixed as he put his arm around her, and she leaned into him. They strolled down the hall to their chambers. When they arrived outside their bedroom, Lee opened the door.

"Looks like a threshold, Mrs. Franklin." He lifted her off her feet and carried her inside. Dim lights lit the bedroom while saxophone music played softly.

The happiness that encompassed her the entire day filled her eyes, and tears streamed down her cheeks. *He's mine for all eternity.*

Lee closed the door.

CHAPTER 33

Once their plane touched down in England, inside the airport door where everyone greeted their loved ones, Lee and Hayley were met by a man wearing a dark blue suit and carrying a sign with their names written across it.

"I'm pleased to meet you, Mr. and Mrs. Franklin. I'm your estate overseer, Mr. Cooper. Don't worry about a thing. I have someone getting your bags for you. If you'll follow me, please." He led them outside to a car parked by the curb.

Hayley and Lee stood, admiring a metallic gray and black classic Bentley.

"Nice car you have here," Lee said.

"It belongs to your estate, sir," Mr. Cooper replied as he opened their car door. "Mr. and Mrs. Newton bought it. It's a 1955 Bentley R Type Saloon."

"This is grand," Lee said.

"I wonder if that's what Matilda was trying to tell us," Hayley said after Lee slid into the backseat with her.

"Sounds like something he'd do," Lee told her. "Cool. I'll call and thank them."

From the airport, they drove away from the city lights and into the countryside lit by the full moon. Hayley rested her head on Lee's shoulder after her eyes blurred from gazing out the car window at the moonlit gray silhouettes of trees and fields streaming by. After the nine-and-a-half-hour flight, they found the time difference had moved the clocks ahead four hours, and midnight would soon be upon them.

The Georgian Gothic-style lamp posts lighting the long driveway leading to the manor received a nod from Lee. "I left the choice of lighting up to Jim. He's always been drawn to the bygone era, hence his collection of old classic cars, his interest in restoration, and his choice of these intricate old style lamp posts."

"Reflections from his past lives probably," Hayley said. "Thank goodness he has good taste. Some Gothic styles can be a bit gaudy."

Mr. Cooper reached the opened security gates, drove forward, and the gates closed. The paved drive led to a turnabout where he parked by the front door, got out, ran around to the other side, and opened their car door.

They slid out of the backseat and, in the warm night air, stood examining the changes that had been made to the property. Security lights lit the home, allowing them to clearly see the renovated exterior. The red-brick had been painted the shade of expresso cream. The slate-tiled roof matched the gray-colored shutters that dressed each of the black framed windows. The all-encompassing vegetation had been cleared away, and new plants filled the beds.

"What do you think?" he asked Hayley.

"A combination of old and new. I like it."

Mr. Cooper and a woman waited outside by the open front door.

"My husband and I stayed to greet you and make sure you have everything you need," Mrs. Cooper told them after being formally introduced as the head of housekeeping.

"Thank you," Hayley said. "We really appreciate your thoughtfulness."

"Our pleasure." She looked at her husband. "I'll show them inside."

Mr. Cooper proceeded to retrieve their luggage.

On the floor inside the entryway, a braid of silver, gold,

and bronze inlay encircled a silver F in the white marble floor with a wrought iron chandelier hanging above.

Mrs. Cooper followed them in. "All lights are motion activated, sir. And a computer butler, as Mr. Newton called it, has been installed to assist you with your needs. I've never seen anything like it. Would you care to have a looksee at your new estate before settling in?"

"What do you think, Hayley?" Lee asked.

"Tomorrow, if you don't mind," she said. "I'm dying to take a shower and get comfortable."

"Would you care for a late-night dinner, Mr. and Mrs. Franklin? Or maybe a snack? We have a variety of cakes and cookies that would go smashing with the champagne in your room."

"No, thank you," Hayley said.

"It's late," Lee said. "You and your husband can leave for the night."

"Thank you, sir. The staff will arrive at 8 a.m. And meals will be served according to your time preference. Have a nice night, and we will see you in the morning." She scurried off.

Hayley walked hand-in-hand with Lee to the dark oak staircase. He led her upstairs, opened the bedroom door, and allowed her to enter first. The room looked as she had pictured it in her mind. The pastel blues with pale yellow accents went well with the oak flooring. And the size of the furniture fit the proportions of the large room perfectly. Their luggage sat at the foot of the bed. A bottle of champagne rested in an ice bucket on an Italian classic chest in front of a large gold framed mirror. Each of the unique hand-picked furniture pieces complimented the room, giving it an eclectic elegance. They worked over the months on interior design, collaborating through internet video meetings with Kathy and Matilda. Each piece of furniture and décor throughout the home had been thoughtfully chosen and arranged to Hayley and Lee's liking in order for the home to reflect both of their tastes.

"Stylish and not over the top," Lee said. "It feels like home."

"I like the color choices," Hayley said. "Jim, Matilda, Kathy, and Thomas did an amazing job."

Lee lifted their suitcases and placed them on the suitcase racks in the walk-in closet.

"Is this the bathroom?" Hayley opened a door off the bedroom. The lights came on when she entered, illuminating a spacious bathroom with a shower large enough for a half dozen people and a bathtub she could swim in. "Beautiful," she said, surveying the room. "Dim the lights," Hayley told the computer butler.

She began filling the huge bathtub and added a little bubble bath. A basket filled with candles and a book of matches sat on a stool close by. Hayley smiled. "Thanks, Kathy." She lit all of them and placed them around the room. "Care to join me?" Hayley called to Lee as she disrobed. She climbed into the tub and sank into heated waters, warmth covering her shoulders and bubbles tickling her ears. She relaxed, feeling the heat melting away her stiffness from the long flight. *Heaven.*

Lee came into the room carrying two long-stemmed glasses filled with champagne, handed one to her, set his aside, and undressed while she sipped her drink. He moaned as he sank into the heated bath.

She sat in front of him, her head against his chest. While he tipped his head back and closed his eyes, Hayley glanced out of the open door leading into the bedroom. She swallowed hard, trying not to let Lee sense her alarm as she watched a translucent female figure gaze out the bedroom window, looking toward the full moon. *I was wrong. That's what she was trying to tell us. It's haunted.*

When the ghost turned away from the window, Hayley recognized her face. *The woman that owned the brooch.* She focused on the rim of her glass and kept her thoughts to herself. *Should I tell him?* When she felt his hands discovering the intimate curves of her body, and her desires flared, she knew the answer. *I'll tell him tomorrow, maybe.* She stood, soapy water streaming off her body, and offered him her hand. They stepped out and dried off.

Hayley led him into the bedroom, casually glancing around the room. The resident ghost had vanished. "Lights out," she said. They stood alone in the faint glow of moonlight that streamed in through the bedroom windows.

In the dimness, Lee tenderly embraced her. When his lips met hers, she felt an eternity of love fill her. While their bodies and souls melded into one, she thought, *I'm yours forever and ever and evermore.*

The End

About the Author

Shirley lives in Northeast Ohio. She turned to writing after taking an early retirement to care for her mother, who had been stricken with Alzheimer's. While writing first started as a pleasant form of stress relief for Shirley, it soon became her creative passion. She thanks God for her family and her close friends, who have given her support and inspiration.

www.ingramcontent.com/pod-product-compliance
Lightning Source LLC
Chambersburg PA
CBHW030115180626
46812CB00002B/429